D0423714

Mandatory
Release

ISBN: 1484081870
ISBN-13: 978-1484081877

Mandatory Release

a novel

JESS RILEY

For my parents, who met in prison.

They worked there together.
But for a second it was pretty exciting, wasn't it?

Also by Jess Riley:

Driving Sideways

All the Lonely People

Closer than they Appear: A Novella

1. GRAHAM

When do you suppose it's a good time to tell the woman you've been flirting with for a month online that you're actually in a wheelchair? And probably won't be running the Full Moon half marathon with her like she thinks? I used to run half marathons. Back when I was married and had much less limited mobility.

That's what I am now. A single guy with "limited mobility." I am also a liar, if your definition of lying includes the selective withholding of information.

I wish I could tell you that I was paralyzed during a prison riot. That I was stabbed in the spine with a shank made from the sharpened end of a toothbrush while trying to rescue eight of my coworkers from a burning unit. Or that I was paralyzed in a rock climbing accident in southern Utah. Or during a motorcycle race in Germany, or a firefight in the Korengal Valley. But what really happened is much less sexy than a prison riot or rock climbing fall or bullet through the spine in Afghanistan. It was actually one of the more than five million car accidents that happen annually in the U.S. My ex-wife was driving us home from a wedding. I probably don't need to tell you we were both drunk. Or that she swerved to miss a family of raccoons crossing the road and the car tumbled down a ditch and gracelessly ejected me into a field.

Basically, I lost my dick to a family of raccoons. Bet you've never heard that before.

So now I'm glib when I should be reflective. I'm caustic where I should be smooth. I'm half when I should be whole. And I'm being perfectly honest about my feelings here, which is something I've supposedly had trouble doing. Just ask my ex-wife.

Anyway, right now I'm on a first date with the marathon runner I met online, and she doesn't know any of this. Her name is Rachel, and she's an accountant. With a name and occupation like that you'd think she wears pearl earrings and Isotoner slippers, right? But she's got five tattoos and rides an Indian. No, I don't mean "East Indian" or the catch-all name rednecks give American Indians. I mean the motorcycle. A Scout, no less.

She doesn't have a sidecar.

We're at a restaurant called O'Clancy's, and its German proprietors have definitely done their part to keep the knockoff movie memorabilia industry alive. To give you a feel for the joint, think Groucho Marx meets Vin Diesel. Everywhere you look there's a framed B-movie poster or black-and-white publicity shot of an actor who hasn't done much since the early nineties. We're sitting beneath a clapperboard that looks as if it may drop onto Rachel's head the next time a server marches by.

I tap the laminated menu against the table and clear my throat. "The Caesar salad is good here." I've said the exact same thing to two other women I've met here in the last six months.

Rachel smiles tightly. She doesn't look up from her menu. "Is it?"

I know I'll be ordering the perch, like I do every time I eat here. And if this date goes anything like the last two, Rachel will next place her menu on the table, sigh deeply, look me in the eye and say, *"Why didn't you tell me you were paralyzed?"* Then she will say, *"You could have told me; I wouldn't have judged you"* or *"If you can't be honest about something this big, I don't see a future for us."* At least these were the responses I got from the last two women I met for dates.

"The perch is good, too." Another lie. The last few times it's been kind of bland and rubbery, about as appealing as a baked eraser. But I keep ordering it because I like perch, and I keep hoping that one of these times they'll get it right again. My job and physical situation have conspired to turn me into a glass-half-empty kind of guy, except in two key areas: dating and perch. Because despite the dim prospects for both, I keep coming back for more.

Rachel doesn't respond. "Take on Me" by a-ha dribbles from the speakers overhead. *Take me on, Rachel,* I think. *Stranger things have happened.*

The date was doomed before it started, but only I knew it. This is horribly unfair and wrong on all kinds of levels, I know. So here I am, pretending everything's cool because I avoid conflict like Ted Nugent avoids vegan restaurants. And a tiny, twisted part of me is really curious about how and when the shit will hit the fan. Poor Rachel. She's uncomfortable, and by now I'm extremely uncomfortable that my disinformation campaign has gone so far. As I have in the past, I tell myself that I'm only screening for women with a good sense of humor.

And like before, of course I don't believe myself. Because while I occasionally do dabble in self-deception, even I know when I'm truly and completely full of shit.

This is bad. Why do I do this to myself?

I'm not sure when it's the best time to tell someone you've connected with online that you're not everything they think you are. It's definitely too late the fifth time you talk on the phone. What am I going to say? "Funny story! So, I didn't put this in my profile, but I'm in a wheelchair? Yeah, pretty paralyzed over here. Still want to hit the water park on Sunday?" Or, "The good news is I'm not married, there are no outstanding warrants for my arrest, and I don't have herpes. The bad news is my house is handicap accessible for a reason. See, I didn't tell you because I really liked talking to you, but you know how these online things go. You're lucky if you make it two weeks. I used to be honest in my profile; funny about it, even. That went over well. You can imagine. Basically, I'm really fucking lonely." I'm going to have to reassess my strategy when these things actually result in a date, because panicked silence/winging it/hoping for the best doesn't seem to be working.

Rachel plays along, pretending nothing is out of the ordinary. But I can feel waves of discomfort radiating from her. Our waitress senses it, too. I make a mental note to leave a bulky tip as compensation for this table of awkwardness.

I order the perch, and Rachel orders the walnut-crusted chicken. The period between ordering and the delivery of our meals is always tricky. But I take heart in the fact that none of my previous dates (the ones where I neglected to mention the whole wheelchair thing, anyway) even lasted this long. Adrenaline simmers in my gut while I wait for her to say something. It's the kind of feeling you can get addicted to, if you're not careful.

While we wait, I tell Rachel an inmate story. At first I'm tempted to tell her the one about the guy who intricately fashioned an entire chess set from his own feces, but that's kind of an appetite suppressant. Instead I tell her about a guy who ate an entire computer keyboard, letter by letter. She smiles politely, and I notice that she blinks a lot. She's got this tic thing that she does, where she continually opens her eyes really wide, but just for a split second, as if to clear them of some debris.

Or maybe this is how she always reacts to what must at first seem like an optical illusion. The waitress appears from stage left, our meals balanced in each hand. She swoops in, and steaming plates clatter into place before us. It feels like a rescue. I smile at her: slight gap between her teeth, black pigtails, eyes spaced too far apart, breasts small but perky. They make me think of nectarines. "Careful, those plates are real hot!"

I wonder how many times she says that in the course of one shift.

Rachel asks for another iced tea, and then we're alone again. I rub my hands together to indicate how psyched I am to dig into my perch, painfully aware of the uncomfortable weight my false levity carries. I've become a one-man show playing to a hostile audience.

We listen to "99 Luftballons" while we chew our meals, and I watch a couple laughing and sharing entrees across the aisle. *You could have that*, I think. *If you stopped lying.*

The silence at our table is palpable. *Think. What did you two discuss in your e-mails? In your six phone conversations?* An idea burbles up as I glance at a poster for *The Godfather II*. "Have you seen the latest De Niro movie?"

She shakes her head and chews, her eyes darting around the room between blinks. I notice that she chews very quickly. Almost as quickly as she blinks.

"I didn't much care for it," I answer for her. "I found it disingenuous and predictable."

Her left eyebrow shoots up, as if to say, *Well, you're certainly disingenuous, but definitely not predictable.* I spear a chunk of perch and dredge it through some tartar sauce. Is fish supposed to be gray? I wish I'd gotten the fajitas.

"Yeah," I continue, ignoring her eyebrow. "His films are so pandering lately. So formulaic. Whatever happened to taking risks? Whatever happened to *Taxi Driver? Raging Bull?*" I chew a mouthful of breadstick and add, "He's really been coasting with his last few roles."

She blinks at me again and shovels a forkful of rice into her mouth. It's a look I take to mean: *Coasting, huh? You would know.*

The discomfort level has inched up, but I take it in stride. No pun intended.

Think think think. Ask her about her family.

"So how's your mother?" During one of our earlier conversations we'd bonded over our mutual family dysfunctions and misfortunes. She told me about her mother's multiple sclerosis, and I told her about my brother's Asperger's syndrome.

Apples to oranges, I know. But it was all I could come up with at the time.

She shrugs and extends a see-sawing hand to indicate "so-so."

A weightless feeling begins to rise in me. Maybe she won't say a thing about my chair! *Maybe she hasn't even noticed.* But she shortly dispels this notion by saying, "Graham, you know, this is probably the biggest thing anyone I've met online has ever attempted to hide from me." She begins ticking bad dates off on one hand. "I mean, there was the guy who was a foot and a half shorter than he claimed, and the one who wore a toupee. And one guy who was probably sixty pounds heavier than his online profile would have led me to believe. Don't get me started on all the married ones. But this is really a bit more than a toupee, isn't it?"

My cheeks burn. "I wanted to tell you, but I—" *I'm not one of Those Guys. Really, I'm not!*

"Honest to God, I waited this long to say anything because I didn't even know where to start." She crumples her napkin, tosses it on her plate, and gives me a look of contempt that I thought only my ex-wife had mastered. "Running a marathon? Give me a break!"

"You're right," I say. "I'm sorry. I should have told you. I didn't know—" *How? When?*

"It's a little late now." With this she scoots back, her chair squawking angrily. By the time I think of my follow-up, she's four tables away.

I toss out one final question, though what good it will do me now is of dubious value. "Would you still have gone out with me if I told you?"

She pauses and turns around, gives me a cold, calculating look. "Probably not."

Well, I had that coming. Hours later, before I fall asleep, I replay the night in my mind. This time, I change a few key details. The fish is fresh, perfectly cooked. Rachel laughs at my jokes and doesn't storm out. Instead, she leans toward me and gently asks The Question. The Question I'm still amazed actually applies to me: *"Why didn't you tell me you were in a wheelchair?"*

But I don't have a good answer to this.

Because whenever I close my eyes, I'm not.

2. DREW

Drew studied the man sitting across the desk. Richard Steffes, Educational Director of Lakeside Correctional Institution. She wondered if he went by Rich, Rick, or Dick. Ricky? He didn't volunteer the information. With his pressed slacks, honest chin, and fastidiously trimmed beard, he looked like the kind of man who sings in the choir on Sundays and never forgets a lawn maintenance chore. Richard it probably was. He shuffled through a stack of papers on his desk and withdrew her resume while she scrunched into her chair. He put on a pair of glasses and began to read, moving his lips slightly as he did. He stopped and glanced up with a thin, teasing smile. Drew knew what he was about to say next, perhaps even before he knew. "Your mother told me you were a state spelling bee champ in your younger days."

It was only a matter of time before he brought up her mother. And sure enough, thirty seconds into the interview, they'd arrived at that moment. Her mother, the icebreaker. Her mother, the revealer of personal information, the champion of non sequiturs, and now, the potential coworker.

Drew forced a grin. "Yep, that's true. T, R, U, E, *true.*" She was embarrassed at her attempt at humor. Job interviews could do this to you. But yes, she once was a spelling bee whiz. Back then, the words weren't as complicated. Neither were the relationships, the finances, or the living arrangements.

He cleared his throat, still smiling—perhaps at the idea that when spelling bee champs grew up, they became civil servants. "Well, I've just got a few questions for you that are more formalities than anything. First, why do you want to teach here?"

She hated this question. She couldn't tell him the truth, so she regurgitated the lame response that most people gave in answer to an interview question like this. "I'm ready for a new challenge. I …" For a weird and horrible moment she could only think *Fame! Fortune! Valuable office supplies!* "I want to reach those students who have fallen through the cracks."

I want to sound like a rejected Miss America contestant.

This seemed to satisfy him. While he shuffled through his interview paperwork, Drew surreptitiously closed her right eye, and he disintegrated. His face became a peachy blur, his hair a foggy cloud of gray bobbing somewhere above. Drew was nearsighted in one eye, farsighted in the other. She didn't have to wear glasses, because with both eyes open, they worked together to keep her from stumbling into gutters or jogging into walls. But if she closed just one eye, everything dissolved into soft focus.

Drew snapped both eyes wide open as Mr. Steffes began the interrogation.

She smiled and smiled. She maintained eye contact. She leaned forward and nodded where applicable. She felt impressively—no—*spectacularly* inept.

"Starting salary is thirty-eight thousand. Full benefits including health, life, dental, and retirement through the Employee Trust Fund."

There it was. They had arrived at the next logistical reason why the applications she picked up yesterday from Beachside Bagels and Piping Plover Books were still floating around the back seat of her car.

"There is a six-month probationary period. As anywhere, common sense applies to attire. No above-the-knee skirts, sleeveless tops, excessive jewelry. No cell phones beyond the gatehouse. You'll have to lock it in the trunk of your car. That'll all be in the employee handbook." He paused, adjusting his glasses. She was already dreading the next question. "I don't mean to sound inappropriate, and please tell me if this is out of line but … are you ready for this?" Meaningful pause and on with the rest: "This will be quite different from your last teaching experience."

Drew knew exactly what he was alluding to, but she wasn't giving him an inch. The local news had already given everyone more than a mile.

Was she ready for this? No. Not really. But she needed the job. More importantly, she needed something distracting and challenging that might restore the faith she once had in herself. Something to offer a foothold; a chunk of driftwood to cling to in the sea in which she'd been treading water for the last few months. It was a curious investment, but one that suddenly felt critical. So Drew beamed. She tried to look convincing. "Absolutely." She sat up straight. It was amazing what good posture and a deep breath of fresh air did for one's attitude. She could teach in any military academy in the United States. She could certainly teach a classroom of convicted felons how to spell "restitution."

After what happened with Ben, she felt ready for anything.

After the interview, Drew got the official tour. Mr. Steffes introduced her to the office staff, which consisted of four friendly older women and one who looked about Drew's age. Her name was Lisa Crane and she had hair the color of applesauce. She wore a scowl and purple knit stirrup pants tucked into cream pumps. Drew hadn't seen someone wear stirrup pants—let alone those tucked into pleather pumps— since 1989. This impressed her, and she felt a natural affection for such a girl.

After the halls cleared between periods, Mr. Steffes escorted Drew into the school's main artery, which looped around the open courtyard in the center of the building. Gray lockers lined the halls, like in your typical American high school. He pointed out the Title I classroom, the vocational tech wing with its auto detailing, welding, woodworking, custodial arts, and drafting classrooms. They peeked into the computer lab, said hello to the teacher, and strolled to the gym. Inmates gawked at her everywhere they went. *Having rape fantasies,* she thought wildly. But for the moment, it felt good to be surrounded by daily, tangible reminders that there were worse things to endure.

Mr. Steffes introduced Drew to the guidance counselor, William Bishop, who was en route to an inmate GED testing session. Drew could hardly believe a prison would even employ a guidance counselor. She doubted there were many college catalogs in his office. Next she met an inmate maintenance worker running a squeegee down a windowpane near the school office. He wore a yellow sleeveless smock over his prison coveralls with the number 14 written on the front and back in black permanent marker. It was the kind of smock, covered in tiny holes, that elementary school gym teachers hand out to distinguish opposing teams for dodgeball.

As they walked, Mr. Steffes said, "A philosophy I adopted when I started here was to treat everyone with the same amount of respect, regardless of offense. It makes things so much easier. But never tell them anything personal. If they ask, you just tell them it's none of their business. And if anyone harasses you, let me know right away."

Drew nodded, scratching an imaginary itch on her arm, trying not to smile at the way he'd pronounced "harasses," with the emphasis on the first syllable.

"We've had some problems in the past with staff fraternizing with inmates." After he said this he cleared his throat, seemingly to underscore the message.

Drew knew about some of these mysterious instances. Her mother told her about one unit officer who brought in fast food and beer for some of his pet prisoners, and about a recreation leader caught engaging in an "inappropriate act" with an inmate in the showers. She didn't clarify what the inappropriate act was, exactly, but Drew could certainly guess.

They stopped at a door, which Mr. Steffes unlocked and pushed open. "This will be your classroom." Drew surveyed the gloomy room. Add a few construction-paper instructional and seasonal displays, and it could be a classroom in almost any public school in the nation. A row of windows overlooked a woodsy courtyard. Four dark computer screens stared blankly from their desktop perches in front of the windows. In the back of the room, a private office bulged with scuffed filing cabinets. In the front of the room, a chalkboard framed by bulletin boards faced sixteen empty desks. The alphabet in cursive upper and lower-case letters was posted above the board. Drew wondered briefly about the man or woman who taught in this room previously. She made a mental note to ask her mother later.

Back in the main office, Mr. Steffes phoned the administration building. He covered the mouthpiece with a hand to ask if she'd like to see the rest of the complex.

"Sure," Drew said, with much more confidence than she actually felt.

He turned back to the phone. "Send a patrolman to pick up Ms. Daniels. Admin building." He smiled at her. "An officer should be here any minute to take you to the administration building. Mr. Bailey will meet you there to show you the rest of the institution. Sound good?"

Drew nodded. What *really* sounded good to her was a grilled cheese sandwich. A dirty martini. Maybe a vacation home in Maine. Somehow touring a medium security men's prison didn't make the list.

She walked out of the school, relieved to have the interview behind her, and waited for the patrolman to pick her up. Inmates followed the yellow line along the shoulder of the road by the school, heading to and from class. Most of them stared at her. She pretended to rummage through her shoulder bag for something—an excuse to avoid their cutting stares, though she could still feel the weight of their eyes crawling over her body. Right before her eyelid did that nervous tic thing it sometimes did, a blue van pulled up. She opened the passenger door and greeted the driver, relieved to escape the gaze of the inmates. First she noticed the clear Plexiglas partition separating the front and back seats. Next Drew noticed that the officer in the driver's seat had mismatched eyes. His left eye was deep brown, his right eye pale hazel. A large tattoo covered his right forearm: Marvin the Martian with gloved hands planted on his tiny cartoon hips, standing on the moon.

The officer shifted the van into drive. "So what brings you here?"

"I'm trying to think of something clever to say, but all I can think of are Girl Scout cookies."

He grinned, and it transformed him into an understudy for a small role in an indie flick about drug smuggling in the seventies. "Hey, I'll buy whatever you're selling." Drew blushed and snuck a few more looks at him from the corner of her eye. Was it possible to look like both the logger and the tree-hugger? The criminal and the cop at the same time? *Guess which I am*, his grin said. "I hear you had a job interview."

Drew found it disconcerting that rumors of her presence, and the intent of her presence, had been circulating. Had she thought she'd escaped workplace gossip? "Yes, that's right," she finally said.

"Oh yeah? Did you get it?" He flashed a smile that made her want to respond with sarcasm and a Kegel exercise.

"Get what?"

"The job!"

She blinked. "Um, I don't know yet."

"So what is it?"

Drew paused, knowing her next question would not be popular. "What is what?"

He shook his head, impatient yet amused. "The *job*."

"Oh right," she stammered. "Special education. Teaching, that is. Teaching special ed."

Technically she'd be working with inmates deemed as having "Exceptional Educational Needs," which meant she was the new EEN teacher. But not everybody knew what an EEN teacher was. So she usually just said, "Special Education." State law required that an education be provided to all such identified students, even if incarcerated—and if incarcerated, that education may be provided up to the age of twenty-one. Since this was an adult institution, her students would be between the ages of sixteen and twenty-one. The fun years. But not so much for them.

"I'm Joe Simon, by the way. And you are?"

"Drew Daniels."

"I heard about you. Moffatt said you were pretty. You'll have to be careful in here."

"Uh-huh." She stole a glance at his forearm again. It was well-muscled, dappled in freckles, with just the right amount of hair.

"Your mom is Sara Daniels, right?"

"Yeah," Drew said, looking out the window at more inmates trekking around the recreation field in their drab green uniforms. "Hey, why do the inmates wear green? Seems like they'd really blend in with the woods if they escaped."

Joe shrugged. "They wear orange if they end up in the hole. Beyond that, I have no idea." He pulled up to the administration building's main entrance, parked, and turned to face Drew. "You know? You kind of look like your mom."

"Thanks for the ride," she said, fumbling with the door and nearly tripping when she jumped out.

He nodded and pulled away, and she glanced back to see his odd eyes watching her in the rearview mirror. She imagined telling their future children how funny it was that Mommy had eyes that didn't focus, and Daddy had eyes that didn't match.

Get a grip, she told herself. She took a deep breath and tried to focus on something calming. The glint of sunlight on a coil of razor wire. The ringing of some far-off bell. Men pounding on the tiny windows of the segregation unit.

She gave up when she realized she could hear her heartbeat in her ears.

Frank Bailey, the prison security director, met her in front of the administration building to continue the tour through an inmate unit. Most maximum-security prisons and several other medium security prisons in Wisconsin housed inmates in cells with bars, like you'd see on any self-respecting movie about a prison. But here inmates lived in rooms that reminded Drew of those in her old college dormitory, minus the neon Grateful Dead posters.

Each inmate had a key to a room containing a bunk bed, desks, closets, and footlockers. Mr. Bailey said that only the segregation unit had barred cells. As he walked her through the unit common area, inmates looked up from games of ping pong and Chinese checkers to watch their little parade. So many people were staring at her chest that Drew's first instinct was to look down and check for a stain.

"The inmates eat their meals here, in their units. We don't have one large dining hall, which reduces the chance for any problems."

"Problems like riots?"

"Problems like riots." They were quiet for the next few minutes, perhaps pondering their individual fates should a riot erupt at that very moment. Or maybe he was wondering what was for dinner.

They walked into unit seventeen, the inmate reception barracks, Drew taking two anxious steps for his every confident stride. "Most people call this 'The Warehouse,'" he said with authority. "First stop before assignment to a unit." .

Inmates wandered around the cement floor, staring at her. Some lay on their bunks; others sat in a cluster of resin lawn chairs in the corner, watching a television set bolted to the wall. *Judge Judy* was on. A tall inmate wearing nothing but a towel strolled past and stared her down. His stringy red hair hung like a grubby cape down his back. Drew looked away, wishing she hadn't made eye contact. She didn't even want to know what he was in for. Making Mrs. Benson's cows sterile with just a glance?

Drew met Pastor Luke at the chapel. He'd wrapped his few remaining wisps of hair up and around his shiny scalp, round and round, giving his head the general appearance of a cinnamon roll. "Are you Sara's daughter?" he asked.

Drew smiled. "Yes." She predicted, based on this morning alone, that she would be asked about her mother and regaled about her wonderfulness sixteen more times before leaving that afternoon.

"Oh, she's wonderful. Well, I'll cross my fingers that you get the job. We need new talent for badminton at lunch."

Lunchtime badminton in prison? Her life was awfully close to becoming an offbeat BBC comedy series.

Back at the administration building, Drew stopped by her mother's office. Sara looked up from the glow of her computer screen. "So how'd it go?" She offered Drew a strawberry from a container on her desk.

"I think it went okay. He's going to call me when he makes a final decision."

Her mother nodded, bit the tip of a strawberry, and grimaced. "These berries aren't ripe at all." She tossed the half-eaten berry into the garbage and wiped her hand on a napkin.

"So if I get the job we could be spending a lot of time together," Drew said.

"Yep."

"We'll be carpooling every day." Drew didn't like the sound of her voice: needy and overeager, a child fishing for attention. The adult version of flailing about in the kiddie pool and shouting at the parents sunning in their lounge chairs. *"Hey Mom! Watch! Mom! Watch me! Are you watching?"*

Drew's mother, eyes glued to her computer screen, ignored her and clicked her mouse several times. Her phone rang and she picked it up. "Sara Daniels, Personnel." She covered the mouthpiece with a hand and whispered to her daughter, "Drew,

I'm sorry, but I've got so much work to do. Can we talk about your interview after work?"

"Yeah. Sure." Drew glanced around her mother's office, approved of the family photos on her desk (equal representation for each child), and left. She wondered when she'd stop feeling eight years old in front of her mother.

Not moving back home would probably help.

3. GRAHAM

I didn't set out to be a social worker at a medium security men's prison. In college, I always thought I'd study biology, maybe end up working for the Wisconsin Department of Natural Resources. Doing water studies, busting poachers, stocking lakes with trout. The kind of masculine, outdoorsy thing that shouted, "I shop at Fleet Farm! I tar roofs in hundred-degree weather without a water bottle!" But then I met a girl, and because I had limited self-confidence in those days and went about my daily routine with a perpetual boner, I rearranged my plans around hers. I didn't want any part in a career with a path of study that required I attend a university she wasn't enrolled in. If I could have majored in her, I would have.

Ten years later I've lost the girl, but I've gained a career trying to keep felons from returning to the regular ingestion of heroin, crack, meth, alcohol, pot, and various household cleaning substances upon their release. It's not exactly trout-stocking, but it beats a Swiffer duster up the ass.

Working in a prison is nothing like the creators of *Oz* or *Prison Break* would have you believe. It's actually more like

19

accounting. You have your piles of paperwork—reports for the program review committee, the parole board, and courts, treatment and release plans—phone calls and e-mails pinging in all day, stacks of hand-scrawled kites from inmates (kites are interview request forms), a stale office that smells of industrial cleaners and old paint, and have I mentioned the routine? It's an endless Sahara Desert of routine peppered only by the occasional oasis of interest—sex scandals, the specter of a riot, the new hire that everybody wants to screw.

"So have you seen her yet?" Andy Moffatt asks, his smile giving his question a suggestive, eager tone that makes me want to shower. Andy Moffatt is the guard on duty in the gatehouse. Oh wait. I'm supposed to call them Correctional Officers. But you know what, PC Police? I'm not going to call Mr. Moffatt a Correctional Officer, or even a CO. I'm not going to call the warden's secretary an "Administrative Assistant," and I'm not going to call myself physically challenged, or worse, "differently abled." You don't have to either. I'm fucking handicapped, and the sooner we get that cleared up, the better. Which brings to mind a line from an old George Carlin bit about euphemistic language: "We're not handi*capped*, we're HANDI-*capable*!" God bless that man. May he rest in peace.

"Seen who?" It's barely eight in the morning and already I'm exhausted. Can I go home yet?

"Drew Daniels! Sara's daughter." Andy's halitosis is so strong it could haul a snowmobile to Rhinelander and back. I begin breathing through my mouth, which I hate to do because it makes my ears plug up and aggravates my sinuses. I shake my head and wheel to the end of the conveyor belt to wait for the metal detector to spit out my briefcase and insulated lunch cooler. Despite the nugget of surprise and pleasure that has formed in my gut, I try to maintain a cool, impenetrable expression.

"She's the new special ed teacher. She started this morning."

Ah, special ed. One of the few teaching options here at LCI. Your other main option—if you teach—is ABE, which stands for Adult Basic Education. This entails trying to plug the gaping academic holes left by sporadic school attendance and an adolescence spent sniffing lighter fluid for inmates who enroll in the prison school.

Drew Daniels. We went to the same high school. We were in the same graduating class, to be more specific. Chemistry lab partners for one semester, even. And to pinpoint things further, I had something of a crush on Drew back then. I know, big surprise, what with my eternal hard-on between the ages of thirteen and twenty-five. To be fair, we were all flooded with hormones back then, obsessed with who was getting laid, determining how to get laid, and developing techniques that could improve the experience of getting laid once we actually *were* getting laid. So I'm hardly an anomaly.

I heard the basic story about what happened to Drew from a mutual high school friend. The rest filtered through the Laurentide Bay rumor mill, picking up distortions and exaggerations, and the current version is probably not even in the same solar system as the actual truth. I suppose I could have simply asked her mother Sara about all of this, since she is the Director of Personnel and I see her almost daily, but it's a touchy subject, and I don't want to seem like an insensitive, nosy asshole.

But why Drew's working here is the real mystery. I'll find out sooner or later, I suppose. I'm definitely hoping for sooner.

I've already told you how I ended up in this chair. Maybe you're wondering if I've always been a compulsive, perhaps even pathological, liar as well. In all honesty, I can't remember lying this badly before the accident. And when I say, "in all honesty," I really mean it. Right now, anyway.

And no, I don't see a therapist or counselor about this. I *am* a fucking counselor.

So it's interesting (to me anyway) that as a result of the accident, I have lost my ability to climb a ladder *and* tell the truth in a dating situation. But I try not to let it interfere with my clinical service delivery as a social worker.

Most of my twenty-five colleagues in Lakeside Social Services run one of two drug abuse and addiction treatment programs: the Nexus program, aimed at higher-functioning inmates, and the STOP program, for the sixty-five percent of inmates who read below a sixth grade level or qualify as Special Ed. My former boss affectionately called the STOP program "Detox for the Delayed." He was later "released from service" due to an "unprofessional attitude."

STOP is an acronym for "Special Treatment Options Program," and I've yet to come across a more meaningless and nauseating bit of jargon. In moments of breakroom levity, my colleagues and I come up with new and improved acronyms: JUMP (Just Us Macho Pimps), WATCH (We're All Totally Crazy Here), and my personal favorite, ECHO (Everyone Can Handle Opiates). Becky Fineman came up with that one, which I suppose made it especially amusing to me since she's one of the best treatment specialists you'll ever meet.

It's been said that you can't joke about "taboo" subjects like death or paralysis or drug abuse or crime. But I believe that you can and should, because laughing at these kinds of things makes space for candid discussion of them. It robs them of their power and allows for frank and realistic development of solutions. Sure, laughter encourages both coping and avoidance. And sometimes it's hard to find the humor in certain situations.

Nuclear war? Maybe. But I'll take *Dr. Strangelove* over *Testament* any day of the week. Life is depressing enough.

Those of us not running the drug and alcohol abuse stuff lead a grab bag of support programs: anger management, grief and loss, incarcerated veterans, and release programming on things like interview dos and don'ts and family reintegration strategies. I'm currently running a program called "Self-Help, Inc." for a dozen inmates. It consists of twenty-six lessons on resolving conflicts without using kitchen cutlery and establishing healthy interpersonal relationships that don't result in burning profanities into a love interest's lawn. The lessons have names like *Responsibility vs. Shame, Winning Comes Second, Freedom as a State of Mind,* and *Choosing Happiness.* This week we're on *Choosing Friends.* It's supposed to help the guys pick "healthy" individuals to establish friendships with: people who are gainfully employed, pay their child support on time, and don't drive the getaway car or stab elderly people to death on their front porches.

"The boring ones," as one of the inmates in the group said yesterday.

I corrected him. "No, the responsible ones. Ones that won't tempt you with situations or substances that could land you back in prison."

When I consider the people I'm friends with, I believe that I could also benefit from this lesson, should I choose to apply it to my own life. Take, for example, my friend Trevor. Trevor is so cheap that despite breaking his computer chair months ago, he hasn't replaced it, instead perching precariously at an angle atop the broken seat. If he leans too far in any direction, there is an excellent chance he will accidentally sodomize himself. He has trouble making and maintaining eye contact, which doesn't play well with the opposite sex. In fact, his self-esteem is such that should a woman agree to screw him only if he wore a paper bag on his head, he would. He inherited enough money from a great-uncle to open a hobby shop in Laurentide Bay, peddling Marvel Comics-themed chess sets and Star Wars paraphernalia. He hasn't intentionally eaten a vegetable since childhood, which probably contributed to his recent scurvy scare. Every Sunday evening we participate in collective online gaming experiences on Xbox Live with a community of men who are also in their early thirties and appreciate a good old-fashioned Bettie Page-inspired look on a woman. Trevor will never land me in prison, but he could contribute to my never leaving the house again and ultimately dying alone in my own filthy couch indentation.

No. If any of my friends were going to land me in prison, it would be Kevin Lipton, who also works here at Lakeside—a third-shift Sergeant on Unit Six. A traditional jock in high school, he was a staple on the baseball, football, and basketball teams. Now a jock in the modern sense, he enjoys participating in tavern-sponsored sport tournaments aimed at nostalgic thirtysomethings: kickball, dodgeball, rock-paper-scissors, pitcher and case races, barstool racing. Yes, there is such a thing. And that's the problem, really. Kevin loves to drink. And drive. It's only a matter of time before the bill arrives for that lovely combo platter.

Kevin and Trevor inhabit two very different social circles, which if drawn on paper would never overlap, except for me.

But back to *Choosing Friends*. I'm alone in the room before the session begins, organizing my handouts and wondering once again if I should change the sun-faded inspirational cartoons and posters tacked onto the bulletin boards, knowing almost immediately I won't because I'll forget. The first inmate arrival is Rodney Gardiner. And it just so happens that Mr. Gardiner is also in a wheelchair. In fact, he came to prison in a wheelchair, and will leave prison in the same wheelchair two years from now, after he finishes serving his sentence for forgery. We greet one another and other inmates begin to file in. One of them, a man doing three years for possession and delivery of marijuana compounded by gang association and a string of prior felonies, collapses into a chair and looks around the room, picking his afro. "What is this, a wheelchair convention?"

You'll hear plenty of this kind of wit in prisons and check-cashing shops around the nation. He quickly segues into a snotty, "So is this lesson gonna be like *Winning comes second?*"

"Even better, Mr. Carver. You're going to love it." He rolls his eyes but cracks a smile, softening around the edges. I know he received a conduct report for lying earlier in the week; another so soon on the heels of the last could land him in the hole. I wonder how long until Mr. Carver begins calling me "Graham Cracker," as some of his peers have been doing "behind my back" for years. Annoying air quotes intended.

More inmates filter in. Most have dual disorders, which means that not only are they addicts, but they are also mentally ill to some degree. Take the range of mental health disorders these guys have been diagnosed with—ADHD, bipolar disorder, schizophrenia, depression, anxiety, avoidant personality disorder, et cetera ad nauseam infinity squared. Add the major recreational drugs in which they dabble—crystal meth, alcohol, pot, cocaine, crack, heroin, LSD, inhalants, steroids, and a bushel of pills regulated by the Controlled Substances Act—and you can understand how any one of them could be found wandering naked through a Veteran's Day Parade, brandishing a turkey baster and babbling about meeting Jesus in a Taco Bell bathroom that morning. I use the present tense because while the bulk of inmate drug use happened prior to arrest, any inmate with money, canteen goods, or services to trade can wrap his veins around a needle this evening if he's so inclined. In a supposedly secure facility, for Christ's sake. Basically, I'm one of those AODA counselors who thinks the war on drugs is the Crystal Pepsi of national initiatives.

I do believe that *some* treatment practices can work, but once you short-circuit your brain chemistry with a drug that, say, lists Drano as a primary ingredient, you'd better clear your calendar for the Bataan Death March to rehabilitation.

I snap out of my thoughts as Mike Sheffield from the Hope Center trips through a sea of inmates and stumbles into the room, as smooth as Newt Gingrich at the Source Awards. He's a community volunteer who helps deliver some of our self-help lessons. He follows almost every statement with, "You know what I mean?" or when he wants to establish a rapport with the inmates, "You know what I'm sayin'?" He's also fond of novelty ties and plastic bracelets for the cause of the week. His car is emblazoned with bumper stickers ordering people tailgating him to save, pray for, support, or have awareness of one irritating cause or another. I sometimes wonder if the treatment supervisor approved him because he thought Mike might inspire the guys. As in, "Well, I may be bipolar, serving thirty years for negligent manslaughter, and recovering from a heroin addiction, but at least I'm not a big sheet of dick skin like Mike Sheffield."

"Graham, my man. What's the word?" Mike sinks into a chair next to me and hunches over, elbows on knees and hands clapped together in can-do stance, his pleated khaki slacks bunching and stretching, cuffs riding up to reveal stripes of blinding, hairy calf. If I lean back I am confident that I will see BVD or ass cleavage. I wish to see neither, so I inch forward slightly. There is a company that makes pants for people who spend the bulk of their days sitting in chairs, wheeled or otherwise—tagline, *USA Wheelchair Jeans. Pants Designed for Sitting.* They ride low in the front, high in the back, and have an ass and legs baggy enough to facilitate some serious shoplifting. I believe that with the sedentary lifestyle of most Americans, this company is compromising some major profits by limiting their target demographic. I haven't yet purchased a pair of USA

Wheelchair Jeans, because would you fuck a guy in those pants? I didn't think so. I appreciate the hell out of the fact that someone came up with the concept, but come on now ... you don't see a guy walking down the street in USA Parkinson's Anti-shake Testicular Stabilizing Briefs.

"Hey, Mike. We'll get started in a minute."

After I take attendance I slip two fingers between my lips and whistle to interrupt the chatting. An inmate named Trolley Winkler claps his hands and offers a helpful, "Okay, guys, let's get down to brass tactics." I cock my head and grin, consider correcting him, but don't.

The inmates sit in a circle in the whitewashed cinderblock room, learning the script for the fabled productive life after prison. Fluorescent lights gleam industriously on the polished tile floor. Mike and I role-play an interaction between a recovering addict and his co-dependent, still-using buddy, a scene that is too mortifyingly embarrassing to even describe. Let's just say Mike hams it up, getting all into the street lingo and using exaggerated body language. The inmates love it, laughing-at-him-not-with-him. Afterward, we discuss taking inventory of and developing personal strengths to build self-esteem. We suggest tactful yet empowered responses to old friends trying to pull you back down. We work to develop problem-solving and coping skills. We outline how to set appropriate boundaries.

It's grueling and redundant work, like crab-walking backward up Pikes Peak, but by the end of the session, most of the inmates seem reluctantly inspired. One of them, a pedophile recovering from an Oxycontin addiction, even shakes my hand on his way out. Inmates always want to shake your hand, like you're closing a real estate deal with them or something. And since the hygiene of many inmates is questionable at best, most prison employees wash their hands with the frequency of Marc

Summers and the intensity of a surgeon doing a pre-op scrub. You can't be too cautious. No one wants to catch a robust, itchy case of pubic lice without an orgasm as a consolation prize. I remind myself to stop at the staff men's room to wash my own hands immediately after class.

Will any of this programming stick? I'm not sure. I've seen the revolving prison door in action—the latest from my own caseload being Miguel Herrera, released last Easter and back by Memorial Day Weekend for parole violation: manufacture and possession of methamphetamines with intent to deliver. But when I listen to myself talk in-session, it all makes perfect sense. These are the keys to happiness—and how simple! Setting boundaries ... Focusing on your ability to make people laugh instead of your ability to pick locks at lightning speed ... Solving problems without throwing an ashtray across the room. Choosing the Sprite instead of the vodka stashed in the glove compartment.

I too could learn from the self-help lessons I deliver three days a month. Unfortunately, like the advice-giver stuck in a bad relationship or the insecure bully taunting the easy mark, it's much easier to dish it out than it is to actually take it.

4. DREW

Much has been written about coming home again after an absence, most famously by Thomas Wolfe. He was of the opinion that you couldn't. If you defined home as the home of your youth, of your childhood memories, probably de-clawed over the years if your childhood was mostly happy, then he was right. Your parents would be different, if they were still together, if one or both were still alive. Some, possibly even all, of your siblings would be gone—away at college, attending PTO meetings in New Jersey, making documentary films about penguins in Antarctica. They could be doing almost anything, because they got out. But you were here again. Home. In your old bedroom, unless your parents had converted it into a sewing room, or an exercise room, or the room in which they hid the evidence of your mother's QVC addiction.

Drew was home again, now. Lying in her old bed in her old bedroom, which had been purged of her personality and transformed into a new and improved bedroom: the sanitized version 2.0 for company. The room had cornflower blue walls and was devoid of personality, as if staged for a Pottery Barn ad.

The yellow bedspread was new and scratchy, the pillow overstuffed and stiff beneath her cheek. Her youth was boxed up in the garage, and an American Robin was singing in the backyard. She knew it was a robin, because her father had trained her to recognize almost every common Wisconsin bird song by ear by the time she was four. He tried teaching her to identify native Wisconsin trees too, but Drew wasn't into trees. They didn't go anywhere.

Drew looked up at the morning sun streaking across the ceiling. It used to be one of those popcorn ceilings, but it too, was new and improved.

Her alarm went off—an old familiar beeping. Because her mother wouldn't purchase a new piece of technology until it actually broke, this particular appliance was neither new nor improved. Because of this, Drew was surprised to feel a slight fondness for her scrappy little alarm clock.

She was normally a huge fan of the snooze button, something Ben had hated. But today she turned her alarm off immediately, wide awake, panic mushrooming in her stomach as she remembered what day it was. Her alarm clock may as well have been a recording of Gilbert Gottfried yelling, "Wake up! It's your first day at work! In a prison! With your mother!" The polar opposite of the Now & Zen alarm clock that eased you awake with soft, progressively louder chimes.

She rubbed her eyes and swung her legs out of bed. Nine months ago, Drew was a public school teacher with seniority and friendly coworkers in a smallish city across the state. A city large enough to anchor two high school campuses and an annual jazz festival, but small enough that you regularly ran into people you knew at the grocery store. She shared an apartment with a modestly attractive fellow teacher named Ben. They made quiche on Sunday mornings and signed cards together when their friends got married: *Congratulations! Love, Ben and Drew.* She drove a sensible car, one with good gas mileage and excellent resale potential. She still had the car, but the rest?

"Drew? Are you getting in the shower? Because if you don't, I will!"

Her mother's voice echoed down the hallway dotted with framed photos taken when Drew's brother Nick, sister Wendy, and Drew still believed in the Tooth Fairy. Nick and Wendy were both in college now—Nick studying veterinary science in Michigan, Wendy six hours away in Iowa City, in training to become the next Marisha Pessl. Her last short story featured two sisters who shared a remarkably familiar relationship. One of the sisters—the older one—was a kleptomaniac with misshapen breasts. It was hard not to feel annoyed by that. Drew was fairly confident that her breasts were evenly sized (although she became horribly paranoid about it for months afterward), and she never stole so much as a candy bar in her life. She'd had friends who shoplifted—her friend Paula Becker once so daring as to actually wear a bikini out of Macy's under her regular clothing—but Drew? Stolen glances were the extent of it.

Drew was seven years older than Wendy, nine years older than Nick, yet as neither had returned home this summer, she was the only one living with their parents again. *Drew Daniels for the win! Does this girl know how to party or what?*

She sighed and padded down the hall to the shower she used through her elementary, middle, and high school years. How did the saying go? To get to heaven, first you have to go through hell? Well, how about this: to move forward, first you might have to move backward.

But she supposed, then, that you would remain in the same place. Just kind of shuffling back and forth in fits and starts. Moving away from home, moving back home, finding soul-searing love, losing it again, giving up a tenured position at an award-winning high school across the state, accepting a job teaching felons how to diagram sentences in a medium security men's prison. It was a messy kind of foxtrot, for sure.

"Are you excited for your first day of work?" her mother shouted over the NPR *Morning Edition* theme music.

"Can we turn that down?"

"What?"

Drew reached over and turned the volume down.

"Hey, I wanted to hear that part."

Drew gave in and nudged the volume up a hair, and her mother hummed along with the final snippet of melody. After she finished, she smiled contentedly and glanced at her daughter to gauge her response.

"So are you?" her mother continued.

"Am I what?"

"Excited! For your first day of work!" Her mother viewed every day as an adventure and was so cheerful you almost had to wear sunglasses in her presence. She made small talk with everyone—the girl bagging her groceries, the elderly man in line before her at the DMV, the cranky sales clerk at the Gap. She could be a motivational speaker if she didn't pretend to be an airhead for the laughs.

Drew knew her mother was pretending, even when she told someone to "throw her down the stairs a towel," even when she yawned and wondered aloud if she were possibly a necrophiliac when she meant narcoleptic, even when she said, "Shhhh! I'm just trying to … wonder" when the word she was searching for was "concentrate." You'd think someone who's worked in a prison for twenty-plus years would have developed an impenetrable veneer over his or her emotions. Some kind of tough outer rind. But not Drew's mother; she was still kind, still believed in the power of rehabilitation and redemption, still donated time and money to the Salvation Army every Christmas. If you were one of those people who judged a person's character based on their exterior, for once you'd be right with Sara Daniels—because she truly *looked* nice, wearing matching pastel sweater sets, deep laugh lines, and the optimistic expression of a gardener paging through a seed catalog in February.

Today she was wearing a twin set the color of fresh honeydew over cream pants, but no open-toed shoes. That was against prison regulations. Her cropped reddish hair, tucked around her earlobes, made her look like an earnest and practical pixie—one that granted the desperate, final wishes of suicidal people, perhaps. People said Drew looked like her mother, but Drew didn't think these people were very detail-oriented.

Drew was staying with her parents until she could save enough to get herself back on track emotionally and financially, at which point she planned to sign a new lease for her own apartment and pull her furniture from storage. There were some money issues after she lost Ben. She wasn't in the red yet, but she could see it from where she stood.

She was also staying with her parents because her mother felt she shouldn't be alone after what happened. Especially since those early days without Ben had been filtered through an ugly new lens—one that distorted every day into something numb to be endured. Drew wanted to eat well-balanced meals cooked by her mother and use silverware that hadn't touched Ben's lips on a daily basis. She wanted to feel protected, to have her mother take care of her—the way she did when Drew had the flu as a child and her mother brought her cool washcloths for her forehead and flat 7-Up with a bendy straw. Perhaps most of all, Drew wanted to put some space between herself and the furtive and not-so-furtive looks of pity and shock she'd been fielding from colleagues, students, and neighbors back in Eau Claire.

At first, her father hadn't been too thrilled with the idea of her moving home again. He believed children should be independent, supporting themselves with a paper route and lawn care service two hours after they dropped from the uterus. But her father was also twenty years older than her mother, so most of the time he did whatever his wife said. With age and high cholesterol came wisdom and for some people, the realization that "*Yes, dear*" was better for the circulatory system than "*What do you mean, you want to mount it to the wall?*" Drew's father retired from the U.S. Postal Service five years ago and now spent his days tracking family genealogy, filling the armada of bird feeders he maintained in the backyard, and stuffing the garage with cast-off household goods he picked up at estate sales. He attended one nearly every weekend. Once he brought home a five-gallon bucket of pencils, replacing Drew's years of childhood constipation as the most frequently tapped source of family jokes.

There was a vaguely uncomfortable silence in the car that Drew was tempted to fill, but her mother stepped in first. "Are you sure you want to do this?" She shook her head and pursed her lips. She opened her mouth as if to say something else, but didn't.

Drew's cheeks began to flush. She blew on her coffee to cool it, hoping also to disperse the fear leaking from her heart.

Then, her mother let it slip. "God, if there was ever a riot, the school is where it would—"

"Mom?"

"Well, it would!" She drummed her fingers on the steering wheel to the beat of a jingle for another NPR show.

Drew could feel the old roles they'd played years ago, waiting, ready to be stepped into once again to resume the show. "I'll be getting the same security training that you did."

"That's what worries me." This was a funny thing to say, but whenever Drew used to ask her mother about working in a prison, one of her more popular responses was an enthusiastic, "It's awful!" accompanied by an expression of wide-eyed terror. When prompted for the juicy details, she'd add, "Oh, I don't mean the inmates, I'm talking about the staff."

Sara slammed on the brakes and swerved to miss a rabbit darting across the road, throwing her right arm across her daughter's chest in the universal Mother Seat-Belt move. Drew gave her a measured look and said, "I think we have a better chance of being maimed or disfigured on the way to work."

"I never wanted any of you kids to work at a prison."

"So it's okay for you, but not for Nick or Wendy or me?" They'd recycled the basic plot of this argument at least a thousand times over the years; it was the old *Do as I say, not as I do* routine.

Her mother took a curve too sharply and a splash of hot coffee leapt from the travel mug to Drew's lap. "Mom!"

"Sorry." Sara abruptly glanced out her window and said, "Awww, that's so sad!" She was looking at wobbly veal calves tethered to their tiny white shelters in a farmer's yard.

"Mom? The road? In front of you?"

"Oh, sorry."

"I'm going to start spiking your coffee with Ritalin."

Sara giggled, pleased that they were back in their comfortable routine—Drew playing straight man George Burns to her mother's airheaded but sweet Gracie Allen. Old and consistent roles they'd had for ages.

But honest to God, Drew had almost forgotten how this drained her personality. Maybe moving home wasn't such a hot idea. Living *and* working with her mother? It was a test even Job would have refused: *Good luck with that, Sport! You're gonna need it.*

Lakeside Correctional Institution, a converted boys' reformatory, lay smack-dab in the heart of a state forest ten miles from Lake Michigan. People driving down the highway splicing into the forest after a long day at the beach were often surprised by the sudden glare of the orange prison searchlights rising over the tree line. Tourists thought it odd and somewhat offensive that a prison had been built in the middle of such pristine beauty.

The prison housed 1,753 inmates, but was built to hold only 1,400. If not for the eight armed guard towers, double fence, and coils of razor wire, it could have been an army base: non-denominational chapel, general store, sprawling administration building, clinic, school, sixteen housing units. Picnic tables and playground equipment identified the outdoor inmate visiting area near the gatehouse. Someone had planted petunias and geraniums along the walkways.

Drew took it all in after her mother parked next to a sign that read, *Lock your car and remove all valuables. The State of Wisconsin is not responsible for any damage or theft.*

The lot was full this sunny Thursday morning. She began the short walk to the prison gatehouse on unsteady legs. One of the guard towers loomed over the small building, casting a thick shadow into the parking lot. Drew swallowed hard, and her throat made an audible click. She fought an electric urge to grab the keys from her mother and sprint back to the car. She opened the pneumatic glass door, the first of two, and gazed into a cool, rectangular room. Small lockers, the kind you could rent at Skateland to store sneakers in, lined one wall. Two officers clad in blue shirts sat behind a counter running the length of the opposite wall. A conveyor belt and walk-through metal detector stood at the end of the room.

One of the officers, an older man wearing square-framed glasses, pushed a button under the counter and waved them in. He was shaped like a yardstick. His ears flared from the sides of his head. The second glass door before them clicked, and they entered the gatehouse. They were greeted by the younger officer, who had the benign face of a guy all the girls considered a friend but never a boyfriend. His name tag read *Moffatt*. "This your daughter?" he asked Drew's mother, grinning.

"We found her on the back porch thirty years ago. Just can't seem to get rid of her."

Drew ignored this and offered the guard a clear, professional smile. "I'm Drew. The new special ed teacher?"

He squinted at her. "I recognize you from last week. When you came in for your interview."

She grinned and felt stupidly exposed, like a daydreamer tapped at a celebratory dinner to make an impromptu speech.

A phone rang behind the counter, and the older guard in glasses answered it. "Gatehouse." He laughed at something the person on the other end of the line said.

Drew watched her mother send her lunch cooler and purse through the bag-check X-ray and then step through the metal detector, no muss, no fuss. Drew followed suit, removing her watch and earrings and placing them in a plastic tray. She slid her purse onto the conveyor belt of the bag-check and walked through the metal detector holding her breath. It beeped angrily. Officer Moffatt studied her. "Hmmmmm. Got a metal belt buckle?"

She shook her head anxiously, looking at her waist.

"What about your shoes? Any metal down there?"

She shook her head again, feeling a bead of sweat trickle down her side. "Wait! I've got an underwire bra on. I don't need to take it off, do I?"

He smirked and nodded. Was he serious? Yes, he was.

"Sorry. I forgot to remind you," Sara said. "Is this really necessary?" she asked the guard.

"It's policy," he replied, still smirking. Her mother clucked and shook her head. Drew suspected she found this whole situation amusing. It would make great fodder for the annual Christmas letter: *The kids are doing great. Nick has a new girlfriend, and Wendy just published her first short story! Also, Drew went braless in a prison this past July. We're so proud of them all. Except maybe Drew.*

Another drop of sweat rolled into Drew's waistband. "You have got to be kidding me," she mumbled, turning her back on Officer Moffatt. She quickly unhooked her bra, yanked the strap over her right elbow, and pulled it out through her sleeve as discreetly as she could. She balled it up and set it on the conveyor belt, where it unfurled into a pink flower with two modest (but uniform!) petals. Her cheeks felt radioactively hot.

The officer grinned nonchalantly while he watched Drew fish her Victoria's Secret bra, the one Ben used to call her "egg carton bra," from the heavy plastic curtains. "I'll call a patrolman to take you down to the school."

Relieved, Drew stuffed the bra into her purse. She glanced at her chest and felt dim gratitude that the room was warm. A half-hearted joke about the difficulty of smuggling drugs in an A cup came to mind, but she didn't share it.

They waited for the third air-locked door to click, and Sara pushed it open. A lone officer in a golf cart zipped up the road to the gates and parked behind the second fence. Drew glanced up at the tower; another guard, hidden in the shadows, lifted a hand. There was a loud buzz-click as the last door before them unlocked. They waved back at the mystery guard and entered the prison. *I'm in prison without a bra on,* Drew observed. But at least this new humiliation provided a small distraction from the knot of dread pulsing and roiling in her stomach.

"Have a good day," her mother said. She didn't kiss or hug her daughter. Instead, she waved brightly and took the sidewalk to the right toward the safe, air-conditioned administration building. And Drew was alone again.

"Are you my ride?" she asked the officer waiting in the golf cart. He had a black beard that spread over his jaw like a well-kept patch of lawn. Behind him, an inmate on his way to the administration building stared at them, an avid look on his face. He wore an olive-colored prison jumpsuit. Drew blinked her right eye and he became a green blur. The officer in the golf cart—Jim Espinoza, according to his nametag—gunned the tiny engine.

"Sure. Where you want to go?"

"The school." She climbed in, and the cart lurched as they took off. Buildings flew by. Inmates on various errands turned to watch them zip past.

"So what's your name?" Officer Espinoza asked.

"Drew Daniels." She decided to save him the trouble of asking. "Sara Daniels is my mom."

He turned to scrutinize her, one eye on the road. "You look a lot like her," he concluded.

Drew greeted the office staff after entering the school, seized by a sudden shyness. Sharon Leslie, the blond office manager, introduced her to a cluster of teachers checking their mailboxes in the key room. Drew's cheeks began to ache from smiling too much. Sharon handed Drew a clip full of keys, opened a closet full of office supplies, and began adding things to a cardboard box: paper clips, pens, tape, notepads, a ruler, pencils, a small stapler. Scissors with rounded tips.

"This should hold you for now. Remind me to get you a key for the supply office. Till you have your own, just let me know if you need anything. Sorry to jet, but I've got to make morning announcements on the PA." Sharon squeezed Drew's forearm and grinned, revealing a smudge of lipstick on one of her front teeth.

When she registered Drew's face, she froze. "What? Do I have something in my teeth?" she asked, covering her mouth with the palm of her hand, eyes wide.

Drew pointed at her own teeth. "Um, a little ... lip ... yep, there."

Sharon rubbed her front teeth vigorously with an index finger and whispered an emphatic "Thank you!" before zipping off to her next destination.

After Sharon left, another woman entered the key room. "Hi. You must be Drew." The woman had thick black hair in a short, boyish cut, and tiny teeth like two neat rows of pearled barley. She wore glasses, corduroy pants, brown clogs, and a white polo shirt. "I'm Janet Sutton. I teach Adult Basic Education."

ABE, Drew thought. *Abe Lincoln.*

She clasped Drew's right hand and pumped it firmly up and down twice. "I believe my classroom is across the hall from yours. I'm headed there now, if you'd like to walk with me." As they made their way down the hall, she shared some advice. "Try to get to work during first count at seven-thirty. Then you can walk down to the school across the athletic field undisturbed. Oh, and if you get a chance, you should send your car through the inmate auto detailing program. They do a great job and the price is right." She took a breath. "Let's see. What else. Rich showed you the call button, right?"

Drew shook her head, aware on some distant level that her shoulders were bunched up around her earlobes.

"We all have call buttons near our classroom doors. They're direct links to the office. If a guy gets ugly, hit the button and ask for an officer. He'll haul the guy out. You might have to write a conduct report, but don't worry about that now. Next time I write one, I'll show you how."

They arrived at their neighboring classrooms, but Janet didn't enter her own. Instead, she waited for Drew to unlock hers, and followed her in. Drew set the box of supplies on her new desk and surveyed the room once again. Bleak wasn't the word for it. Sterile in the figurative sense, perhaps. But what would help? Motivational photos? Holiday decorations? A poster featuring that bedraggled *Hang in there* kitty? *Hang in there, you're eligible for parole when you're eligible for Medicare!*

"I love the view you have," Janet sighed, walking to the bank of windows that overlooked the birch-studded courtyard. "My windows give me a view of a brick wall." She walked over to a bookcase and changed the subject abruptly. "Most of the guys are studying to earn their high school equivalency diplomas. Sally kept the study guides here." She pointed to a closet in the back of the room. "I think you'll find practice tests for math, language arts, and social studies in there."

"So why did Sally leave?" Drew couldn't believe she forgot to ask her mother this. When Janet paused, her forehead furrowed with concern, Drew tried to withdraw her question. "You know what? Forget I asked. I don't really need to know. It's not important."

"No, it's okay. She wasn't here that long." Janet leaned against Drew's desk and composed her thoughts. "Basically, she got scared. The inmates liked to mess with her. She was like having a substitute teacher every day. She had no boundaries. Couldn't control them. They would say to her, 'Don't come to work tomorrow. Don't come in. There's going to be trouble.' And nothing would happen, of course, but they'd keep it up, threatening to call her at home, come and find her when they got out, that kind of thing."

Janet flapped a hand dismissively. "Anyway, she wasn't cut out for teaching. Here or in a regular classroom. You do have teaching experience … ?"

"Six years in a public school."

Janet gave Drew a measured look: *Whatever made you leave, it must have been some kicker for you to end up here.*

She didn't ask. Instead, she pushed away from Drew's desk and said brightly, "Well, if you need anything, don't hesitate to ask. I'm right across the hall."

The speaker above the call button clicked, and Sharon's voice summoned Drew back to the school office. Drew spent the remainder of the morning in a back room swimming in paperwork and reading Sally's old files. She'd spend the afternoon alone in her new classroom, organizing books and making some sense of the filing cabinet. And she was perfectly happy to do so. She became gun shy when the first bell rang and inmates poured into the halls, swearing, hooting, and strutting. She peered through the window blinds and watched them shouting and laughing in the school courtyard before the second bell rang. Clusters of men in all shapes and colors, some dressed in the drab green prison uniforms and others wearing T-shirts and jeans. It was like parachuting into a closed social experiment, all the mice in the maze just a little bit rabid.

At noon she walked to the administration building to eat lunch with her mother and realized too late that she'd taken the wrong route, winding up somewhere behind unit fifteen. A group of inmates playing basketball noticed her and began yelling.

"Here, kitty-kitty-kitty!"

"Why you so shy? Come on over here and say hi!"

"Hey, baby, I got a present for yooooou!"

They laughed and whistled. She strode blindly past, fear souring her stomach. One of them rattled the chain link fence. "Hey, bitch! We're talking to you!"

"Shake that ass!"

She heard a van pull up next to her. It was Joe Simon, the officer with the two-hued eyes, but Drew barely noticed.

He rolled down the window. "Hop in."

Drew stepped in gratefully, still hearing the inmates jeering through the walls of the van. Her hands trembled. This was already light years from teaching in Eau Claire, which was what she wanted, she guessed. She was surprised, and maybe a little alarmed, to discover that though her hands were shaking, she was also strangely excited.

"The animals are restless today. You okay?"

Drew nodded, heart pounding in her ears. "Thanks for stopping." She shifted her lunch bag and struggled for normalcy.

"Well, you looked a little lost," he said. "Heading to the admin building?"

"Yeah." *But I really just want to go home.*

As they pulled to a stop, Joe pointed out a pair of pheasants venturing out of the dark woods on the other side of the fence. They watched the birds strut through the understory shrubbery for a few seconds: a mother hen and one gangly teenage chick. After five seconds that felt more like half an hour, he said, "A bunch of us are going to the fireworks this Saturday, if you want to come."

"Thanks, but I'm spending the day with my family." His timing was off. Drew suddenly imagined Joe as a paramedic, hitting on accident victims as they bled to death in the back of the ambulance. As the world washed in and out in those final moments, they'd look up and see his mismatched eyes, and the last emotion they'd feel before the lights faded would be utter confusion.

"Some other time," he said, smiling.

Drew wobbled into the administration building and fell into the nearest bathroom, locking herself in a stall. Three other women used and left the lavatory while she hid, her pulse finally slowing to a more reasonable pace as the hot air hand dryer cycled down for the last time.

By late afternoon Drew met all but five of the thirty-five teachers, got fingerprinted and photographed for her ID badge, and filled out more paperwork in her mother's office. She felt oddly thrilled, anticipating the reactions she'd get when she told people she worked in a prison. Not everybody could say they worked with thieves or con artists. Except maybe paralegals and political interns.

Drew busied herself making copies, selecting books she wanted to stock her bookshelves with, learning the layout of the prison, watching William Bishop administer a GED test to nine inmates. She would enter the classroom next week.

It was Thursday, July second. Friday was a holiday for Drew and every other non-security employee—the kickoff to a long Fourth of July weekend. For the first time in her life, she had no plans for a vacation day. For the second time in her life she felt completely lost, with no map in the glove compartment.

5. GRAHAM

I'm okay-looking, I think. Girls tell me I have nice eyes. I wasn't a big jock in school, but I wasn't a couch potato, either. I've got decent arms and shoulders (thanks, chair model Invacare Compass XE!) and my teeth are straight and only three shades away from the maximum whiteness possible, according to my Crest White Strips chart. My hair looks like it's been taking diet pills, but my head is smooth, well-shaped, and unblemished. I don't have nostrils you could store bowling balls in. Most importantly, my features are symmetrical. Isn't that supposed to rate highly among the opposite sex?

But here I am, divorced, no real romantic options in sight. Not even any curiosity or pity sex prospects, which aren't that hard to find in some dark corner after last call. I know, it wouldn't matter if I were Bradley Cooper. I've got deeper emotional and honesty issues to deal with. But when you consider my inability to be forthcoming all of the time in the grand scheme of personality defects a person could have, it barely registers. I mean, I could be a member of the Westboro Baptist Church. I could litter, hand out raw onions on

Halloween, lean on the horn when I drive past golf courses or outdoor Jenga tournaments. I could wear pinky rings and bow ties and think I actually looked good doing so.

My biggest problem is that sometimes I get a little bitter. Even incidents of *timing* in the historical record can do the trick. For example, I feel pretty gypped by the kind of music that was popular in my formative years. Marcy Playground has nearly ruined sex and candy for a lot of people, and the summer of 1998 was exceptionally cruel, thanks to Ace of Base. And I know hair bands are enjoying a resurgence, but let's leave Poison and Slaughter where they belong: in the novels of Chuck Palahniuk. Don't get me started on what people wore back then. Zubaz tiger-print pants, denim overalls, neon Hypercolor shirts, and multicolored silk shirts? For men!? Had everyone developed brain damage from hearing Urkel's catchphrase one too many times? Did the mirror industry bottom out between 1990 and 1995? It's amazing the birth rate didn't drop completely off the charts back then, because I can't imagine anyone fucking a guy with Billy Ray Cyrus hair and a tendency to call his friends "fartknockers." Yet it happened. And often, if Generation Y is to be explained.

Of course my parents, who came of age in the early seventies, had no appreciation whatsoever for the kind of music that formed the soundtrack to their youth. Zeppelin? The Who? The Stones, Rush, Pink Floyd, David Bowie? Forget it. You could safely bet your firstborn child that the hi-fi in their first apartment was playing songs by groups that could have been named for dishes served at a Tupperware party: Peaches and Herb, A Taste of Honey, Ambrosia, Bread. Auditory laxatives designed to propel the status quo into a sunset of mundane.

Where was I? Right. Bitterness. I try, I really try not to get bitter and pissy about people, but I make an exception for Joe Simon. You ever hear those ads on the radio for local jewelers selling long-stemmed roses that have been dipped in gold leaf and retail for fifty-nine dollars? You ever wonder who actually buys that shit? Joe Simon. That's who. I don't like stereotypes, but you're going to get a certain image in your mind when I tell you he hunts, is on a first-name basis with all the girls at The Tilted Kilt, gets shitfaced at Packer games, and owns a four-wheeled all-terrain vehicle he uses to "tear it up."

Excuse me while I puke into next Thursday.

He's also screwed half of the single female employees at Lakeside, and a few married ones too. He's clearly someone trying to get the most out of his youth before it evaporates, leaving him gassy and paunchy in an easy chair before a football game on Thanksgiving, or drunk and sentimental at the local tavern, reminiscing about a 2007 football game with an arm slung around the shoulders of old high school friends while they sing along to Springsteen's "Glory Days," playing over and over and over on the juke.

Okay, maybe this is a little too bitter.

But does his youthful vitality have to be so in my face all the goddam time?

I go to the admin building after my final group session of the day to get a Coke from the break room. Joe Simon is there, of course, because I have the luck of an Indian cotton farmer in debt to Monsanto. I catch the tail end of a conversation in which another officer named Tony Kaplan is chiding him about how long it'll be before he gets Drew Daniels in the sack.

"I give you seven days, tops," Tony says. He clasps his hands behind his hairy neck and kicks back against the white cinderblock wall.

Joe makes a smug face like, *We'll have to wait and see!* and I want to punch him right in his disgusting Skoal hole. Drew, if she's anything like she was in high school, has better sense than to bottom-feed with a guy like this. Back then she was an A student, making better dating decisions than most of the girls in our class. We flirted shamelessly in our chem lab, trading enough sexual innuendoes to stock a complete season of *Family Guy*, but it never really progressed beyond that—a fact that still disappoints me. Back then, she dated a guy two years older than us. He was away at college in La Crosse, which made flirting remarkably pressure-free, because hey, she already had her man! She was emotionally available but physically unavailable, and I found her irresistible. Unfortunately, we never became more than lab mates, our breezy friendship limited to playful hallway smacks, bad jokes about Bunsen burners, the occasional beer bong at a party.

Well, aside from one night at the beginning of our junior year, when Drew came over after a fight with her boyfriend. We watched *Good Will Hunting* in my basement, sharing a bottle of peach schnapps that we hid behind a throw pillow every time my mom came down the creaky stairs. Ostensibly, to do about seventy loads of laundry. Drew was curled up on the other side of the old orange sofa, but an hour into the movie, she leaned back against one of the armrests and casually lifted her feet onto my lap. Her calves, really, and she had a skirt on. Bare legs. I immediately began to panic. Didn't know what to do with my hands. It was the kind of friendly, affectionate thing girls might do with any of their friends, but I felt a big question mark on the end. She may as well have punched me in the balls, because I sat there for the next hour with the most painful hard-on I'd ever had in my life, compounded by the fact that my jeans were too tight and there was no way I was giving away my state with even a subtle adjustment. I have no idea how the movie ended, because a 3-D porno had begun to play in my head, of me pushing her skirt up and doing hot, filthy things to her that would have been scrambled on cable. But I just sat there frozen like an idiot, my dick an iron rod in my pants, wondering if I should try to kiss her, paranoid that my breath smelled like Cool Ranch Doritos, wanting her to stay forever but also wanting her to leave so I could breathe again. The next weekend she took a road trip with Brooke to visit her boyfriend in college. When she returned, she was wearing a new pair of diamond earrings. She never came back to my house, which was just as well, because I had no idea how to handle a girl like Drew when I was sixteen.

I move smoothly to the vending machine and plug in a few quarters. While I make my selection I toss over my shoulder, "She's a bit out of your league." My soda tumbles to the bottom and I reach in to retrieve it.

Though I can't see them, I can tell Joe and Tony have exchanged looks. "How would you know, Wheels?"

Yeah, did I forget to mention they sometimes call me "Wheels?" Oh, the wit. See how it soars! I crack open my soda, take a sip to prolong the suspense, and say, "I went to high school with her."

There's a beat of silence, and then Tony jumps in. "D'ja bang her?" I can almost hear his future children eating dirt in the front yard, wiping the boogers they don't eat on lampshades, and throwing bits of eraser at children who are much smarter and more sensitive than they.

I turn to face him and roll my eyes. "Grow up."

"What for?"

She'd better not sleep with him. I will lose the last remaining molecule of faith I have in humanity if she does.

God, I can't wait to see her again. And I'm not even that bitter about the timing.

As I pack my bag to leave for the day I think about Joe, and guys like him. This town breeds two kinds of men: guys like Joe who end up working the trades or becoming keepers of the human zoo here at Lakeside, and guys who grew up near the beach and left long ago for Big Ten schools, after which who knows what. Careers on Wall Street maybe. Apartments in Manhattan, Chicago, or Boston. Vacations heli-skiing in British Columbia or ascending Mount Kilimanjaro, returning home only reluctantly for the occasional holiday or funeral.

Situated on the western shore of Lake Michigan and named for the glacier that covered Wisconsin during the last ice age, Laurentide Bay is *the* summer destination for many of Chicago's and Milwaukee's wealthy. Their homes—some vacation, some permanent residences—loom from the dunes and woodlands beyond. Tourism, as you might have guessed, is big here, and many of the year-round residents depend on area motels, restaurants, shops, and sport fishing charters for income. The rest of us work at Lakeside Correctional, on the west side of town. To us, it really is a company town. To most everyone else, it's a nice place to go for seafood and beachfront sunrises. Hardly anyone cares that at least one inmate manages to escape every ten years or so. It's never an inmate from an urban area, though. They don't hit the fence because *"There's bears and shit in them woods."*

Because commuting an hour between Laurentide Bay and Green Bay or Milwaukee isn't completely unfeasible, a surprising number of the town's wealthier residents live here permanently, enrolling their children in the local public elementary school. And for a while, a kid who lives in a duplex on the west side of town has things in common with a kid who spends Christmas break at a lodge in Aspen. Sure, the kids from the east side have more toys, but at that age there are things everyone can agree on: Girls are gross, farts are hilarious, and games involving rocks, spray paint, and fire are much preferable to checkers. The class tension lies dormant until puberty, when most of the beachfront kids have been packed off to prep schools, only returning only for Christmas and easy summer jobs.

At that point, when it becomes cloyingly obvious who the haves and the have-nots are, you can guess with a high degree of accuracy who will buy their living room furniture from *Dwell*-featured designers in fifteen years, and who will rent theirs from *Get it Now!* Futures have been charted. Anyone who diverges from their pre-packaged path becomes a local celebrity, as Rick Holmen did when he joined the crew of *Bath Crashers*, lending his carpentry skills to various surprise home improvement projects on national television once a week. The trick is that you have to leave Laurentide Bay for this to happen.

I zip my duffel bag shut and lock my office behind me—always a task that brings me a measure of relief until I remember that I'll be returning to unlock the door and repeat my day all over again in fourteen short hours, seven of which are reserved for sleep, thirty minutes of which are lost to my commute, another thirty minutes of which I spend eating a single-serving frozen entree, and roughly two hours of which I devote to personal hygiene (which takes a lot longer when you're in a wheelchair, believe me) and the opening and reading of mail. Which leaves a few brief hours to lead some kind of life. Usually, I spend those few hours watching TV or sucking fantastically at the latest game I've picked up for my Xbox. Sometimes I do a little mate-shopping on the various online dating sites I subscribe to, although that activity has lost its luster of late.

In short, my life is a cautionary tale, if you could stay awake long enough to listen.

Which is why I'm looking forward to seeing Drew. She is someone who knew me as a completely mobile, truth-telling young man with a full head of hair. She is someone who knew me when I had a life and she is someone who could possibly resurrect that life. She represents sheer *possibility*: of happiness, of adventure, of the new and improved, even the possibility of heartbreak. And when your life has become as predictable as mine, even the possibility of heartbreak is welcome. Anything to shake up the soul-sucking routine.

I push down the shadow-laced hall, say goodnight to the second-shift guards in the control room, say goodnight to our perky slip of a warden, Leslie Atkins. Yes, our warden is a woman. The State of Wisconsin is big on diversity, and Lakeside is a case in point. While ninety-nine percent of clerical staff is female and eighty-five percent of security staff is male, gender equity is making great strides in the institutional white collar careers left for the rest of us. The gender split for social workers and teachers, for example, is pretty much fifty-fifty. And though only ten percent of Wisconsin residents are minorities, about a quarter of Lakeside staff is. Unfortunately, seventy percent of inmates at Lakeside are black, Hispanic, American Indian, Asian, or other—not exactly consistent with larger state population trends.

And as for diversity in hiring, I'm practically their poster boy. I've been in two publicity photo shoots in the past five years alone, along with second-shifter Nick Nguyen and Keisha Martin from the Program Review Committee.

I wheel toward an inmate in standard-issue prison greens. He's carrying a manila folder, headed my way. When he sees me, his face breaks into a broad grin. "Mr. Finch! Howzit rollin'? You still teaching that anger management class?"

I scan my mind as I try to place him—*one gold front tooth, neat corn rows, chubby cheeks, loping gait*—I think I had him in that very class last fall. My mind clicks, and now I even have his name: Dante King. I smile back. "Hey, Mr. King! How's it going?"

As I watch his grin slide into disappointment, I realize I've gotten his name wrong. "It's Dante Hargrove," he says flatly.

Fuck. Watch me demonstrate an attitude that most black inmates suspect all white people share: *Y'all look alike anyway; why don't we just call you Toby?* Fuckety-fuck. I close my eyes, shake my head, and tap my temple. If I could have managed another gesture that conveys my embarrassment and desire to right my mistake, I would have done so. "Damn. I'm sorry, Dante. My brain is fried right now. Long day."

"S'aight. Hey, you have a good one," Dante Hargrove says, tipping his folder at me as he passes. I know most people wouldn't give a shit about hurting an inmate's feelings, but Christ, sometimes it's all they've got left.

Right at that moment, when my face is warm with shame and I'm feeling mentally askew, I spot Drew, her low heels clacking across the cool tile floor, her shiny dark hair parted on the right and pulled into a straight ponytail against the nape of her neck. I used to fantasize about pressing my lips into the slow curve of that neck, inhaling the cherry almond scent that sometimes drifted my way during chem labs. She's wearing appropriate prison attire—khaki dress slacks and a white short-sleeved blouse—that on anyone else might look unimaginative and even frumpy, but on her, underscores the clean, long lines of her frame. Then I zoom in on her individual features: her slightly crooked but proportional nose, her narrow wrists, the freckles that dapple her tanned forearms. It's hard to tell from this distance, but it appears her nails are still short, though from pragmatism or the nervous chewing habit she maintained in high school, I can't tell.

I wonder if she's in the building to find her mother. I wonder if I'll always want her. I think the answer to both is "Yes."

"Drew!" I wheel toward her, my mouth curving into a reflexive smile. "Drew Daniels!" My pulse begins to jog.

She freezes, confusion flashing through her wide brown eyes.

"It's me—Graham. Graham Finch." I wait for a beat, not wanting to embarrass myself by having to add, *"From high school?"* My gut twists as another second passes in which she fails to recognize me.

Finally a warm look of recognition seeps into her features while our eyes connect. The look morphs to surprise when she takes in the rest of me, and my chair. "Oh! Graham! Hi! Is it really you?"

"I was going to say, 'Just kidding, it's Pedro Martinez,' but I didn't want to confuse you more." Oh my God. Weird much? But she laughs, and it's like a tinkling of tiny bells, a skipping of happy children, a sprinkling of fairy dust.

"What are you doing here?"

"Earning a meager paycheck. The real question is, what are *you* doing here?" She even *smells* pretty—clean and subtle and soft, like the perfect kiss goodnight.

She sighs. "Long story. I'll tell you about it sometime over lunch."

"Sure." *Lunch is too short. How about dinner? How about a long weekend in Vermont? How about the rest of our lives together, over breakfast?*

"Wow, it's been a long time," she adds, studying me. Her forehead scrunches slightly, and I know she's wondering whether or not to ask The Question. I decide to save her the trouble.

"Car accident. It's *my* long story."

"I'm so sorry. God, Graham, I'd heard something about the accident, but I …" She lets her sentence drift away.

I shake my head. "Thanks, but I'm fine. No worries."

Three pregnant seconds tick by. An inmate singing a vibrato-rich R&B song at full volume breaks the spell as he passes us on his way to the health services unit. Drew's eyes widen. "Hey, I've got to run. My mom and I drove together, so I've got to catch her before she leaves without me. But it was great to see you again." She pauses and then makes my evening by adding, "Want to meet for lunch next Monday?"

Are Japanese game shows goofy?

6. DREW

On the way home from work, Sara Daniels pulled up to a stop sign at an intersection and waited. Eight cars passed, with nearly forty seconds between vehicles. The blinker tick-tocked, tick-tocked.

"Punch it!"

Drew's mother squinted. "No, there's a car coming."

Drew craned her neck to see tiny headlights over a mile away. "Where? In Delaware?"

Tick-tock-tick-tock.

"Okay, go now! Go!"

"I can't! Don't you see that car?"

"You mean the one pulling out of a driveway in Fargo right at this very moment?" She scanned the highway. "Okay, it's clear. Go! Quick!"

Sara, startled, hit the gas pedal and the car jerked ahead. Drew slammed back into the passenger seat. Just as quickly Sara stomped on the brake, and Drew lurched forward, her head snapping toward the windshield. The seat belt locked painfully against her ribs and Sara's right arm swung out over her daughter's chest. "Drew, do you want us to have an accident?" After a tractor trundled past twenty seconds later, Sara finally decided to turn, in a wide, cautious arc. "There," she said with a nice chunk of self-satisfaction in her tone.

"I think you might need to get your eyes checked."

"My eyes are fine," Sara said dismissively. She looked at Drew and smiled. "So," she said, "I saw you talking with Graham Finch after work."

"So," Drew replied in return, "do you find this interesting?"

"As a matter of fact, I do. I like Graham. He graduated with you, right?"

Drew nodded.

"I thought so. Didn't he drive an old DeSoto?"

She turned to catch her mother's eye. "How do you remember that?"

"I don't know. Not everyone drives a DeSoto, I guess."

"Yet you forgot to tell me when Frank died." Frank had been their family cat for ten years. He was black and white and a little brain-damaged, and the whole family loved him, especially his lopsided gait and the way he'd sometimes lose his balance and fall face-first into his food while trying to eat. He may not have been the brightest bulb on the Christmas tree, but he was the prettiest, with long, fluffy hair and clear green eyes. The neighborhood female cat posse loved him, and once Wendy and Drew were shocked to observe him mating with one of them—not because they didn't think he had kitty urges like his smarter feline peers, but because he was doing so lying on his side. Frank died under a hosta one warm June morning, and Drew's mother forgot to tell her until a month had passed.

"I don't forget these things on purpose! It just happens. I have too much on my mind."

In all fairness, she probably did. She extended herself at work, often putting in overtime and volunteering for assorted committees on her own initiative. She donated what was left to her various charitable causes, which had recently made more demands on her time since she was elected Sergeant at Arms of the Daughters of Saint Catherine Holy Family in the Name of the Good Shepherd Relief Society. When Drew asked what her Sergeant at Arms responsibilities entailed, her mother had quipped, "Smack down any old ladies that talk too much at meetings. Oh, and I lead the opening prayer."

They pulled into the driveway to find Drew's father in the garage tinkering with his latest cowsucker: a 325-piece thimble collection he bought at a recent junk sale for twenty-five dollars. A cowsucker, as defined by Drew's family, was a senseless contraption cobbled together, usually with duct tape, to yield some kind of questionable function. Wire hangers and tinfoil bent onto an old television set to improve the reception? Cowsucker. Wooden heel glued onto the sole of one shoe to facilitate walking for someone with a lazy hip? Cowsucker. The dickie? Ugly cowsucker. Nearly everything labeled *As Seen on TV?* Major cowsuckers, all.

Here, her father's thimble collection served three functions. One, it gave him more items to hoard and fuss over; two, since he hoped to catalog and then re-sell the entire collection on eBay, it might provide a small return on his initial investment; and three, it gave the rest of them something new to tease him about. In Drew's family, this was considered more valuable than a Kate Jackson sighting at the Laurentide Bay Fourth of July Fireworks Spectacular, or good ventilation during a visit with Grandpa Jim.

Drew climbed out of the car. "How's your hobby in a bucket?"

"Good, good," her father replied, nonplussed. "Come check this one out. A commemorative thimble from the 1939 World's Fair! That's probably worth a lot of money. If you're lucky, I'll leave it to you in my will."

"Truly, I am the luckiest girl alive."

"Say, how was your first day? Did they put you on the fast track to warden?" He suddenly cocked his head. A bird was warbling in the shrubbery behind the garage. "Do you hear that?"

Drew smiled. "Northern Cardinal."

He nodded, eyebrows raised expectantly. This was her prompt for the rest.

"*Cardinalis Cardinalis.*" There was a long stretch between the ages of twelve and twenty-five where Drew didn't indulge him like this, but it made him happy. The fact that she didn't even pretend to be embarrassed by this now made her suddenly feel old. She had reached the gray, nostalgic wasteland behind Too Cool For Your Parents, where it finally hits you that they won't be around forever, and neither will you.

"That's my girl."

"Just call me Charlie McCarthy."

"Okay, Charlie. Hey, tell Mom I put the hamburger in the sink to defrost like she asked."

Drew's parents had been calling each other "Mom" and "Dad" for years, which struck her as creepy when she actually thought about it. As for the hamburger, you could rest assured that it wouldn't find a home in ketchup-drenched loaf-form, doing the heavy lifting for the noodles in Hamburger Helper, or even pressed between a bun, the way God intended. At Drew's house, meat rebelled against conformity. Having seen the weekly dinner menu taped to the fridge earlier in the day, she knew that tonight's meat would take the shape of bierock: a pastry pocket stuffed with cabbage, onion, and hamburger. You cut your bierock in half and butter each steaming cone of meat, like it's a dinner roll.

That last part bears repeating. *You butter the meat.* Fine Wisconsin supper clubs have been buttering prime rib for years, having no need to keep kosher, as perhaps one Jewish person has dined at the Fin & Feather since 1978, and that was the result of a wrong turn off I-94, but it just seemed ... *wrong.* Drew hated having friends over for dinner in grade school because inevitably, the menu would include old favorites like crockpot pizza festooned with green peppers the size of solar panels, or creamed chipped beef on toast. And when her friends balked at eating the latter, her father would say, "What? You don't like Shit on a Shingle? Everybody likes Shit on a Shingle!"

While her mother went upstairs to change into after-work sweats, Drew picked up a bag of Chex Mix and plopped onto the couch, flipping through afternoon television. She felt like she was back in high school, which was actually a relief after the year she'd had. Through some miracle of syndication, *That '70s Show* was on every channel. When Topher Grace grew bewildered about something it reminded her of Graham. She'd heard about his accident after it happened and remembered thinking, *How awful!* over and over again. When she told Ben, that was his reply, too. "How awful!"

But he hadn't known Graham, and there was this bright undercurrent beneath his statement: *Thank God it wasn't me.* Drew wondered what being confined to a wheelchair would be like. She closed her eyes and imagined she was paralyzed, right there on the couch. She made her legs dead weight. Pretended she couldn't move them. What a claustrophobic sensation! She wondered if he could have sex. Well, probably, but could he feel anything?

At that moment her mother entered the living room wearing a small pink and white T-shirt. When Drew realized what the shirt said, she sat up, alarmed.

"Where'd you get that?"

"From the T-shirt fairy!"

"I thought I threw that out."

"Now you see what happens when you let your parents clean up after you."

This was a loaded statement.

Her mother was wearing a T-shirt that Drew had been given by an Emergency Medical Technician when she was fourteen and needed medical evacuation by helicopter after drinking enough brandy to kill herself. The T-shirt read, *I took a mediflight and lived to tell about it.*

A warm wave of studio audience laughter washed from the television. One person was laughing above the crowd with a booming, obnoxious chuckle. Sara bebopped around the living room, clapping her hands and electric sliding into an end table.

"Why are you wearing that?" Drew was too exhausted by the day to hide her annoyance.

Lost in a bad, imaginary audition for *So You Think You Can Dance*, Sara raised the roof for a few seconds before shifting into a new move that made her daughter blush. "The inmates call this 'crunking.'"

"If you ever do that at a wedding, we don't know each other. I don't know you, you don't know me. We leave at different times, in different vehicles."

"By the way, I saw Brooke Walters at Festival Foods last week. Wonder if she still has her T-shirt?" Sara did the Hustle on her way into the kitchen.

Drew was with Brooke the night she drank enough brandy to pickle her liver. Enough brandy will kill a person, but invincible fourteen-year-olds don't dwell on such inconvenient facts. Luckily Brooke's mother returned home from her Lady's Sodality meeting to find her daughter and Drew—blanched in booze and vomit, passed out on her white leather couch—before they reached that end. A frantic race to the local emergency room ensued; unfortunately, Laurentide Bay's only ER didn't have the right equipment to run the full battery of tests that would determine all of the substances they'd consumed, so a mediflight had to be called in to transport the girls to a larger, better-equipped facility in Green Bay, where it was determined that they'd ingested only a toxic amount of alcohol. No heroin, no cocaine, no MDMA, no prescription drugs. Initiate stomach-pumping sequence. Activate home-bound punishment term.

The phone rang, and Drew's father stopped flipping through the day's mail to pick it up. A second later he held the receiver out for her. "It's for you, Charlie."

She went into the kitchen but paused before answering. Everyone of even marginal significance to her knew her cell phone number and would have called that instead. It was probably a plea for money from the local volunteer firefighters' organization. When Drew was in high school, her father always gave her the telemarketer calls, to be funny. "Hello?" She braced herself for the sales pitch.

"Is it a boy?" her mother stage-whispered to her father.

"No," he loudly whispered back on his way to the living room, "it's the Bad Influence."

"Drew Daniels," Brooke said on the other end of the line, "I thought you'd never come back!"

Drew was almost too surprised to respond—how often does someone call right when you're thinking of them?

"Hi, Brooke!" Sara yelled while she rummaged through the refrigerator.

Drew shot her mother a look before returning her attention to the phone. "This is so weird! We were just talking about you."

"Well, I was just thinking about you! Did your mom tell you we ran into each other at the store last week? She said you were home again."

"Yep. And she's wearing my old mediflight T-shirt."

They laughed together in familiar two-part harmony. "Wow, that thing fits her? It's got to be too small for most kids."

"She is very childlike," Drew said, frowning and shooing her mother away. Sara stuck her tongue out at her daughter and finally left the kitchen. "Oh my God, it's like I'm sixteen again, only with my own car and way more baggage in the trunk."

"Can you meet me at Finnegan's at eight?" Brooke asked. "We have so much to catch up on." A memory lit up Drew's mind like a flare: the time Brooke hung up on her in a rage when Drew told her she couldn't go to a party because she wanted to study for her ACT exam.

"I know," Drew agreed. "I haven't talked to you in forever."

She knew on some level that there was a reason for that, but whatever it was felt thin and forgettable. The transient shadow of a dissipating cloud. Years had passed since they'd spent much time together, but people mellow with age. They grow wiser, different.

Don't they?

7. GRAHAM

After I get home from work I eat my freshly nuked chicken pot pie and bathe in the white glow of my computer screen. A cheerful bell indicates that I have two new e-mails in my inbox from women I've "met" online. I'm sure nothing will come of either correspondence, but I roll up my sleeves to read and reply anyway. Autumn is younger—a gamer and former Army brat who has to be one of the oddest girls I've met online. She goes to Comic-Con every year, and I have a feeling she's working up the courage to confess to something really weird, like being sexually aroused by balloons. Or maybe she's a furry. My other pen pal, Kendra, is Autumn's polar opposite. Her hair has never been a bright shade of magenta, and I'm going out on a limb here, but I think I can safely say that Kendra has zero interest in doing the "Run for Your Lives" zombie-infested 5K obstacle run. Which I'd totally do if I could. Benign as a pudding cup, Kendra litters her messages to me with LOLs and exclamation marks and smiley faces. Both girls are cute, if their photos are somewhat accurate, but I don't spend my days wondering if I'll hear back from either of them. Shrug, nod, reply, repeat. *Nothing to see here, folks, move along.*

When I recall what my marriage was like, it sometimes amazes me that I'm willing to dust myself off and get back on the horse that tossed me. The night of my friend Greg's wedding—the night of the accident that curtailed my mobility five years ago—started off innocently enough; in fact, I have footage of it. I'm walking through the house, narrating my way to my wife Caitlin, who was rolling her hair into fat curlers in the upstairs bathroom. "Graham," she scolded around the bobby pin pressed between her lips, "Get out of here! I need to make myself pretty." Caitlin was already very pretty, of course. And like most pretty girls, she knew it. You'd have better luck eliminating malaria worldwide than getting her to admit it, though.

I whispered into the video camera, "Witness the natural habitat of the American female. Her preening is designed to lure the best mate possible. One who will stalk her with a camcorder while she readies herself for a social function."

"Gra-ham," she sing-songed, curling another chunk of her blond hair around a hot roller.

"The female is losing patience. Witness the flushed cheeks, the huffy exhalation—"

She stood, facing me with hands on hips, scowling. Half of her hair frizzed to the left; the remainder trained cylindrically against her soft cheeks. "I'm leaving, I'm leaving!" I said, retreating. "But hurry up, we're running late."

I only remember all of this because I've watched the video dozens of times since. Marveling at how tall I was. How innocent we were at that exact moment, how unaware of the massive changes awaiting us at the tail-end of the evening.

I read Autumn's e-mail first. *Greetings, Graham. What's the news? Sixpence for your thoughts. News here is limited. I anticipate your response. Hammer of Justice!* No concluding thoughts, no signature. Well, maybe that was the Hammer of Justice bit. I'm not sure how I feel about dating a World of Warcraft fanatic.

I knew Greg's wedding was doomed after Caitlin's fourth rum and Coke. She got mean and histrionic when she drank, and already her eyes had that loose, accusatory glint. I don't remember many of the details from earlier in the evening—I remember the bride's grandmother pinching my ass and winking at me (the last woman to pinch my backside), and I remember our waiter dropping a full tray of entrees intended for our table. I spent more than ninety bucks buying drinks and shots for people. I recall slow-dancing with Caitlin to Louis Armstrong's "What a Wonderful World," trading hushed barbs through our smiling lips while we stiffly shifted from foot to foot amidst happier-looking couples.

I read Kendra's e-mail next. *Hi Graham. How are you? I'm fine. Not much new here. What's new with you? We should get together soon. Well, I have to run. Bye!*

Later in the evening I overheard Caitlin saying something salacious to Derek Raddish, who played shortstop for the Laurentide Bay Waves in high school. I leaned against the bar next to her, grinning, waiting for her reaction to my presence. "Well, look who's here," she said. "We were just talking about you!"

Oh really? I thought. *And what do I have to do with the kind of lingerie you prefer?* I decided it was time to leave. We were both drunk, and the further we slipped into that state, the larger our argument on the way home was going to be. We said good-bye to our friends and leaked out the door, boozed up and ready to rumble.

I reply to Autumn first. *Hammer of Justice, huh? No seal of command? I don't think my thoughts are worth sixpence, but I appreciate the thought. How much is sixpence, anyway?* Here is someone who doesn't give a rat's sweet ass what anyone thinks about her. I continue to play along because there's something intriguing about that. It's not every day that you meet someone who could be the runty little love child of Dwight Schrute and Miss Havisham.

"I'm driving, Caitlin. I'm not as drunk as you." Crickets chirped and moths looped around the fluorescent lights illuminating the parking lot. The lights emphasized the dark shadows under Caitlin's eyes and I remember thinking, *This is how she'll look when she's old.*

"The hell if you're driving. You could start a fire with your breath."

I sighed deeply. "I'd tell you to be reasonable, but why start now?" Bass thumped through the walls of the reception hall, the music screaming briefly through the doors whenever someone came outside for a cigarette.

Caitlin walked to the driver's side of her Ford Mustang convertible (an ostentatious car I'd never have purchased for myself) and pulled the keys from her purse in an angry jingle. I remember the way the light bounced from them, glittering and blinding. "I'm driving. Deal with it."

Next I reply to Kendra. *Hi you. I'm fine. Not too much new.* I pause, already exhausted by the inanity of it all. I don't see this one getting weirdly entertaining. This is a woman whose answer to my every question would be, "I don't care. Whatever you want to do." I foresee a future of couches encased in clear plastic, of foundation hedges trimmed to within an inch of their lives, of dry turkey and enough routine to erase my entire personality, and I almost hit delete, but I don't. Maybe she's not an e-mail person. Maybe she's scintillating in person. I type, *Would you like to get together for coffee next week? My schedule's pretty open … whatever works for you.* I let my fingers hover over the keyboard for a few seconds longer and add, *I've got something I need to tell you.* I press the enter key and close my eyes. If I listen closely, I can hear my life swirling down the kitchen drain. I decide to pour myself a drink, and do so. Jack Daniel's and Coke. *Fuck the bladder, we've got a catheter!* It could be the next big slogan. I settle back in at the computer and go shopping for love.

Journey's "Girl Can't Help It" was playing on the radio. The red lights from the dashboard were reflected in corners of my glasses, and I stared through them thinking, "Damn right, she's just that way" in the melodramatic way you do when you're drunk, when the world is buzzing around you and you're the most insightful, soulful bastard on the planet. *Hell yeah, Steve Perry.* The cold night wind whipped through our hair. I think Caitlin left the top down so we couldn't hear one another. So we wouldn't have to talk.

You never think that you're going to be paralyzed when you're listening to Journey with your eyes closed, thinking back to the first time you heard the song on the oldies station in grade school, when you're annoyed with your new wife but you know you'll make up later. It shouldn't happen that way. But that's how it happened to me. I opened my eyes in time to catch a family of five raccoons lumbering across the road ahead of the car. In the headlights of the Mustang they looked massive, bear-like. "Caitlin, look out!"

I've had months. Years. To reflect on that statement. If only I'd kept my eyes closed. If only I'd kept my mouth shut. What compelled me to say that? Empathy for some goddam raccoons? Habit? Irritation at Caitlin, always headed straightaway for the drama?

If I'd kept my eyes closed, my mouth shut, I'd be walking today, maybe. I'm sure I'd still be divorced. But I'd have walked out of the courtroom an intact man. Physically, at least.

"Oh shit," she said in a monotone, and I remember her voice being calm, the kind of calm laced with icy alarm that means you're really in trouble. Things are slingshotting beyond your control. She stomped the brake, cranking the steering wheel hard left. The tires squealed, the raccoons scattered, the headlights sprayed out across an old hayfield as the car thundered violently into the ditch, careening, hitting a boulder or post or some small piece of forgotten farm equipment, and *God why didn't I wear my seat belt.*

I became a rock flung from a catapult, flying through the field, crumpling, barreling into the earth, my hips twisting and snapping into an absurd origami-angle, my upper body cartwheeling over again, slamming into the earth. The dented car slid to a smoking, ticking stop behind me. Headlights blared into my half-lidded eyes. I found my breath again. Gasping. Pain squeezing me like a lime, urgent and bright. *My head.* It felt like the end of the world, doomsday, a plague of locusts and a rain of fire in my torso, in my arms, in my brain. But nothing in my legs. *Something is broken inside me.* "Caitlin," I wheezed, tasting blood. *Something is very wrong.* "Caitlin." I gave up and slid into the dark, and it was like slipping into a warm pool.

I didn't speak again for four days.

There is a world between that life and the life I live now, and I don't like to revisit that world often. It is a planet of sterile hallways, moaning patients, endless physical therapy to retrain my damaged muscles. I even had a hospital-appointed social worker, which turned out to be one of the few things I found amusing during the whole ordeal.

The verdict? I had a swollen brain, internal bleeding, three broken ribs, a broken ankle, and I was completely paralyzed at my T11 lumbar vertebra: highly unlikely to walk again, but retaining full use of my upper body, including arms and hands. A paraplegic. Which means I'm one of the luckier ones. Every spinal cord injury is different; some people lose only partial movement in their limbs. Others—the quads—can lose almost every sensation from the neck down, save for the occasional spasm, tingling, or phantom pain. But despite my particular good fortune (in the full spectrum of possible outcomes), it took me years to appreciate it.

Caitlin, a creature of habit even when inebriated, had been wearing her seat belt. She escaped with a few cuts and bruises. She was lucky, because she narrowly avoided any citations related to drunk driving. By the time the police arrived and began to piece together what happened, I guess she'd scared herself sober. Or she hadn't been that drunk to begin with …

In the post-accident wasteland where I adjusted to my new reality, Caitlin and I self-destructed. Caitlin wasn't cruel; she would never leave a paralyzed husband for that fact alone. The real reason she left is more painful to admit: After the accident, I became kind of an asshole. A petulant, pissed-at-my-handicap-accessible-shower, my new-assistive-driving-device, and my newly-widened-doorways asshole. I threw things. I cried. I drank so much my hangovers would last for days. I became someone even my mother would rather speak to long distance than in person.

Caitlin tried for a while. But she could only put up with so much. She was young, she still had a chance. We'd been married for one year, shakily for half of it. I gave her an easy out. We hired a mediator for an amicable split, financially and emotionally. I later realized that personal independence was probably one of the best things that could have happened to me at the time.

I last saw Caitlin the day of our divorce. We were in the parking lot of the courthouse after the papers had been filed, wondering how to say goodbye. I handed over Caitlin's final box of stuff—Christmas ornaments, I think—and we hugged one last time. Now she's married to a chiropractor in Boston.

And I'm a wheelchair-bound social worker employed by the Wisconsin Department of Corrections, shopping for love alone on the eve of a national holiday weekend.

8. DREW

Drew met Brooke in Mrs. Miller's rowdy first-grade class of 1988, the year *Big* premiered and Greg Louganis biffed his head on the diving board at the Seoul Olympics. She was the new kid at Wilson Elementary that fall, boarding the yellow school bus on the first day of school with her Pound Puppy, a slick new Lisa Frank Trapper Keeper, and a queasy stomach. Brooke sat in the seat behind the driver, her pigtails shooting like golden sparklers above her ears.

Confronted with such astonishing hair, Drew could only stare, slack-jawed and enraptured. She'd always wanted blond cornsilk hair like that. People with that kind of hair got to be on *The Brady Bunch* and *Full House.* They got to be Barbie, not Midge. They got to be Rainbow Brite and Madonna for Halloween. After introductions, Brooke announced brightly, "We got a new puppy yesterday and she crapped on my pompoms. But she's really cute."

And that was it. Anyone who appreciated a dog that would despoil a cheerleading accessory was someone Drew would like to watch *Punky Brewster* with after school.

Together they believed in leprechauns, redemption by sugarcoated cereal, and that you could never have enough clubs: the detective club, the waitress club, the library club, the charm necklace club, the doing-it club. Although "doing it" was a rather vague notion, possibly involving strenuous stomach-to-stomach gyrating on a bed. At slumber parties they practiced doing it, giggling in their sleeping bags and offending the other girls, who were wholesome and still believed in the Easter Bunny in the fourth grade.

Over the years Brooke bloomed into the best kind of friend to have—especially if you had self-destructive tendencies and an affinity for the backseats of squad cars. At age sixteen she was sent to rehab after her mother found a Baggie of pot tucked in a Monopoly game in her closet. While she never stole any of Drew's boyfriends outright, she did dabble in friend swiping, backstabbing, manipulation, and casual betrayals.

She was a toxic friend. The kind of friend your parents tolerate with tight lips, or forbid you from seeing at all. The kind of friend you pass notes with on Monday and weep over by Friday. The kind of friend who regularly gave backhanded compliments like, "Your perm isn't *nearly* as hideous as Lori made it sound!" The problem was this—she was fun. A visit to the principal's office and a trip to a Six Flags Amusement Park, rolled into one.

Drew was surprised Brooke called her. And she was even more surprised that she agreed to meet Brooke for a drink. Their last conversation had been two years ago, and there were no shocking secrets to reveal; just the generalized catching up that you do with an old friend you see every few years: How's work, how's your family, are you dating, married, or single, and why or why not? Since then, there had been occasional Christmas cards, games of phone tag nobody won—all still warm, but missing the immediacy, the drama, the closeness and trust of real friends.

But it was more than that. Brooke was, despite her trapdoors, *Drew's*. They invented dance routines together to Milli Vanilli songs, performing for Drew's little brother Nick and the neighbor's dog. They babysat together, watching Ned the Dead's weekly B-movie bomb and looking for parent sin stashes after the kids fell asleep. How many photos does Drew have of the two of them together, wearing happy, intoxicated smiles, arms slung over one another's shoulder, confident they'd always be so close? Drew gave her credit for calling. Would she have done the same had their roles been reversed? And now that she had this invitation to a party thrown by all her old vices, should she accept?

As Drew pulled onto Sanderling Drive she impulsively made a quick detour to Target to replenish her dwindling makeup supplies. Inside the store she headed toward cosmetics and saw Joe Simon walking out of the shampoo aisle. He was wearing cargo shorts, sandals, and a black T-shirt that read: "BITCHES AIN'T SHIT BUT HOES AND TRICKS" –GANDHI. He had a shopping basket in his left hand. She ducked behind an end cap, hoping he didn't see her. Should she say hello? If she did, they would probably make small talk for a few minutes, part company, and bump into one another again twice more, saying things like, "You again!" or "Are you following me?," laughing awkwardly, each time more embarrassing than the last. She watched him until he disappeared down another aisle, still pondering the best course of action.

She decided speed was the way to go, tearing down a cosmetic aisle and grabbing what she needed: powder, mascara, eyeliner. As she snuck around the back in an end run to the checkout lanes, she nearly ran into him. He had his back to her as he compared two small boxes, engrossed in product comparison. When Drew saw what he was holding, she laughed. She couldn't help it, really. Joe Simon was holding two boxes of the most commonly shoplifted item in the United States. Hemorrhoid cream. Preparation H and the Target brand, which was twenty-three cents less expensive.

"My grandpa swears by that stuff," Drew said, breaking his reverie.

He jerked and spun around. One of the boxes flew out of his hand, landing on the floor with a slap. His eyes registered confusion and surprise until he recognized her. She smiled at the red flooding his face. He bent down to pick up the box. "Hey! I was just you know, buying a cooler. For the fireworks tomorrow, and some bug spray. For on the beach, and—" He dropped the box again and fumbled to retrieve it.

"I see that." Drew smirked, aware he was mildly interested in her, delighted she caught him with his proverbial pants down. God, he was young. How old could he be? Twenty-two? Twenty-three, maybe?

He smiled and shrugged. "Well," he finally said, "when the barn's on fire you call the fire department." He cradled the box at eye level, an actor doing a lowbrow endorsement.

Drew laughed, glad he could find the humor in the situation.

He returned both boxes to the shelf and grinned. "So what are you doing here? I mean, besides shopping and sneaking up on people."

"Oh, I specifically came here to sneak up on people." Drew cocked her head toward the shelf. "You're not going to buy any?"

"There is no way in hell I could talk to you if I had that in my basket." His ears were scarlet, and she realized she'd truly humiliated him, even though he looked somewhat pleased by the whole business. "I so wish you ran into me when I was buying protein powder or a giant box of extra-large condoms."

"We could play that game, where you bring three things to the cashier to freak him out. Like laxatives, plastic sheeting, and a giant canister of cheese puffs."

He laughed, and they began to walk toward the checkout lanes. "So you grew up here?"

"Yeah, but I lived in Eau Claire for a while. I taught there for a few years."

"Why'd you come back?"

"Oh, you know. The usual. Doomed relationship, squandered hopes and dreams." She cracked a smile and added, "It would make a great T-shirt: ASK ME ABOUT MY SQUANDERED HOPES AND DREAMS. And then in tiny font below it would say, *If you want to slit your wrists.*"

He laughed again, and she realized with some dismay that she liked the sound of it a bit too much. She was, in fact, doing a compulsive, manic little stand-up routine to hear more of it. "Doomed relationship, huh? We could compare notes." Suddenly he paused and added, "Walk with me to the pharmacy? I have to pick up a new glucose monitor."

"Oh?"

"I have diabetes."

She wished he hadn't told her that, because now he had the sympathy factor working in his favor. If he also volunteered with the Special Olympics or visited Children's Hospital with therapy dogs, she could be in some real trouble.

"Hey," he said, "what are you up to tonight?"

"I'm meeting a friend at Finnegan's."

"Really." One corner of his mouth curled into a grin. "We were thinking of going there later." He didn't specify who comprised this mysterious "we."

Drew adopted the same flirty, noncommittal tone. "Maybe we'll see you there. Classy shirt, by the way."

He glanced down, grinned sheepishly, and shrugged. "Well, it's been a classy kind of day."

She laughed. She should not be using this tone with a coworker. She should not be using this tone with anyone right now. This is exactly the kind of tone that got her in trouble to begin with.

It took a few seconds for her eyes to adjust to the off-color, smoky interior of Finnegan's, but her nose instantly recoiled at the scent of wet ashtrays, mummified popcorn, and stale beer. Drew scanned the bar. All the familiar props were there, but she still wasn't sure she was in the right place. The white, punched pseudo-tin ceiling was suspended far above the scuffed plank wood floor; neon beer signs cast glowing blue and yellow shadows on the burgundy walls, on which hung dozens of framed black and white photos of Laurentide Bay's early days as a shipbuilding town. Miniature red Leinenkugel's canoes fixed with fluorescent lights hung upside down over the pool tables, illuminating the green felt below. The television bolted above the bar was tuned to a baseball game. A few older men hunched over the bar, nursing pints of beer. Two couples wearing grim faces shot darts in the back of the room. This was the place that used to turn people away from the door to avoid a fine from the fire marshal?

It's funny how small a place seems when you revisit it years later. In high school they spoke of the bar in reverential language; while Drew and her friends shivered in a cornfield, shotgunning lukewarm cans of Milwaukee's Best and peeing in the ditch, their older brothers and sisters were peeing in climate-controlled bathrooms with actual toilet paper at the first place in town to have The Strokes on the jukebox. Over the years Finnegan's became *the* Thanksgiving Eve reunion spot for students home from college, so nearly everyone in town has been to the bar at least once, standing on a barstool to autograph the ceiling tiles with a black Sharpie. Drew's signature was above the foosball table. She could see it from where she now stood: *Brooke & Drew – 2004.*

After a cursory glance around the room she spotted Brooke sitting alone at the opposite end of the bar, swinging her feet and chatting with the young bartender. She looked exactly as she did when Drew last saw her, four years ago—trim and fresh, with the same fall of straight, fine blond hair Drew had so envied in their youth. Someone with that kind of hair could come across as either vacuous or icy, but Brooke was neither, when she liked you. She was wearing jeans and an airy short-sleeved blouse with pearl buttons. You could tell, even from a distance, that the pearls were real. A pair of angular tortoiseshell glasses perched on the bridge of her nose, though Drew didn't recall Brooke having anything but 20/20 vision.

When Drew had bemoaned her own comparatively plain looks during adolescence, her mother had taken Drew's cheeks in her cool palms, looked her daughter directly in the eye, and said, "Brooke might be beautiful, but she's so beautiful she's boring. You, on the other hand, are unique."

Brooke hopped from the stool and smiled magnanimously. "Darling," she said in her Eva Gabor voice, throwing her arms out. "Look at this gorgeous girl."

Drew smiled and glanced back over her shoulder to determine the whereabouts of this gorgeous girl.

"Cut it out and get over here!"

"It's so good to see you," Drew said, stepping into Brooke's hug. Her hair smelled of rosemary and mint. *My hair smells like nachos and inmates,* Drew thought.

"I invited Lori Beuchel to meet us later. You don't mind, do you?"

And Drew was reminded of another reason why their friendship gradually dissipated. She grew tired of their every activity turning into an excuse to throw a party. She feigned enthusiasm. "Of course! It would be great to see Lori again." Lori Beuchel, an even more fickle friend who'd gone from chucking soggy toilet paper onto the ceiling of the girl's bathroom to shuffling legal files in the law offices of McCready, Weaver, and Bright.

Brooke held Drew at arm's length and shook her head, smiling. "I can't believe you're really here."

"Neither can I."

Drew slid onto the stool next to Brooke, who adopted a solemn expression. "I heard about what happened."

Drew forced an artificial smile and decided that in this case, the best response was levity. She leaned in to whisper, "So did I."

"I'm so sorry, Drew. God, I don't know how you handled it …" She placed a graceful hand on Drew's forearm—a gesture of literal support to underscore the emotional. The gentle, unexpected touch was another of Brooke's guiles. If you weren't careful, those fleeting physical connections could make you forget she canceled your last three dinner dates for unconvincing reasons.

Drew shrugged, hoping it conveyed a healthy, resilient attitude about the whole incident as well as the fact that she really didn't want to talk about it. She changed the subject with a bright smile. "How's Mark?"

"Oh, he's fine. Nothing new there. My mother? That's another story entirely."

Brooke and Mark had been high school sweethearts, but she shelved him in college so she could explore her options.

Mark left for culinary school and sous chef gigs in Seattle but never stopped pining for Brooke, calling and e-mailing weekly; they even spent several winter breaks home together as if nothing had changed. But back at Marquette University, Brooke would forget all about Mark and start seeing some tie-dyed guy obsessed with Phish, or a Delta Chi with a giant sense of entitlement and date rapey eyes. Drew had always wondered what kind of man Brooke would end up with, but part of her suspected he'd be a man that could walk into a jam-packed restaurant on a Saturday night and instantly be seated at the best table—the one that had been reserved for a state senator. An international traveler with a smile for everyone but time for no one. A narcissist who never passed a mirror without checking his own reflection.

In the end, Brooke shocked everyone by returning to the dependable, considerate man she'd spent the majority of her time in college denying. It was as if she'd hit senior year, looked back at the uninspired castoffs cluttering up the last four years, glanced over at understudy Mark waiting in the wings, and said, "Okay. Time to grow up. Shall we?"

Drew smiled. "Now what's your mother up to?"

"The latest is grandbaby this, grandbaby that. Do you know what she said to me the other day? She said, 'Well, they've made so much progress with special-needs babies since I was your age. I guess I shouldn't worry so much.' Who says that kind of thing? I'm barely out of my twenties!" She rolled her eyes and took a long sip of her drink.

Drew frowned and shook her head, as she was expected to. But Brooke's mother's comment was nothing new; in high school, Brooke's mom stopped speaking to her for days when Brooke was elected prom queen. But that may not have been a bad thing, because when she *did* speak to Brooke, she dipped into an impressive arsenal of passive-aggressive and cutting remarks.

As surprised as Drew was when Brooke married Mark, she was even more surprised that they hadn't yet had children. It was the next step after you got married and bought a house in Laurentide Bay. Growing up, Brooke frequently referenced her future children, usually in protest at some irritation or another: *"When I'm a mother, I'll never force my kids to tithe ten percent of their allowance to church"* and *"When I'm a parent, I'm going to trust my daughters"* and *"When I have kids, we're going to live in a city where the idea of culture isn't a giant fish statue."* Yet here she was, with no kids to deprive of church, no daughters to trust, and a giant fish statue on the next corner.

"Anyway. So you're working at Lakeside?" Her blue eyes flashed with the unspoken: *Remember when you used to say you'd never end up working there? Like your mother?*

"Yeah." Drew forced a chuckle, hoping it sounded natural. She decided to confront the unspoken head-on. "Remember when we used to say we'd never work there?"

"So what happened?"

Drew sighed and shook her head, settling on the easiest response to rattle out. "Life. But what about you? How are things at Roots?"

Roots, located in 130-year-old former dockworker housing, was Laurentide Bay's premier restaurant and wine bar. Mark was owner and executive chef, and Brooke served as general manager in the family business. Someone once told Drew that Brooke did cocaine on the bar with the bartenders after hours. *Travel and Leisure* named Roots one of the region's best restaurants last year, and *Chicago Magazine* hot-listed it in "Where to Eat this Summer: Vacation Edition." A photo of Brooke and Mark accompanied the article; in it, they leaned comfortably against the polished mahogany bar, toasting their success with

PR smiles and Pinot Noir. The menu was seasonal, featuring local seafood, produce, and artisanal cheeses to the extent possible.

It sounded pretentious, and much of the clientele was. But the food? One bite of the vegetable tart baked with roasted eggplant, caramelized onions, sautéed mushrooms, lentils, sun-dried tomatoes, and butternut squash drizzled with a balsamic reduction and you'd beg autumn to last forever.

"Oh, fine. But Mark's gotten it into his head that we should branch off and start a brewpub on the docks. Grilled sandwiches and casual alfresco dining, gourmet burgers and some kind of signature side. Homemade beer-battered fish on Fridays, some kind of fruity drink in a novelty glass or something. You know, gourmet casual. Just tossing around ideas for now."

"You'd totally get traffic from all the boat people," Drew said. "Tired, huddled masses and all." It was a joke for her own benefit, because she knew Brooke wouldn't get it.

"Ugh, I don't even want to think about the logistics of this yet."

"We'll have to think of a clever name."

"Dockside Bar and Grill."

"No, too easy. I'm kind of drawn to 'I'm on a Boat, Motherfucker!'"

"Hit the Deck." Brooke looked miserable. "Maybe you can talk him out of it. I'm getting a headache."

"Oh, it'll be fun. Think of all the Parrotheads who'll come! Hawaiian shirts, piña coladas, getting caught in the rain."

Brooke groaned and put her head on the bar, then quickly looked up again, inspired. "I know exactly what we need."

"A reincarnation?"

"Some people call it that. I call it tequila."

"I don't do tequila."

"You do tonight!"

Brooke summoned the bartender, who ambled down and leaned toward them, crossing his thick forearms on the bar. A toothpick dangled from the left corner of his mouth. "Let me guess. Two shots of tequila."

"Jared," Brooke said coyly, "am I that predictable?"

"Not really. I just know what you like." His smile had a suggestive, knowing residue that made Drew look away.

While they watched him work, Brooke leaned in to whisper lewdly in Drew's ear, "Jared has a *huge* penis. We're talking, like, *ginormous.*"

Drew checked Brooke's hands to see if they were actually cloven hooves. "How do you know that?"

"I know a lot about Jared."

Her gourmet husband would have happily eaten only Wonder Bread and Spam for the rest of his life if it meant Brooke's loyalty and enduring love. It was a stark reminder to trust Brooke at your own risk. "I should point out," Drew said, "that nobody says *ginormous* anymore."

"Well, what should I say?" Brooke huffed.

"How about roomy? Jumbo? Hefty!" Drew began to enjoy herself. "My, what a hefty penis you have. Does that count as a carry-on? Do you need a small, wheeled cart for that? *A license?* Do people get altitude sickness at the tip?"

Brooke rolled her eyes. A few minutes later they were licking the salted heels of their hands, swallowing burning gulps of tequila, squeezing lime wedges into their mouths, and grimacing. "I'm getting too old for this." Drew's mouth watered, but not in anticipation of a delicious meal. It felt like someone had slung her GI tract onto a taffy-pulling machine.

"You're never too old for tequila."

"Will you say that when you're ninety?" Drew shuddered and arranged her empty shot glass on a cocktail napkin.

A shadow fell across Brooke's face. "If I make it to ninety."

"Oh stop. You'll probably outlive us all."

"I hope not," she said.

Drew took a good look at her friend. This was *not* something the Brooke she once knew would say.

Brooke clasped Drew's shoulder with fingers that were too bony and cool. "Let's just have fun tonight and save the heavy stuff for later. I haven't seen you in forever." She pressed her lips into a thin smile. There was no arguing with her when she smiled like that. Well, there was never really much arguing with Brooke, period.

"Check," Drew said. "Heavy stuff saved for later. Gives us something fun to look forward to." She ordered a vodka tonic, Brooke ordered an Amstel Light, and Jared delivered promptly. Drew skewered her lime with the cocktail straw. The alcohol swirled, amoeba-like, through the ice cubes. "Kind of quiet here tonight."

Brooke took a sip of beer and shook her head dismissively. "It's early. People are still out on their boats."

"Boat people," Drew murmured.

And she was right, of course. Two hours and three vodka tonics later, Finnegan's was mobbed with both tourists and year-round residents of Laurentide Bay, young and old, rich and poor alike. Drew watched Brooke hold court, watched people she passed notes to fifteen years earlier bask in the glow of Brooke's smile and laugh at her effervescent jokes. Brooke was a small sun, the rest of them mere space debris in her orbit.

Lori Beuchel arrived with her husband Paul. She and Drew exchanged polite hugs. Drew once had a profound, secret crush on Paul. She could barely look at him whenever they got together for cookouts or drinks. Sometimes Drew would imagine Lori dying in a plane crash and Paul turning to her for comfort. But there would be trouble in their new relationship.

Drew would imagine herself saying to him in a moment of difficulty: "Paul, I'm not like Lori. I'm complicated." Paul would take her hands, look deeply into her eyes, and say, "We're all complicated." Then Drew would snap out of it and think, *Wow, I'm such a jerk. I really like Lori. I'll have to make her cheat on him in my next fantasy instead.*

Before long, Drew felt the tequila and vodka catching up with her, boosting her confidence, slowing her reflexes, polishing the edges from the night. She had the same conversation about what she was "up to these days" with too many former high school acquaintances who looked at her expectantly, searching for common ground, hoping she too was married or engaged or remodeling a kitchen or planning a vacation to Cabo. Drew told people she was teaching, but she didn't offer the name of her employer. Only a few asked, and she answered honestly. They looked at her differently afterward, their eyes glazing with something like disappointment. She wondered yet again if she'd made a huge mistake in moving back home. Most of her friends would rather drink Windex than live with their parents again. She had no mortgage, no spouse, no children. Why was she not flirting with a stranger in a Parisian café?

Maybe because the available balance on her Visa card now limited her travel options to the Herbster Annual Smelt Fry. The Wisconsin Gourd Festival. The Spectrum Brass Quintet performing "Who Could Ask for Anything More?" (*Drew could!*) at the Stoughton Opera House next weekend.

Or maybe—more truthfully—it was because some people might go to Paris when they had wounds to lick, but Drew wasn't one of them. Home was her comfort zone, with the gravitational pull of Jupiter.

An hour later, after a vacationing middle manager said to her, "I'm sorry, could you repeat that? I was too busy staring at your breasts" and she spilled a White Russian on her black Cambodian-sewn shirt, Brooke suddenly materialized and threw her booze-loosened arms around Drew. Brooke swayed and peered at her, trying to focus on Drew's face. "I'm so glad you're home. Just like old times."

"Ah yes, the good old days," Drew said. "When our dreams were bigger and our pores much smaller."

Brooke suddenly pinched Drew's cheeks, hard.

"Ow!"

"Don't worry, you won't need Botox for at least ten years. Come on, let's go talk to Owen."

"Who's that?"

"The bald guy at the end of the bar who's buying our next round. He has more money than God."

9. GRAHAM

On Monday morning I run into Kurt Gregory, a new psychologist at Lakeside, washing his hands in a men's bathroom in the admin building. "Hey, Graham. How was your Fourth of July?"

"Not bad, yours?"

"Took the boat out to watch the fireworks on Lake Michigan. We set off a bunch of our own, too. The kids still have all their fingers and most of their hearing, so I'd say the weekend was a success." The faucet squeaks in protest when he turns the water off.

"I didn't know you had a boat."

"We inherited it from Liz's uncle. Not too flashy, but it runs." As Kurt dries his hands on institutional brown paper towels he chuckles. "This is the only job where you have to wash your hands before you take a leak."

It's an old joke, but still I smile. I hold up my palms, speckled with prison floor grit picked up by the tires on my chair, wet from the freshly mopped bathroom floor. "True. But *I've* got to wash them before I do almost anything."

Kurt chuckles awkwardly. "It is what it is."

I don't know if people say this where you live, but they say it all the time here and it makes me want to disembowel myself. What is *it*, exactly? A pile of burning tires? A three-legged panda? A maraca full of Tic Tacs?

Honestly, I couldn't care less about my entire morning, which consists of one anger management session with an amiable crew of miscreants and program review committee reports to write for a half-dozen offenders on my caseload. I'm feeling cynical about all of them: two armed robbers, a vindictive creep who molested his own daughter, a rapist who loves to appeal conduct reports, a smartass burglar with an eating disorder, and an inciter of racial discord serving a three-year sentence for battery. All have addictions to various mind-altering substances. I have meetings on deck with two guys on my caseload who need refresher courses on DOC disciplinary codes. I also have a stack of kites on my desk. One is from Gerald Redfeather, who is requesting a meeting to demand more Native American food options, such as "pemmican and hot dogs." I didn't realize hot dogs were traditional for the Oneida, but what do I know?

If Drew hasn't forgotten or decided to blow me off (wouldn't that be entertaining in the literal sense), we're having lunch together at noon. I pay an unusual amount of attention to the clock all morning. When 11:50 finally rolls around I try to compose myself, put on a nonchalant face. I push to the admin building's expansive main reception area, which doubles as the visiting room, to wait. The well-buffed green tile floor gleams like a mellow lake beneath the visiting area, which is stocked with chairs where later today inmates will flirt with their girlfriends, console their worried mothers, or try to bond with their sullen and possibly doomed children.

Now, unless you're a committed single or met your spouse in the second grade, you know how exhausting it is to play the game. Which is why most guys I know don't even bother; they simply switch off their brains and think with their dicks. I may have gone that route as well, if I had much of a dick to think with. In case you're wondering, yes, it gets hard. But no, aside from the odd phantom sensation, I can't feel a thing. Which really hampers masturbation as a cathartic activity.

I pretend to examine some inmate handicrafts locked in a trophy case—colorful knit mittens and scarves that will be donated to a local homeless shelter—while I eavesdrop on a conversation between four women from the records office. They perch in the stiff, scratchy lounge chairs that will be filled with inmates and visitors four hours from now. The lobby fills rapidly, especially when the guards go on break, so people tend to squat and eat wherever they find space. One of the women is on the cabbage soup diet and another is nibbling a triangle of cold leftover pizza. I feel small and sweaty, like I'll be accused of doing something unsavory any second. Luckily, the cube drones are too busy gossiping and mechanically chewing their lunches to notice me.

Maybe Drew forgot about our lunch date. I strain to remember if we'd made definite plans, of if I'd simply tossed out a meaningless, "We should have lunch sometime!" Which could be interpreted as, "I like seeing your face around, but not enough to commit to seeing it more often!" I'm about to give up and return to my office to eat my ham sandwich alone at my desk when she pulls open the glass doors and steps into the administration building.

"Graham! How are you?"

If I listen closely, I can almost hear an angelic choir belt the chorus of Handel's "Messiah" while a diagonal blade of sunlight pierces the gray clouds and lands in my face. "I'm great! How are you?"

She leans down to kiss my cheek. A new development! When did she become a cheek-kisser? Not that I mind. When she pulls away I'm a bit dazed by our recent proximity. I want nothing more than to be alone with her (the laws of physics permitting), so I ask, "Want to eat lunch outside? There's an open picnic table in the back."

"Sure." As we head for the back courtyard, I ask, "Did you go to the fireworks?"

She shakes her head. "No. I watched them on TV with my parents." She pauses and gives a small laugh. "I suppose this means I'm officially lame." We find the picnic table indeed vacant and settle in, unpacking our lunches in the sunlight. Al fresco dining is preferable, even in prison.

"Probably. But you're in good company. I watched my redneck neighbor set off cut-rate fireworks in his driveway." I guess this means I'm literally *and* figuratively lame.

Drew takes a sip of water and favors me with a sweet smile. "So what makes your neighbor a redneck?"

"Well, he wears the same dirty undershirt almost every day. And he quotes both Jeff Foxworthy *and* Larry the Cable Guy. He has a mountain of discarded tires and farm implements behind the barn, and he makes his own beer, laundry soap, and jerky. Often from the same ingredients."

"That's not so bad. My dad makes his own jerky with a dehydrator."

"From possum meat?"

"No. But did you really just say 'farm implements?'" We both share a warm laugh at my expense.

And it was a damned good investment on my part, I might add.

It's nice being on the same level as Drew. That is to say, seated. There's a brief moment where our attention is again directed to the fact that I can only get around in a chair with wheels when I apply hand sanitizer to my prison-dusted hands so I can eat my sandwich without contracting the norovirus or some such delightful germ. When I first started using hand sanitizer I felt like everyone was looking at me like I was *Brokeback Mountain* personified, complete with real broken back, but now I don't really give a shit what anyone thinks. I work in a prison, for Christ's sake. Accidental ingestion of inmate spooge is not a personal goal of mine.

"Wow," she says, watching me. "I never considered that part of being in a wheelchair."

"Tip of the iceberg, Drew." She gives me a look I hope isn't pity, but I suspect it may be.

For a while we gossip about what our old classmates are up to, and Drew tells me she met up with some of her old friends on Friday night.

"Brooke Walters, huh?"

She smiles and swallows a bite of pasta salad. "She's still the same, only with a different last name. Sullivan. But you probably knew that already."

I nod. Brooke Walters-Sullivan was, and still is, a sloppy, slutty drunk, but since she and Drew are friends, I simply say, "So I hear." *Shared history,* I think. *Mutual acquaintances to trade snarky anecdotes about.* Not a bad way to begin a relationship.

"Anyway." She flaps her hand and smiles politely. "You got married, right?"

While she finishes her pasta salad I give her the honest if brief overview of my marriage. "We shouldn't have. We were too young, with about as much in common as Quentin Tarantino and Pat Robertson. Not so married anymore."

"I'm sorry, Graham. Any kids?" She doesn't give me time to ask the relationship question of her, though I think I already know most of her answer.

"Nah."

"Me neither. I did have a cat, though. Named Blindey."

"Blindey?"

"Yep."

"Was he deaf?"

She laughs the way girls do when something's cute yet sad. "Poor guy got hit by a car."

"I'm sorry."

"It's okay," she says. "Little Blindey had a good, long life."

"All right," I say, brushing potato chip crumbs from my fingers. "I have to ask the obvious, annoying question."

Her lips lift into a muted grin. "What I'm doing working here, right?"

"Right."

She hesitates, eyes cast down at the table.

"You don't have to answer if you don't want to," I add, beginning to wish I hadn't asked.

"The simple answer is that I didn't want to stay at my old job. Too many memories, too much baggage. After … everything that happened, I just wanted to move home again to regroup and be near my family. I needed a living situation I could afford, and I didn't want to live alone or with some random roommate." She shifts in her seat, unable to make eye contact with me. This is clearly a discomforting topic.

"I did apply at a few other school districts near here, but you know how it is these days. Budget freezes and cutbacks. Anyway, I don't know where I want to be in a year. I needed to buy some time to think." She unfolds her napkin, smooths it out. "My mom worked here, so I thought I'd apply. And here we are."

I nod, processing all of this still too-vague information.

"Anyway, blah-blah," she says, making an effort to rearrange the mood.

I suspect it was difficult for her to even share this much with me, so I decide to help by changing the subject. "Do you know what Lakeside is most famous for?"

Her face melts into a grateful smile. "That you work here?"

"Unfortunately, word has yet to leak through the fence. No."

"That Jeffrey Dahmer was once transferred here?" She crunches a carrot stick.

"No, even Lakeside has standards. And we're medium security. No serial killers allowed."

"Then what?"

I pause for effect. "We're famous for worm composting and—" I jiggle my wheels to emphasize my next point— "wheelchair recycling." Oh, how I love the irony of the latter.

She stares at me, completely still for two beats, then bursts into laughter.

"You think I'm making that up, but I'm not. Hey, don't laugh, it's all about specialization. Fox Lake can have their college credit courses. We've got worm shit for the Lakeside garden." I finish my last bite of sandwich and add, "Oh, and if you order early, the guys in Mike Bruin's woodworking class will make you some nice little reindeer you can put on the mantle this Christmas. For cost. Contact Harold Weber in Hobbies if you want some scarves or mittens. Also for cost. But you have to hurry, most of those are donated to local shelters."

"Stop." She presses a hand to her chest, smiling. "You're joking."

I relish the delighted expression on her face. "I'm not. Janet Sutton does almost all her Christmas shopping here. Not everybody can say their garbage bin was painted by a convicted murderer."

She's shaking her head, still wearing that bemused, amazed smile.

"You're making your Christmas shopping list in your head, aren't you?"

"Heck yeah, I am!" She laughs. "I always get my dad some kind of banjo music on CD, but a birdhouse made by an embezzler would be so much better."

"Banjo music?"

"He likes these really under-the-radar groups that he hears on public radio, like they're a guest on *Prairie Home Companion* or some random program you'd catch by accident. They're usually so indie you can only buy their music on their website."

"So what are you listening to these days?"

"You wouldn't like it," she says, a blush spreading into her cheeks. "You'd call it vagina music."

"Is that the iTunes category?"

"No, but it would be hilarious if it was. What do you like? I mean listen to. What do you listen to." Her blush deepens. If I were more optimistic, I'd wonder if she was flirting with me.

"Depends on my mood. Are you familiar with a group called Storyhill? I just heard them on public radio. Your dad would totally dig them."

"Oh my God, I'm sorry." She laughs, and I join her.

"So if you were in a band," I ask, "what would you play, and what would your band be called?"

She plucks a chocolate chip cookie from my crumpled brown bag and considers it. "Lead guitar for the Trans-Fatty Orchestra. We'd do pompous Christmas music for people who like croissants. Can I have this cookie?"

"My mother made them, so it may not be entirely edible."

"Your mother made this? Aw, that's so Donna Reed!"

"You have no idea. If my mother could live life in black and white, she would. Okay, here's a band: Honest Bob and the Factory to Dealer Incentives."

"Did you just make that up?"

"Yeah," I lie, watching her laugh wind down into a sigh. I remember when making stupid puns about the periodic table comprised our humor repertoire. For a minute I don't regret that we never went on a real date in high school, because we have no past relationship muck between us; just pure, goofy memories. But the nagging fear behind this optimistic thought is this: If she didn't find me sexually appealing enough to pursue *then*, what in the hell possesses me to think she might now? Lowered expectations? Declining standards?

I ask about her family, teaching in general, even our respective religious upbringings—anything to keep the conversation going. In Wisconsin, you basically have two choices: Catholic or Lutheran. No big news flash that we were both raised on a healthy, guilty diet of Catholicism. Where binge drinking is encouraged and masturbation is not. While she talks, I listen. I'm not even tempted to interrupt or daydream.

Have you ever had one of those moments where you just knew the person you were sitting across from could be happy for the rest of her life, if only she spent it with you? Not like you personally are the key to her euphoria or something, you're not that ego-centric, but she would be happy because you *adore* her. You complement one another. You're on the same team. And you *know* there's chemistry there because sometimes she looks at you a beat too long, but it's also a look of affection ... of easy, effortless kindness. And you can feel all of this in your gut, in your heart, in your bones, in every muscle fiber and every molecule of your body.

Some people would say this is what it feels like to find your soul mate (Mike Sheffield might even use the nauseating term "soul twin"), but let's leave those people in their patchouli and sandalwood haze and get on with it already.

You *know* that you and this person were *made* for each other.

Forget hormones, forget our biological drive to replicate ourselves, forget having things in common. I'm talking about *destiny*. I'm talking about a *deeper connection*.

And then ... and *then*, when it's all making sense, the person you're meant to share orange juice and oatmeal with each morning for the rest of your lives screws it all up by saying, "So hey. I've been meaning to ask. What do you know about Joe Simon? He's an officer here. You know him, right?"

I blink. I think it goes without saying that this isn't how I imagined the last five minutes of our lunch date going. She didn't ask it in a pointed, *I now want to gossip about this jerk I met at work* way; she asked it in a shy, *I'm interested in this individual in a romantic way and would like your honest assessment of his character before I make a fool of myself* way.

Before I can say anything she blushes and shakes her head quickly, as if to clear it. "Never mind. It's nothing. I'm not interested, or anything. I just ran into him this weekend at Target."

Her mouth says one thing, her eyes say another. It's nothing men haven't been dealing with for thousands of years. I choose my words carefully. "Target, huh?"

She chuckles and blushes more deeply. "Yeah." She then starts laughing silently, her shoulders shaking, and tears actually well in her gorgeous, expressive eyes. "He was buying" —she pauses for a breath— "*hemorrhoid* cream." And she dissolves into full-scale buckets of laughter.

I feel better knowing she sees him as a man capable of having an inflamed rectum, but only a little.

The rest of my day is a tapestry of aching tedium so dull my eyeballs throb; I almost put my head down on my desk for a nap, twice. But my day won't end when I return home. Oh no.

Social butterfly that I am, I made dinner plans for the evening. With Kendra.

I could weep.

Kendra's okay. I mean, she's about as exciting as a documentary on the history of Styrofoam, and the only photo I've seen of her hovers uncomfortably between Tina Yothers and Melissa Joan Hart. But a date is a date, and I've got to suck it up. Because roll up your sleeves, polish the silver, guess where we're going? That's right, kids, we're going to Country Plate! It's nothing but first class for Graham Finch and his dates.

I'm early, of course.

Normally I would assume that all of you have eaten at a Country Plate near you, but some people like to say, "When you assume you make an 'ass' out of 'u' and 'me.'" The same people probably eat at Country Plate all the time and should be beaten and robbed of the things that mean the most to them.

Anyway, how to describe Country Plate. Well, do you like pie? How about sticky benches upholstered in vinyl? Do you like waiting in line between people who smell of kitty litter to eat soggy bacon and burned hash browns while experiencing a hangover with more staying power than William Shatner? Do you like people vomiting onto their plates next to you at three-thirty in the morning? Then you'll love Country Plate.

It wasn't my choice to come here, if you can't get that from my description. I glance around the restaurant to see if I can at least engage in some interesting people-watching. The clientele is what you might expect on a Monday evening. A few teenagers wearing heavy eyeliner and black T-shirts drinking coffee and staring morosely at their placemats, three elderly couples fussing over their soup and paying their bills entirely in change, a handful of weary parents with small children shrieking and smearing grape jelly over everything within five feet. Everyone is white. Probably half vote for Democrats, half vote for

Republicans, and 95 percent consider themselves Independents. If I were a Hollywood set designer charged with composing a background for a restaurant scene set "in the Midwest on a weeknight," I'd take the crew to a Country Plate in any town in Wisconsin.

A waitress with a rather aggressive smile seats me. (Well, she leads me to a table and kind of "parks" me.) She hands me a laminated menu larger than a sheet of drywall. I order a Mountain Dew. Seconds later it arrives in a clear bucket with a straw you could ride a bike through.

As I pretend to survey the menu I spy a girl who could very well be Kendra.

I don't know what it is, but something about her reminds me of Malt-O-Meal. She's attractive in that vague, wholesome, cheese-fed way many Wisconsin girls are, and I know immediately that I won't see her again after this date. I'm not surprised to see that her jeans ride too high at the waist. Luckily, my expectations were about knee-level. At this point I reprimand myself for being such a judgmental prick. I'm not exactly guest-star material for *Mad Men*, unless I'm playing some schmuck paralyzed in a skiing accident who reminds everyone how lucky they are that they can still walk on the beach hand-in-hand with a date.

She scans the room, but her eyes skip over me. Probably because I haven't told her I'm in a wheelchair.

Wow. When I say it like that it sounds so awful. At this point I'm ready to wave and shout, "Hi, Kendra! I'm your date from hell—the one that will provide you with a lifetime of amusing anecdotes!"

So I wave. How else will she realize it's me?

She'd been wearing an expression of nervous anticipation, her head swiveling while she tried to find me amidst the Country Plate patrons. When I wave her eyes lock with mine and register

... nothing. I imagine she's in shock. Then a corner of her mouth curls up, and then an eyebrow. The other eyebrow joins it. It has the overall effect of making her look like a clinically insane clown.

She cautiously walks over to me. "Graham? Is that you?"

I nod, smiling as much as my guilt allows. "Yeah."

And here's where it gets complicated.

"You're in a wheelchair?" Her face is frozen in that awful expression of shock, but it's an amused kind of shock.

I shrug. At the last second I decide to go for honesty. "I didn't know how to tell you."

She's silent for so long I fear she's lost the power of speech.

Things suddenly catch up to me and I feel my shoulders slump. "I'm sorry, Kendra."

This seems to do the trick because she falls into the chair next to me. "Well, this is a surprise. But you know, I had a date last week with a guy who told me he was a doctor. He actually drives forklift in a factory. It's almost like you go on dates just wondering what kind of crazy shit you'll run into. After a while you even make a game of it. Like, I wonder if he's bald, or has a prosthetic hand, or what do they call it when someone replaces their Rs and Ls with Ws?" She snaps her fingers quickly.

"A speech impediment?" *Like when someone forgets the article between "drives" and "forklift"?*

"Kind of. But it's something else." She shakes her head. "It's like they talk like this: 'I wheewy, wheewy wike you, Kendwa. You'we a beautifuw guw.' Anyway, it doesn't matter. Nobody I've met online is remotely close to their profile. It's all part of the game. Has everyone you met online been one hundred percent honest? My guess is no."

I never spend enough time with anyone I meet online to get to that part, actually.

"I mean, I was mostly honest, but everyone exaggerates a little."

"So what did you exaggerate about?"

She smiles mischievously. "Oh, you'll figure it out. Maybe."

I'm not quite sure how to respond, because I'm not usually on the receiving end of the weirdness. Which doesn't say much for me, but there you have it. And by the way, this is sweet, dull, innocent Kendra? Never trust that someone can be well represented by an electronic medium. Never.

"I'm sure you have at least one dating horror story," Kendra continues. "Man, where's the waitress? I'm starving!"

"So you're okay with this?" I gesture downward. It can't be misinterpreted.

"Well, it would have been nice to have had a heads-up." She makes that face. The one you make when you're trying to convince someone you're both earnest and interested in his plight when you're really neither. "But I get it, I really do."

We watch the other diners for a moment and I clear my throat. "So I guess this is the part where I change the subject."

She brightens. "Excellent! What should we talk about?"

"Um, have you read any good books lately?"

"Yeah, I don't read books. I don't have the patience for it."

I'd say I lost a bit of respect for her, but that would be coming from someone who doesn't tell his dates he's in a wheelchair. I try again. "Movies?"

"I haven't seen anything in the theater since I signed up for Netflix. I refuse to pay for the privilege of hearing some dillweed talking and kicking my seat behind me."

"Okay, so what's the last movie you watched on Netflix?"

"*Donnie Darko.* My cousin recommended it. I thought it sucked. But then, there aren't many movies I love one hundred percent." She examines the laminated dessert flip-book on display behind the salt and pepper shakers. "I guess I'm really picky."

I guess I'm not.

The waitress comes around again and Kendra orders a coffee. "And a basket of mozzarella sticks?" I add. I'm a little taken aback by Kendra's frankness. I'm both fascinated by and afraid of it, like how I feel about those frogs that give birth through pores on their backs.

"Oh, I love cheese! I know it can bind you up, but I don't mind. What follows is one hundred percent so cathartic."

I blink. A sliver of fear sinks into me, and I begin to suspect that perhaps Kendra ingested one hundred percent of a gallon of deck stain as a child.

"Oh, you'll get used to me. Did I ever show you pictures of my cat?"

When our waitress returns with Kendra's coffee and our mozzarella sticks I want to press two twenties into her palm, politely excuse myself, and leave. But a sick part of me also wants to know exactly how freaky this girl is. So instead, we place our entrée order. Or as one of Kendra's recent dates would have said, our *ontwhey owdew*.

Kendra orders French toast with sausages and I order a Western omelet. "So what makes it Western?" Kendra demands of our waitress, scowling skeptically.

Our waitress blinks. "Uh, it's got taco seasoning in it? And Monterey Jack cheese? And jalapeños?"

"Huh. And Mexicans slapping them together in the back? Which reminds me. Last time I ate here there was a huge, curly black hair in my Monte Cristo. Let's cut back on the pubes this time around, m'kay?"

At this point I want to shout, *"Thank you for coming, good night Laurentide Bay!"* and roll right the hell out of here, but I just sit and smile like a game show host, like I'm privy to this kind of conversation every day. The waitress backpedals to the kitchen, mouth agape. If I were a betting man, I'd put money on a loogie being hawked into Kendra's French toast batter.

Kendra hums along to the ambient music for a few bars, her eyes skipping over the other dining patrons, before they settle back on me. Her lips curl ever so slightly, and I can almost feel what's coming next; the air over our booth develops a lascivious weight. Her curl becomes a full-on lewd smile and she raises her eyebrows. "So I know you're not supposed to ask these things on the first date, but I have to know. You can't feel anything ... down there ... right?"

I cringe and patiently match her smile. "No, but please don't stab my thigh with a fork to prove my point."

She leans forward, tracing a coy finger through the condensation on her plastic cup. "But I bet you've found ways to compensate, right?"

I sigh and close my eyes.

"Oral sex," Kendra stage-whispers, one hand cupping the side of her mouth in an empty homage to privacy. A kid, maybe nine or ten, spins around in his seat and stares at her.

"Yeah. I got that." I shake my head and give her a bracing grin. "*Born on the Fourth of July*?" I ask. Surely she'd gotten that idea from the infamous line, "If ya ain't got it in the hips, ya better have it in the lips!"

"No, October eighth."

After her meal arrives Kendra slides the sausage between the slices of French toast, drenches her makeshift sandwich with syrup, presses it flat, and lifts the entire stack to her mouth with her bare hands while I watch in horror. "I know! I have a huge mouth, right?" She follows this with a wink. God help us, an actual *wink*.

I lean over the table toward the nightmare that has assumed the shape and sound of my date. And then I start laughing, and I can't stop. "Are you for real? Is there a hidden camera somewhere?"

"Reality bites, Graham. But this sandwich is pretty good."

I must have been a complete waste in my last life. A real horror to behold. What other explanation do I have, other than karma? I hear it's a real bitch.

10. DREW

It was time for Drew to meet her students.

She'd organized her files and read their IEP reports. She'd written her lesson plans and researched supplemental classroom activities. And she'd found a box of essays, practice GED tests, and spelling tests where her predecessor had written things like *Great work!* or *Excellent!* in the top margin. Did it matter at all to the inmates whether or not they did *Great work!* on a spelling test? As the papers had never been returned to their authors, Drew guessed their former teacher answered that question with a big, fat "No."

She was ready. At least she thought she was.

The bell rang, and inmates wandered into the building, shouting and slamming locker doors. The first inmate into the classroom, eighteen-year-old Marcus Wilcox, panned her blankly. He sat at his desk and began combing his hair. The next two through the door were James McDonald, another learning-disabled inmate, and a white, pimple-faced boy named Mark Heather. Jared Hoffman walked in next, staring at her.

A wiry inmate flashed a mouthful of yellow teeth. "Who you?"

Drew closed her attendance book, stood, and smoothed her pants. "I'm sure you all had a relaxing weekend and are ready to dive into schoolwork again." She smoothed her pants some more, for good measure. And to give her hands something to do that didn't involve shaking or sweating.

This was met with good-natured protests, eyerolls, and some muffled swearing.

Someone shouted, "You be playin' with us, new teacher."

Her pulse was surprisingly regular. She felt as if she'd transcended panic, as if she were coasting on Paxil or codeine. "Not playing at all. If you treat me with respect, I will return the favor. My name is Miss Daniels. Our main goal will be to prepare you to earn your high school equivalency diplomas. It won't be easy, but it will open certain doors for you. And if you're not planning on staying here forever, you're going to need those doors wide open." It was a bit different from her standard greeting in the public school system, but she was happy with it nonetheless.

Drew was met with mostly vacant stares. A few of the inmates grinned for no apparent reason. One was missing his two front teeth.

Drew hopped up onto her desk and sat, like John Keating from *Dead Poets' Society*. "I know Miss Rindo had you keep manila portfolios on your progress." Drew gestured to the file organizer on her desk. "Because this class is based on your own educational goals, we'll continue to work this way."

Blank stares.

She cleared her throat. "Let's begin with attendance."

Most of the guys raised a reluctant hand when she called their names. A few bellowed, "Here!"

"Howard Bell?"

Her words echoed in the classroom before being sucked into the box fan chugging along in the back.

"Howard Bell?"

A lanky boy, all limbs and ankles and elbows hunched over a table in the back of the room let his hand fall off his desk. He didn't look up. "Thank you," Drew simply said. She remembered from her prep work that he was severely cognitively delayed. But she couldn't recall his offense.

"Until I can meet with each of you to learn a little more about your IEPs, you can pick up your folders and continue with what Miss Rindo had you working on." She frowned at the sound of her voice. Her plan had been to strike a balance between professionalism and friendliness, confidence and empathy; but somehow, she'd completely overshot her mark and landed somewhere near "soulless cog in the machine." She chalked it up to nerves.

While she slid the attendance slip into the folder outside the door for the school clerk to pick up, most of the inmates sauntered up to her desk and made a display of plucking their folders from the wire organizer. Drew could tell by their wary silence that they were sizing her up, looking for chinks in her armor. After they returned to their desks they began to work quietly on GED practice tests. Several sat before computers and played interactive learning games. *Eight plus seven is fifteen. Six plus five is eleven. That is correct. You pass to the next level.* So far so good.

Drew approached the table occupied by Howard Bell, pulled up a chair next to him, and opened the phonics book he was staring at. "So this is what you've been working on?"

He nodded. "Yeah. I don't know what the hell's going on. It don't matter though. They releasing me in a month."

Drew swallowed hard. She felt acutely white, prim, and middle-class. "Well, what page were you working on last?" she asked gently.

He shrugged. Cognitively delayed. You could drill a concept into his head for hours and he would have forgotten it by the next day.

"Let's start at the very beginning." *A very good place to start.* She cleared her throat, silently cursing Rodgers and Hammerstein and their catchy songs.

He agreed with an indifferent shrug. They spent the next half-hour going over rhyming words: *log, dog, bog, fog ... rat, cat, bat, sat ...* Drew listened patiently as Howard wrestled with the words, trying his best to get firmly hooked on phonics. She helped him sound out the letter combinations, and he struggled to spit them out. The rest of the class, engaged in practice GED tests, seemed indifferent to Howard's Sisyphean task. Finally Howard slammed the book shut. "Fuck this bullshit baby-reading anyway!"

Drew blinked and tried to remain calm. "I know it seems hard. But you've got to try. I know you can do it. We'll have you reading an entire book by the time you leave." She felt awful encouraging a man not that much younger than herself to read a page of three-letter words.

He narrowed his eyes at her but continued, plodding along until the bell rang. The class exploded as the inmates leapt from their desks and filed into the hallway.

Howard stood and muttered, "Thanks." And abruptly, his expression brightened, as if struck by a grand idea. "So are you really gonna have me reading by my MR?" *MR.* His Mandatory Release date.

"We'll give it our best shot." It wouldn't be pretty. It would be more *Runaway Bunny* than *Rabbit, Run,* but if they kept working, maybe it could happen.

After the classroom emptied, she exhaled. She forced her shoulders to relax and stretched her jaw, realizing she'd been clenching it for most of the hour. She looked around the empty classroom and almost smiled. *One class down.* She wandered back to her office and stared at the manila folders littering the counter. Paper spilled haphazardly onto the floor. She waded through the clutter to the filing cabinet at the back of the room.

She found Howard Bell's file almost immediately. The face sheet presented her with neatly compartmentalized facts and figures. *Battery to Law Enforcement/Firefighter* and *Third Degree Assault* had been typed in a box marked "offense." He was sentenced to sixteen months.

According to the report, he was nineteen. He had anger management issues and five children, but no gang affiliations. He smoked marijuana on occasion, but the same could be said of most men she'd dated in college.

On the night of February 7, 2012, an unidentified black male later identified as Howard Tyrone Bell was apprehended after striking a police officer with a baseball bat. The officer had been trying to contain a crowd that had gathered at the scene of a recent shooting. Mr. Bell insisted that the victim of the shooting was his brother, and that he (Mr. Bell) was only trying to find the rest of his family. The officer sustained minor injuries trying to restrain Mr. Bell and was sent to the hospital; he was released shortly thereafter. Offender has no prior record.

Drew heard a jingle of keys, and Janet Sutton poked her head in the open door. "How's it going?" Even from twelve feet away Drew could see something black stuck between her front teeth. She was wearing a silky blouse with starchy knee-length shorts over ivory tights, the same kind Drew routinely wore to piano recitals in her youth.

"Great!" Drew realized she was simply staring at Janet with her mouth open and shook her head to clear it. "Sorry. I'm feeling a little overwhelmed right now. First day and all."

Janet nodded. "I understand completely."

Drew tapped Howard's file. "This guy can't even read the word 'cat,' yet he has five children." Drew knew she sounded naïve, but she'd taught in an upper-middle class, homogeneous classroom in Eau Claire. Her old school district had its flaws, but she was pretty sure most of her students were able to read three-letter words by their eighteenth birthdays. And she knew none of her former students were parents five times over when Selective Service came to call.

"Oh sure. You'll see a lot of that here. And with your guys, they can't even enroll in the parenting program. Got to have a third-grade reading level to be in that."

Her guys. That implied an ownership of—a *responsibility* for something (or rather *someones*) she wasn't sure she was ready to take responsibility for. But she signed up for this. She now earned a paycheck for this, didn't she? And then the question that had been washing up on her mental shores for days dried out and demanded sudden attention. She asked before she could stop herself. "Janet, has there ever been a riot here?"

She heard the clock tick behind her, so loud she could nearly feel it in her chest. Or maybe that was her heartbeat. Janet's brow furrowed. "Not that I know of. But there was a riot in South Bend back in 1993. The skinheads took over the education wing." She paused, and Drew could almost predict Janet's next line. "A teacher was raped. They threw one of the officers out a third-story window."

She felt the muscles in her cheeks twitch.

"I don't want to scare you, but you should always be prepared for anything. Don't let your guard down. But don't be paranoid, either. That's a real mind-eff, pardon my language."

When Janet spun on her heel to return to her classroom Drew spotted a teeny wad of paper—*a spitball!*—lodged in the hair above the nape of Janet's neck. Something about it both comforted and saddened Drew. She imagined Janet shoe-shopping with her aging mother, growing impatient with the jokes told by her daughter's boyfriend, debating carpet samples with her mild-mannered husband. Drew imagined Janet getting ready for bed tonight, brushing her teeth, washing her face, discovering the spitball when she pulled her pajamas over her head.

Drew made a mental note to bring her A game in the classroom. It suddenly seemed imperative to gain and keep the respect of her students, if only so she didn't leave work to meet a friend for drinks with a spitball in her hair.

Then again, in the grand scheme of things, when you could be raped or thrown from a window during a workplace riot, a spitball in your hair didn't seem all that bad.

Drew had been there just two weeks and she was beginning to appreciate both the regimented prison routine and the way surprises sometimes broke it up. One Thursday while eating lunch at a picnic table near the administration building she looked up and saw two raccoons lumbering through the narrow, razor wire-lined corridor between the electrified fences. And then there were the feral cats roaming the grounds. How they got in was a similar mystery. Walking from the school to the parking lot at the end of the day, she often spotted the cats sunning themselves on the cement steps to inmate housing units. Inmates sometimes got conduct reports for raising litters under their bunks. Amass too many conduct reports or even only one really bad one, and you'd end up in the hole with your breakfast, lunch, and dinner ground up and baked into a loaf.

Drew learned that any of the 417 prison employees could bring their cars into the school garage, and for thirteen bucks, inmates enrolled in the auto-detailing program would clean those cars inside and out. She also learned that inmates could purchase anything from candy bars to hair care products at the prison store, Canteen.

Inmates earned between five and forty-two cents an hour, depending on their jobs. If an inmate didn't have a job, he could spend his days watching TV, playing ping pong, or building a model space shuttle out of plastic spoons if he felt so inclined, but he was paid zilch. If he attended school or enrolled in alcohol or drug programming, he made fifteen cents an hour. The best-paid inmates were the barbers.

Some misty mornings a note was taped on the gatehouse door: *Fog Alert*. The inmates were then held in their units, delaying jobs and school, until every guard tower in the complex had a clear view of the next. Fog alerts were perennial favorites of inmates and staff.

By her second week virtually all of the inmates knew her by name, and the catcalls and whistles had become just another part of the daily soundtrack. She continued to work with Howard Bell, who hadn't made any notable progress with his phonics. She was starting to recognize inmates by name as well as by face. Having read most of the files of her students, she also began to associate offender with offense, even though she knew she shouldn't.

Third hour was the worst. Victor Hansen, who had participated in a gang rape of a nine-year-old mentally handicapped girl, sat next to Ricky Lipton, sentenced to two concurrent sentences of eight years each, one for each count of second-degree sexual assault. According to his file, he'd "violated" two twelve-year-olds at knifepoint on a dirty mattress in a cockroach-infested basement. Ricky Lipton had lovely, shining curls that he protected with a clear shower cap if it was raining out.

Then there was Bobby Buchanan, a sixteen-year-old with dimples and attention deficit disorder. He had beaten an elderly woman with a heavy metal flashlight before ripping her purse from her hands. Bobby sat in the desk right in front of Drew and had already passed three of the seven tests that would lead to his High School Equivalency Degree. He was also HIV positive.

Ronald Ulrich and Dale Garvey, both eighteen, had been the class's bosom buddies, but now the two weren't speaking for some reason. Ronald, cognitively delayed and epileptic, was in for shooting a kid in the neck with a nine-millimeter pistol. Dale, emotionally disturbed, was serving a twenty-year sentence for recklessly endangering lives and grand theft auto. He hijacked a car at gunpoint and led police on a high-speed chase through downtown Milwaukee at three in the morning. Dale was born with Fetal Alcohol Syndrome and witnessed his father's suicide at the age of eight.

Barry Gast, in for possession of cocaine with intent to deliver, sat to Bobby Buchanan's right. Barry was studying to take the science portion of his GED practice tests. Right after entering the classroom every day, Barry grabbed his folder, pulled up a chair next to Drew, and said, "Let's hit it" or "Let's roll, Miss D."

Drew was still a bit baffled as to how she was supposed to relate to them, and she guessed that feeling wouldn't go away anytime soon. This wasn't *Freedom Writers* or *Stand and Deliver* or *The Ron Clark Story* or *Dangerous Minds* or *Privileged White Teacher Inspires Troubled Minority Students with Unconventional Methods that Irk Tenured Colleagues*. She couldn't bribe her students with candy bars or ask them to read about Anne Frank and then write their life stories, because she'd already read their files, which were unnerving enough the first time around, and also because most of them had difficulty with multisyllabic words. Plus, if a person's tattoos were any indicator of his belief system, she was pretty sure she had at least one Holocaust denier in third hour.

She wouldn't mind a comparison to *Half Nelson*, because while then she'd be a drug addict, at least she'd have her own apartment. And a cat, for a few scenes. So the riddle was this: How does a young, middle-class woman build an appropriate rapport with and actually *teach* something to a class full of criminals, most of whom have a fairly singular way of relating to women? It had to be a riddle, because she couldn't think of any kind of answer that made sense.

She hadn't seen much of Joe since the Fourth of July, running into him at work only once in the last two weeks. She hadn't seen Graham in at least a week, either. She spent her evenings going for runs down the lazy country roads near her parents' house, gradually feeling more like her old self. She read *Games Criminals Play* based on her mother's recommendation. When they were in high school, Nick, Wendy, and Drew had each received, at one time or another, their mother's classic admonishment, "I can't believe how much you're thinking like a criminal right now!" It was textbook Sara, and now Drew knew the textbook from which it came.

She watched awful reality TV because her own life seemed normal by comparison. Later, she watched Telemundo to brush up on her Spanish to better understand what her Latino students were saying to each other in class.

She barely missed her old friends in Eau Claire.

She hardly even thought about Ben.

Who knew working in a prison could be such great accidental therapy?

Drew liked the feel of her keys bouncing against her right hip, jingling cheerfully as she strode toward the school office. A lone inmate in a blue smock was manning a floor polisher in the cool hallway. Drew smiled politely at him as she passed, and he tipped his head in her direction. "Good afternoon, Miss Daniels." Everyone seemed to know her name, and she hadn't even been there three weeks. Drew smiled and said hello in return. She had no idea what the inmate's name was.

Many of the inmates were so polite that when she actually read their files, their crimes seemed almost make-believe. They could teach etiquette or acting classes, really. Sell Advanage cleaning products door to door.

She entered the break room behind the office, surprised to see Joe seated at the round table in the center of the room. Surprised to see him and surprised at the happy lurch in her stomach.

He was flipping through a tattered magazine, drinking a grape soda. He glanced up and smiled. "Care to engage in a little childish gossip?" He pulled out a chair.

She sat and returned the smile. "My favorite kind!"

Joe said nothing for a beat, just kept smiling.

"So?" Drew's cheeks were suddenly warm. She didn't know where to look. How long would it take to feel comfortable with those mismatched eyes? They were attractive and disturbing at the same time. She forced herself to focus on the brown one.

Joe took a swallow of soda and finally said, "They walked Retanski out."

Alyssa Retanski was a cute brunette officer on second shift. Drew had never actually spoken to her, but she'd seen her tooling around the grounds on a golf cart, always looking unapproachable and important.

"They caught her messing with one of the inmates."

"What do you mean, 'messing with the inmates?'"

"Blow jobs in the laundry room. Sergeant Peterson walked in on her with some new guy in for burglary. These guys are sweet-talkers, that's for sure. Charmed the pants off Alyssa." Joe studied Drew and drolly added, "You should be careful."

Drew let her mouth fall open. "You mean I'm not supposed to have sex with inmates at work?"

"You're young and pretty, and that makes you an easy target. Spend enough time here and you'll see what I mean."

She tried not to roll her eyes. She wasn't like Lisa Crane, who flirted with the inmates and teased them for dirty urine tests. "You called me young! That was so sweet."

He snorted. "Yeah, you're so old. What are you, like, twenty-five?"

"Ha!" Drew was relieved when his radio squawked before she had a chance to embarrass herself by saying something like, "Flattery will get you everywhere," pretending she was joking when really, she wasn't.

He listened to the staticky voice on the radio for a few seconds. "Hey, I gotta run." He shot both fingers at her, à la Isaac from *The Love Boat*, and left the lounge. Drew leaned into her chair and sighed. She picked up the magazine, aware of the warmth where his fingers had touched the page. She was pleased to see that it was *National Geographic* and not *NASCAR Illustrated*. Jesus was on the cover. She closed her right eye, and Jesus dissolved into a blur. What was she doing? She was in no shape for any kind of new relationship, even one that was purely physical, involving lots of steamy, deep kisses and sweaty thrusting and tangled hair and hot, urgent—

Someone was shouting down the hall. Drew threw the magazine across the table and jogged toward the office. Lisa Crane flew into her face, eyes bulging with excitement.

"There's a fight outside!"

The office emptied into the hallway, toward the glass doors. Two inmates were grappling on the ground, a blur of green uniforms and flying fists. A cluster of inmates leaned over them, jeering and shouting. Guards rushed in to break up the fight, their keys jangling frantically.

A second later the crowd dissipated and the fighting inmates were hauled away in separate vans to the segregation unit. Lisa walked back into the building with Drew. "Those two will get banned from school now. Chris Whiteside and James Walker." She clucked her tongue and shook her head. "You just watch."

Drew was mildly impressed. She hadn't known the inmates' names.

"They're lucky nobody had a shank." Drew had a feeling Lisa had been waiting all day to use that word. *Shank*. Which rhymes with *stank* and *skank*, incidentally. She suddenly smirked and examined Drew. "I hear Joe Simon's got the hots for you."

"What?"

"You heard me," Lisa said. "I'd be careful, if I were you. He's quite the player."

Drew frowned and replied, "Well, thanks for the warning, I guess." She imagined Lisa was insanely popular at the age of twelve, but bottomed out a few years later when an actual personality was required for extended human interaction. Drew excused herself and headed toward Janet's classroom. She was hunched over her desk writing an incident report.

"Have a seat."

Drew fell into the chair next to her and made a serious effort to lighten up. "There was a big brawl outside."

"Gee, sorry I missed it." Janet kept writing.

"The whole office ran out to watch."

"I'm sure they did." Janet thrust the report in front of her. "You'll be writing a few of these sooner or later. What do you think?"

Janet was writing up a student from her second-hour class for disrespect, disobeying orders, and disruptive conduct (the "Three Ds"), plus an added bonus: sexual contact and soliciting staff. This incendiary cocktail could result in segregation, loss of good time, and even extension of mandatory release date.

On the morning of Thursday, July fifteenth at 10:14, I noticed inmate James Hustisford drawing inappropriate graffiti in pencil on his desk. I asked him to stop drawing and to erase what he'd drawn. He refused. He also refused to participate in the test I was administering. I asked him twice to begin writing, and he said to me, "You can go fuck yourself." *He then proceeded to unzip his pants and expose his genitals. I contacted Officer Barnes and had Inmate Hustisford removed immediately.*

Drew looked up when she finished reading and smiled. At least it felt like a smile. "Wow," she said. "And it's not even lunchtime!"

Drew caught a glimpse of her reflection in the bank of windows across the room. She was distressed to find that she looked remarkably calm; amused even. This was it, then. She had officially stepped into the career elevator and pressed the "Basement" button. She thought of her friends back in Eau Claire—mostly fellow teachers, but also a nurse practitioner, a yoga instructor, and one probation officer, a tiny girl named Francine, who frequently entertained her friends with stories about her clients. One of them had a glass eye. He liked to pop it out and bounce it on his palm during their appointments. Drew felt a special affection for Francine just then, and made a mental note to call her soon. Compare notes, have a few laughs, shake their heads in tandem wonder at the infinite weirdness humanity could display.

After finishing her sandwich at lunch, Drew declined an invitation to play badminton, deciding instead to clear her head with a walk along the forested stretch of highway in front of

Lakeside. As she walked toward the gatehouse, she heard, "Hey, Drew! Wait up!"

It was Graham. Drew stopped and smiled, genuinely happy to see him.

"Want to go for a walk?" Graham asked. "Well, you walk. I'll roll."

They greeted the officers in the gatehouse, made their way through the gauntlet of locked doors, and headed into the parking lot together. She still wasn't used to seeing him in his wheelchair. Whenever she saw him now, her first reaction was a bit self-centered. As in, *what would I do in a wheelchair? Who would even want me then, beyond some guy with a paralysis fetish?* And then she felt guilty filtering his very personal, very life-warping experience through her own selfish sieve. Her next reaction was always more specific to Graham.

What kind of hell it must have been for him, in the beginning. How did you say goodbye to the most elemental of activities that people take for granted? Walking, for one thing. Standing in the shower, letting the water cascade down the full length of you. Jumping up to take a quick pee between commercials. Taking a quick pee, period. She wasn't even remotely clear on the logistics of that, and she didn't foresee herself asking.

"Hey, come with me for a second," he said. "I want to show you something."

She followed him to his truck (specially outfitted to accommodate him and carry his chair) and waited while he unlocked it and retrieved his cell phone. He queued up a video and handed his phone to her.

Drew began to smile. "What is this?"

"It's a promo video for the Tek robotic mobilization device. On the market in Turkey."

In the video on Graham's phone, a man with a deep, smooth voice narrated while a young man with a T7 spinal cord injury went about his daily routine belted to a pneumatic machine that held him in an upright, standing position or smoothly lowered to seat him at eye level with dining companions. He slid in and out of bed independently, and with ease. He washed dishes at a tall sink. He maneuvered effortlessly through slim aisles in a bookstore, his machine boasting a tight turning radius. He had his hands free to pay for and carry a tray of food in a cafeteria.

"This is amazing! Are you getting one?"

"Well, it's pretty expensive, and I don't think it'll be available in the US for a while."

"How much is it?"

"Fifteen grand. Not too bad, really. Price of a mid-range car."

"It kind of reminds me of a Segway."

"Except it's actually useful."

Drew smiled. "Of course." They continued past the parking lot onto the shade-dappled, paved road. A blue jay gave a series of shrill, prehistoric shrieks somewhere in the woods. "God, what a gorgeous day. Did you eat lunch already?"

Graham nodded, his arms rhythmically pushing himself up a gentle incline in the highway. A Prius materialized behind them and quietly passed, giving a wide berth.

"Jesus, those cars are sneaky bastards."

Drew glanced at Graham's arms, watching his biceps and forearms flex. Modestly covered in hair and muscular, every vein standing out from his efforts. *Push, propel. Push, propel.* There was something nearly sexual about those arms, something rough yet reliable, and she forced herself to look away, at a tar-spackled crack in the pavement. "How far do you want to go?"

"To the top of that hill, and then I'll race you back down."

"I think you'd win." They kept moving, Drew glancing sidelong at Graham, whose breath had quickened from the exertion. "Are you sure you don't want to go the other way?"

He raised one eyebrow. "I'm fine, Mom."

Drew smiled self-consciously. His tone was genial but impatient, and she knew better than to press the issue. "Well, at least I didn't try to push you."

"That'd make me feel like a man." Graham looked up at her, grinning crookedly. A semi-truck was barreling down the hill toward them, blasting its horn. "Thanks," Graham shouted, lifting his hand to wave at the truck as it passed, its hot tailwind lifting their hair and flattening the ditch grass behind them. "Thanks for that. Hearing from the left ear is so overrated anyway." He turned to her and smirked. "Okay then, smart one. Let's see you try to push me. Don't forget, it's uphill."

"Seriously?"

"Yeah. I bet you can't last ten feet."

"What are we betting?"

He paused for a moment, considering his options. "You get me to the top of the hill, I'll buy you a drink. If not, drink's on you."

"You're on," she said, stepping behind him and grasping the small handles on the back of his chair. "Let's see how fast I can get this thing moving." She heaved herself into the first push, taking three deliberate steps forward. He and the chair were much heavier than she'd guessed, the incline much steeper. "Oh my God, do you have the brake on?" A hearty, exasperated laugh escaped her.

"No." He playfully banged the sides of his wheels. "Come on, She-Ra! Push with the legs!"

Two more steps, three, four, five (slowing down now), six, seven, and ... she stopped and bent forward, arms fully extended, elbows locked to brace the chair and keep it from rolling back into her. She hung her head and took a few deep, humbled breaths. "I give up. You win."

He beamed, taking over for her. "Need a towel, Sweaty Spaghetti?"

She patted her brow primly with one hand. "Ladies don't sweat. They glisten."

"Or in your case, drench a shirt and spend the afternoon dehydrated and crampy."

Drew pursed her lips, lifted her left elbow, and flipped him the bird, sideways.

"Gangster finger. I like it. Very fitting. Very feminine. Hey, speaking of flipped birds, did I ever tell you about my mother? She's like the bird whisperer of east-central Wisconsin. Chickadees eat out of her hand. There's this one sparrow with a broken leg that lives in her back yard. She puts out a special dish of birdseed for him because he has to lie down in it to eat."

"Yes, but does she have a life list and go digiscoping like my dad?"

"Nah, she's just a softie when it comes to helping cripples."

"Aw, Graham," Drew said, laughing sadly.

"So what's digiscoping? It sounds like something your doctor would do to your colon after you turn fifty."

"You put a digital camera on the end of a spotting scope. It's a birding thing."

"I always thought bird watching seemed like one of those inevitable hobbies you succumb to in middle age. Like shingles."

She laughed again. "It doesn't seem so bad. It's quiet, you're out in nature taking pictures, on a secret mission to find some rare bird to fill your life list."

"With a bran muffin in your fanny pack for later."

"Sunscreen, binoculars, a prescription for Valtrex ... what more do you need?"

"Your wasted youth back. Maybe a new hip."

They continued for another half mile before turning back when they encountered the stinking, mangled carcass of a dead skunk near the center line. "Dead skunk in the middle of the road," she began to sing. "Did you know," she said, interrupting herself, "that the guy who originally wrote and sang that is Rufus Wainwright's father? Little bit of trivia for you."

Graham gave her a considering look, opened his mouth to say something, but thought better of it and only smiled. They returned to the gatehouse as noon count ended and went their separate ways.

11. GRAHAM

Tonight I have a date with a girl named Abby. I met her online, which should come as no big shock. This time, I learned my lesson. I decided to eliminate the surprise portion of the evening and be completely forthcoming about my spinal cord injury. "I think I should tell you," I blurted on the phone as we made plans, "that I'm in a wheelchair."

Silence. Then, "Wow. Huh. Um, why didn't you tell me earlier?" It was hard to gauge her response, as Abby is the kind of girl who keeps her emotions on a short leash, speaking in a placid, balanced tone even when discussing a topic she's passionate about—say, clubbing baby seals. If I had to guess, I'd say she sounds stunned, and I can detect the faintest whiff of reproach.

"I know, I should probably have put it in my profile. I guess I wanted people to get to know me for me. Not out of pity or some kind of weird curiosity." I didn't mention that I *had* listed my disability in my first profile, and it netted me a grand total of zero winks or smiles or whatever the hell the interest indicators were. "People say they don't discriminate, but …"

"Wow," she said again. "Graham, I would have been okay with it. I wouldn't have judged you." Again, with the even tone. She could do hypnotherapy with that voice.

"I'm sorry, Abby. I really am."

"How did it happen? If you don't mind my asking."

I told her.

"I'm so sorry, Graham." She paused, and I could almost hear my news setting up shop in her mind. I could feel her recalibrating whatever internal mechanism is charged with deciding how to proceed in such strange situations. Go with the flow? Or sever the connection? "Well, that's okay," she finally said. "I have a wandering eye." And she giggled self-consciously.

"Oh!" I said. "Um..." *Wandering eye.* Spinal cord injury. *Wandering eye.* Spinal cord injury. "Well, don't worry. Lots of people have commitment issues."

"No!" she nearly shouted. "I mean, I have a medical condition. It's called Strabismus. It's a visual defect where one eye sometimes ... focuses in another direction."

"Oh," I said again, trying not to laugh. "I'm sorry. I thought you meant..." I laugh for real this time.

"No biggie. As long as we're being honest, right?" She giggled again. "It actually only wanders some of the time. It's temperamental, you might say." She paused before adding, "I keep telling it to settle down, enjoy the life it has, but somewhere along the line it was bitten by the travel bug."

I knew she was blushing now. You could hear it in her inflection. I laughed again, and the sound of it startled me— probably because it was authentic. The girl had potential. "So now that we've gotten our physical challenges out of the way, where would you like to meet?" I hesitated. "Assuming you still want to go out with me." It came out before I could stop it, in that old, familiar tone that always filled me with self-loathing.

"Of course I do," she said, warmly. "And I know a great place downtown. It's called Roots. Have you heard of it?"

I usually avoid Roots, because the food and clientele are a bit too precious for my tastes. I like my food the way I like people: real and easy to digest. Leave the celery root purees and miso-braised sunchokes for people who enjoy TED talks and Wes Anderson movies. I also avoid Roots because of who owns it. Mrs. Brooke Sullivan. And I believe I've mentioned my mild aversion to Brooke Sullivan.

Still, I didn't want to be difficult. "Roots is fine," I agreed in as amicable a tone as I could muster. Abby seemed like a nice girl—with a sense of humor to boot—and I wanted to get things off on the right foot. She manages a daycare in a small town thirty minutes south of Laurentide Bay. If she in any way resembles the photos she's posted in her profile, she's attractive in a non-threatening, friendly way perfectly befitting a woman whose daily mediums include finger paint and Play-Doh: sandy blond shoulder-length hair, thin lips curved into a warm smile, full cheeks framing a nose that's an ounce too large for her face, but cheerful nonetheless.

We arranged to meet at the restaurant at eight.

After parking my truck and getting myself situated in my chair, I wheel to the door. I am out of my element here, among the convention of tea lights, the minimalist furniture upholstered in velvet, the fluttering jazz. It's meant to lull the guests and enhance the dining experience, but it only agitates my already jangled nerves. This restaurant is in an historic building, and the postmodern interior seems at odds with the worn brick exterior. I long for a simple, dark and smoky Wisconsin supper club with fried perch, a baked potato slathered in sour cream, an iceberg lettuce salad drizzled in French dressing, and a whiskey Old Fashioned to wash it down. Hell, I'd take Country Plate over this pompous bullshit any day, but as tonight's location was not my choice, I will hunker down and politely endure my truffled risotto with the summer people.

At the hostess stand I'm greeted by none other than Brooke Sullivan herself, in black-framed glasses that make her look much smarter than she is. "Graham! It's so good to see you," she says, leaning down to kiss the air near my left ear. What a fake thing to do. Something inside of me begins digging trenches, laying sandbags, and unspooling barbed wire around the perimeter. It's going to be a long night.

"Brooke." I fix a smile to my face. "It's good to see you, too."

It's also good to know I can still lie with the best of them.

"Table for ... one?" she asks, wearing a bland service-industry smile.

I try to hide my annoyance. "No, I'm meeting someone. I know it's hard to imagine." That second sentence just kind of slipped out. *Paging Bitter Wheelchair Guy...*

Her expression stiffens and she laughs in self-defense. "Oh! No, Graham, I wouldn't ... I didn't mean ..." Her words disappear into the ambient din of the restaurant. She consults a diagram of the dining room and glances over her shoulder. The bar hums with a lively midweek crowd sipping imported beer and martinis, but only about a third of the tables in the dining section are occupied. She turns back to face me, her expression cool and professional, and says, "We're in luck. A table for two just opened up. Follow me." Her smile falters as her eyes dip to my chair, but it returns when her eyes bounce back up to my face.

Abby isn't here yet, so after I'm parked at the table I pretend to study the menu while checking out my fellow diners. Their faces glow in the candlelight. Every couple seems to be auditioning for a Kay Jewelers commercial, feeding one another crostini and flirting over the duck confit. I'm surprised at how nervous I am. I attribute it to my discomfort at being in such a prissy environment, surrounded by shiny, gilded couples with investment portfolios larger than the gross domestic product of Bolivia. I sip my ice water, which has been garnished with lemon and cucumber slices. Why must even the water be pussified here? I pick the cucumber out, but the lemon has sunk to the bottom of my glass like a punctured boat. There'll be no retrieving that wedge without a major production and ice cubes flipping all over the table, so it's just going to have to stay there.

I pick up the wine list, a cardboard mini-easel in the center of our too-small table, flapping it open and shut. I'm bored. I've already decided I'll be eating the organic roast beef with morel stuffing. It comes with garlic-buttered polenta and maple-glazed carrots, which is the closest thing on the menu to a substance my own palate will recognize and accept. I will not order a glass of the Roots-recommended old vine Zinfandel, as I still have my testicles. Plus, it's fifteen dollars a glass.

While I wait for Abby, I watch the couple to my left. They remind me of wealthier versions of my parents, studiously dissecting and reviewing their entrees. The woman even has hair like my mother: that midlife, chin-length relaxed perm—a shade between honey and overripe banana—that suggests a flustered yet weary surrender in the face of menopause. Which reminds me that my mother is coming over this weekend so I can sign some papers for my parents' living will. Ever since my grandmother died last year of a massive heart attack, my mother's been preoccupied with getting her affairs in order before she exits the planet, stage left. I keep waiting for this morbid trend to end, but I think the Grim Reaper has the advantage here. He's got the advantage on all of us.

As I ponder this cheerful thought I spot Abby at the door. Brooke briskly leads her to our table; en route, Abby offers a brief, shy wave. I smile and nod in return, greeting her with, "I apologize for not pulling your chair out for you."

"Oh!" She giggles self-consciously. "That's okay." She's much cuter in person, and very well proportioned in a form-fitting white blouse and pin-striped trousers. I can't even imagine one of her eyes having a mind of its own. After she sits she extends a hand. "It's nice to finally meet you in person."

I shake it. She has a pleasant, Goldilocks grip—not too hard, not too soft, but just right. "It's nice to meet you, too. And I'm sorry again, for not being entirely honest right up front. When you're in this kind of situation, the 'reveal' becomes this huge deal, taking on a life of its own. I really appreciate your willingness to take a chance on me, especially after ..." I trail off, because I'm unable to finish with, "I lied."

"Not at all. I completely understand." She shakes her head, smiling warmly, and I watch her left eye slowly travel forty-five degrees until it's looking at a painting over my shoulder. "Ah, there it goes."

"Wow," I say, trying to maintain a neutral tone. "Have you always had this ... condition?"

"Since childhood. It comes and goes. It's usually more active when I'm feeling a little stressed."

"First dates can be fairly stressful," I acknowledge. I watch, fascinated, as her eye travels back to me. "I'll try to keep things low-key."

She laughs, genuinely. "I appreciate that."

Abby and I had exchanged a series of cheerful e-mails and two phone conversations prior to tonight, volleying the usual get-to-know-you information back and forth: what we do for a living, a little bit about our families, the things we do to fill our free time. We revisit all of these topics again between visits by our server. I do order the morel-stuffed roast beef. Abby orders the butternut squash and sun-dried tomato risotto. And we do share a bottle of the red Zin. My balls have surrendered and retreated. It's only a matter of time before I purchase a pore-reducing toner that smells of green tea and papaya.

Abby's a nice enough girl. Sweet, considerate, witty … but why does my mind keep traveling back to Drew? To the soft curve of her neck? The dimple in her right cheek, the way her eyes crinkle when she laughs at my bad jokes? As I watch Abby talk animatedly about a recent trip to Italy, I nod and smile at all the right parts. I even manage a relevant question or two. "Oh, wow," I hear myself say in a voice that sounds miles away. "So your favorite city was Venice? Did you ride in a gondola?" I watch Abby gesture as she talks, pausing only for a brief sip of wine before her hands dive into new shapes. Her teeth gleam in the candlelight. I appreciate that she doesn't pronounce the word "Italian" with a long *I,* as in "Eye-talian."

Yet I am not in the now. My mind is wistfully sitting in the bleachers watching Drew running in the sunshine after a soccer ball, her shiny ponytail streaming behind her. It is 1997. I am on the track team, my specialties the 800-yard dash and the long jump. You couldn't turn on a radio without hearing Sublime's "What I Got." And what I got that year, the year I turned sixteen, was a crippling, devastating crush on Drew Daniels.

I will myself to snap out of it. Drew has never indicated that she ever felt anything for me beyond the affable affection of a buddy. I am sexless to her. A rolling, rambling friend, a congenial pal from high school, an innocuous coworker who may as well be a eunuch.

After our leftovers have been boxed and the server lays the check on the table, Abby smiles at me. "I had a good time tonight."

"Me too," I reply. But I'm not sure I mean it. The funny thing is, on paper this is the best date I've had in years. So why does my heart feel like it's on the bottom of the ocean?

After my date I arrange myself on the couch and log on to Xbox Live. According to my friends list, Trevor's playing a game demo. His gamer tag is De4thDicKi3, a reference to the turtleneck dickies his mother made him wear under V-neck sweaters in grade school. It's also a pathetic attempt at being l33t. Loser. I text him a message—*hey man, I see you playing that pussy demo*, send him a chat invite, put my headset on, and flip around the tube while I wait for him to respond. *American Ninja Warrior* is on G4, which I like to call the thinking man's Spike TV. I'm feeling too scattered to actually play anything, and I'm between games I feel genuine enthusiasm for. I realize that my public acknowledgment of this outs me as one who received more than his share of wedgies and swirlies, but hey. If the shoe fits.

And as long as I'm in a public disclosure kind of mood, I'll also admit to owning the complete DVD library of *Family Guy*, *Tim and Eric Awesome Show Great Job*, *Venture Brothers*, the definitive gold box edition of *Twin Peaks*, every episode of *Veronica Mars*, and, tucked away on the back of the shelf, the first full season of *Maude*, which was a gag gift from Kevin that I not only viewed in its entirety, but enjoyed.

As I watch a guy attempt to scale a rope wall, Trevor clicks on with a lackluster, "Hey man. What's up?" His voice is nasal and smothered.

"Wow man, you sound terrible."

Trevor groans. "My jaw's totally swollen. I had a reaction to a local anesthetic."

"You know, too many collagen lip injections are a bad idea for anyone."

"Screw you. I had a root canal today."

Biologically, Trevor is thirty-one. Physically, he is seventy-seven after forty years of working in a coal mine, smoking a high-tar unfiltered cigarette every thirty minutes, and eating lard sandwiches on white bread every day for lunch since the age of two. Last week his tongue was experiencing some kind of bizarre and painful spasm that caused it to stick to the roof of his mouth for hours on end—a reaction to one of the many medications he's taking. A few months ago he had his gallbladder removed. He's so thin his mother once threatened to hospitalize him for anorexia, yet his cholesterol is a staggering 612. *Six hundred and twelve!* In case you don't know, a healthy number is less than 200.

"Jesus man, you're a wreck."

"Tell me about it." He sounds pathetic.

"I guess it could be worse," I say. "I knew a guy in physical therapy, a quad, whose thigh bone burst right through his jeans while the therapist was working with him. We heard a loud CRACK, and then the guy goes, all nonchalant, 'Oh shit. Look at this.' He didn't even feel it."

Trevor grunts.

"His bone snapped almost in half," I continue. Brittle bones are just one of the many fun little aftershocks of a spinal cord injury. *Helll-oooooo, Boniva!* See, there's Glib Me again. Andy Glib, falsetto not included. Mel Glibson, anti-Semitism optional.

"That sounds pleasant."

I can hear gunshots and explosions in the background. "Sick of getting your nub pwn3d by n00bs there, Mr. DicKi3?"

"Whatever. I'd shoot an invite but I'm probably gonna shut it down pretty soon."

I don't bother to tell him about dinner with Abby, and Trevor doesn't bother to ask, though I'd mentioned it to him yesterday. When Trevor's facing his latest health ailment, he's usually not in the best of moods, and can't be bothered to invest much in a conversation. Then again, the same could be said when he's *not* feeling under the weather. Trevor never goes out with anyone (unless you count Rosy Palm and her five sisters), and my dates are usually of the first *and* last persuasion. So until something is worth mentioning, such as we've been happily married for at least a year or two, we don't discuss our romantic distractions and disasters.

We gripe about a glitch in one of the games, and based on Trevor's general disinterest in our discussion, I finally say, "Hey man, you sound awful. Go take a nap. Go sit under a bare light bulb and write some bad poetry."

"Fuck off, I really feel like hell. I'm gonna sign off in a minute. As soon as this round is over."

After I pull my headset off I channel-surf for a bit, not quite ready for bed. My options are thus: a Blaxploitation movie marathon, *Friends* reruns, and a Time-Life infomercial for soft rock classics from the seventies. All the players are at the table in unflattering footage shot at weird angles: Bertie Higgins, Todd Rundgren, Dan Fogelberg. There may have been a law passed in the seventies that all male musical acts must adopt weird, cumbersome names that mimic a Listerine gargle when spoken aloud. I watch the infomercial, hosted by Air Supply, for a few minutes, feeling a weird nostalgia for the days of avocado-colored kitchens, macramé wall art, and shag carpet-upholstered vans—even though I wasn't even alive in that decade.

My cell phone rings. Since it's almost midnight, I'm guessing it's Kevin. Calling late at night after six or seven beers to serenade my voicemail with an entire Bon Jovi or Tesla song is one of his favorite hobbies. A quick check of the screen confirms this. Kevin greets me with a hearty, "My boy!" I can hear the muted din of a moderately busy tavern in the background: laughter and conversation, bottles clanking, Sheryl Crow on the jukebox.

"Kevin." I brace myself for whatever antics he has planned for the night.

"Hey, I was thinking. You remember that time your fart made Don Winston throw up?"

I grimace, smiling despite myself. "You called to ask me this?"

Kevin bursts into his patented maniacal giggle. If my friends were reading material, Kevin would be *Maxim*, and Trevor would be an anime graphic novel with a non-linear plot, magic gemstones, and a talking lemur. If they were animals, Trevor would be a hypochondriac tortoise, and Kevin would be Bugs Bunny on crystal meth. "So I've been thinking," he continues. "I know where you're gonna pick up lots of chicks."

"A poultry farm?"

"A poultry farm, he says." He muffles the mouthpiece and shouts to someone: "A poultry farm, he says!" He returns to the phone. "No, listen." He pauses for effect. "You ready for this?"

"Just get on with it," I say, rolling my eyes and resuming my channel surfing.

"Ready? Are you sure?"

"Don't be an ass."

More giggling. "Okay. We're volunteering at a diabetes fundraiser sponsored by Harley-Davidson."

"What do you mean 'we?'"

"I signed us up!"

"Do you even know anybody with diabetes?" I immediately remember that Joe Simon has diabetes. The prick. Joe Simon and his Screw for the Cure life slogan. Well, to hell with him. I've got a spinal cord injury. I'm the best sympathy fuck around.

Kevin ignores my question. "You have to come, man. There's bound to be lots of dudes in wheelchairs there! Motorcycles, Graham. Think about it." In the background, I hear a woman hooting laughter.

"Your sensitivity knows no bounds."

"Okay, listen. Listen. I'm gonna let you in on a little secret."

There's a long pause, and I finally shout, "What?" I love the guy, but sometimes talking to Kevin can be as mentally fatiguing as taking a standardized test in Russian.

"Okay. Here it is. You ready? Okay." He lowers his voice, serious now. "Chicks love dudes in wheelchairs." More bottles clanking into a garbage can in the background.

I laugh. "Well, this dude in a wheelchair begs to differ."

"Come on, man! You'll have fun. I promise. It's for a good cause. And I'm telling ya, chicks dig dudes in chairs. I'm not talking about those nutcases you meet online. I'm talking about Grade A, high quality hotties. I'm talking about some first class, melt in your mouth and in your hands, prime cuts of *women*."

I sigh and play along. "So what am I, your bait? I lure them in and you take them home?"

"Wow, what a great idea! Why didn't I think of it?" He giggles again, fiendishly. Not many guys can giggle without sounding like the gay Teletubby. But Kevin can, probably because he's got the build of a mixed martial artist and metabolizes alcohol the way the rest of us metabolize tangerines. Kevin is dating a girl named Mandy, whose pastimes include publicly bemoaning her weight and dropping national debt-sized hints about how badly she wants to get married.

Suddenly he shifts gears. "Hey, didn't you have a date tonight? With that chick what's her name ... Annie? Bammy? Clammy?" He giggles again at his own subprime wit. "Clammy, I like that."

"Abby. I did ... it was fine. She's a nice girl."

"Nice!" he practically shouts. "Nice, he says. So did ya toss a little salad? Do some finger blasting? Get a little stank on the hang-low?" Kevin's using the frenzied SUNDAY! SUNDAY!

SUNDAY! voice he pilfered from a dozen used car salesmen and

SUNDAY! voice he pilfered from a dozen used car salesmen and monster truck rally announcers. Once he gets into character, it's hard to pull him back out.

We had actually shared a simple, friendly hug. I haven't kissed a woman in ... shit. I can't even remember the last time I kissed a woman, let alone got a little stank on my hang-low, as Kevin eloquently put it. "What do you think?" I reply.

He ignores this. There's a sharp intake of breath, and Kevin finishes with, "Harley-Davidson. Fundraiser. You. Me. Chicks. Be there or be square."

I sigh.

"Hey, I gotta run. It's my turn to sing karaoke. 'Suspicious Minds' by my main man. I'll do a shout-out for you during the instrumental."

"Is there even an instrumental in that song?"

"Who gives a shit? I'll do it anyway! Because that's the kind of friend I am."

12. DREW

Drew stepped up to the chalkboard and wrote the words "noun" and "verb" on the board, then turned around to face the classroom. The inmates stared at her as a single, bored organism.

"Can anyone tell me what a noun is?"

They shifted in their seats, avoiding her eyes and collectively sweating. A box fan in the rear of the room propelled cool, unpleasant smells in her direction. She was about to give them the answer when an inmate playing a computer game said, "Person, place, or thing."

"Good. Now can anyone give me an example of one?"

Some of the guys looked confused. "An example of a noun ..." Drew said again.

Finally, an inmate in pigtails spoke. "Car."

"Wonderful! Another example?"

They repeated the entire process when she introduced the verb. She was met with even more blank stares. *It's the action part*, she told them.

"Can anyone put a noun together with a verb and give me a complete sentence?" Someone farted enthusiastically in the back of the room and the class burst into laughter.

"That was lovely," Drew said, affecting an air of nonchalance. "A complete sentence, guys."

"*Gonzalez farted in class,*" the inmate on the computer said, bored. A few inmates in the back of the room laughed again.

Drew's face grew hot while she wrote his sentence on the chalkboard, standing slightly sideways, careful to hold her backside still as she wrote. "Another one?"

After a few more sentences, she passed them their homework assignments. To use the term "homework" was a sick joke, because most of the guys wouldn't be going home any time soon. Drew had stapled together eight assignments, each page more difficult than the previous one. Because her classroom contained a mix of abilities, nobody was on that proverbial same page. "Start at the beginning and work as far as you can."

She knew Howard Bell wouldn't bother with the assignment. He couldn't even read the word *down* without a major effort, much less an entire set of directions. Drew had once heard a rumor that at least two states—California and Indiana—estimate the number of prison beds they'd need in ten years by counting the number of fourth-graders who failed to read at grade level. When she looked around the room now, it was hard to disagree with such a method.

During third hour she thought she saw Victor Hansen blowing kisses at her from under his shellacked curls, but every time she looked directly at him, he'd already bent back over his paper, pretending to write. Last week they'd somehow gotten on the subject of firearms. Eight of her twelve students claimed they'd been shot. Some of them lifted shirts or pant legs to reveal gunshot wounds that had recently healed among the crude blue tattoos.

She could tell most of the inmates dismissed her as another spoiled white girl from the suburbs. They all knew she was the only one among them who wouldn't have trouble hailing a taxi or getting a job with benefits, and it was painfully obvious that she was the only one who had grown up with violin lessons, a college fund, and a home devoid of lead paint chipping from the interior trim.

She knew she couldn't help all of them, but she wanted to sometimes. When she saw how shocked Bobby Buchanan had been at the fact that she knew who Kid Cudi was (thanks to her brother Nick), she felt a rush she'd never felt before. Many of them had childhoods that left them shell-shocked, and Drew understood that sometimes their brains simply didn't cooperate, couldn't process consequences for certain actions. She understood that their days were a meaningless parade of case managers, social workers, psychologists, and treatment specialists. She knew solving for x meant nothing when you'd be lucky to get a job mopping urinals in a public bathroom.

Her favorite student was Howard Bell. She'd selected several Dr. Seuss books for him, and he told her his goal was to read one of them to his children when he was released. She had also begun to work with a painfully shy inmate named Leroy Johnson in the afternoons. She coaxed him into taking the first test toward his equivalency diploma. Drew asked him if he read anything for fun back in his unit. After much prodding he finally confessed that he read some Donald Goines and Iceberg Slim. "I don't care if it's the label on the back of the shampoo bottle," she told him excitedly. "Just read. The more you read, the better you'll be. It's exercise for your brain."

And then there was Ricardo Mariano. Bored with simply staring at her, he'd begun whispering in Spanish to the kid who sat next to him. Drawing from her limited Spanish language skills, Drew thought she heard him once say, "I'm gonna get that bitch." When she asked him what they were discussing, he fluttered his eyelashes innocently and said, "I'm asking for help with a math problem." Ricardo had the most beautiful penmanship she'd ever seen.

She guessed that most of the inmates behaved better in her classroom than they had in public schools. They'd used up all their Get Out of Jail Free cards. They could only go to solitary or maximum from here, where they would sit in a cramped cell for twenty-three hours at a stretch, all the time in the world for reading or writing. Problem was, if you couldn't read or write (or were pretending you couldn't), you would probably go a little insane.

Lots of inmates, used to coasting through the system, completed barely enough work to avoid a conduct report for disobeying orders. Lakeside classes were full of this breed. Having read their files, Drew believed that too many of them were also complete sociopaths.

Sociopaths with excellent cursive, badly groomed nails, and beauty parlor hair.

Life at Lakeside had a highly structured rhythm. But beyond the rigid precision of the daily schedule, where every minute was scripted and accounted for, the hours after work were also sculpted by routine. For example, because it was Thursday, Drew was heading to Finnegan's after work for the weekly happy hour soiree. Non-security staff and a few first-shift officers had also been prodding her to join the Wednesday evening volleyball league, in which the games were played at seven o'clock sharp on an indoor sand court at another tavern across town. Drew had already yielded to the lunchtime badminton aficionados, walking through the empty inmate locker room to join them in the gym for three matches so far. She had also, on four occasions, joined Janet Sutton and Ann Bruce, who walked laps down the vacant school corridors during rainy lunch hours while the inmates ate in their units. And during the actual workday, Drew was required to update a daily electronic calendar with details about her schedule. Time was captured and reported upon in fifteen-minute increments. Every morsel of the day accounted for, plotted, managed, and recorded, as if to stave off chaos or lollygagging on the taxpayer dime.

There was little room in her new life for improvisation, but since she wasn't too keen on surprises these days, that suited her fine.

Drew arrived early at Finnegan's and snagged a table in view of the door. She nursed a gin and tonic while she waited for a few familiar faces to arrive, watching a guy named David Harrison, one year ahead of her in school, shake dice with the bartender, a girl who'd been three years behind her in school. David and his father owned a popular sport fishing charter service in Laurentide Bay. Graham entered to the staccato beat of David slamming the dice cup over and over on the bar. "Hey Drew!" he said, giving a little wave before heading to her table. He parked next to her. "What's up?"

The accident may have stolen Graham's legs, but it didn't steal his sense of humor. Drew nodded at his chest, smiling. "I love your shirt."

He looked down at his blue T-shirt, which featured a white line drawing of the familiar wheelchair-bound stick figure posted in nearly every retail parking lot in America. It read: I'M ONLY IN IT FOR THE PARKING. "You like that? My brother picked it out."

"Hey, how is your brother?" Drew remembered Graham's younger brother having some rather eccentric tendencies. Like not understanding sarcasm and refusing to walk in the middle of any hallway.

"He's great. Formally diagnosed with Asperger's about six years ago, which explains a lot. He's a numismatist now."

"A new mith matist?"

"A *numismatist.*"

"Numith. *Miss.* Numishmatist."

"Numismatist."

"Newmismastist."

"Newsmiss. *Snoomiss.*" Graham frowned. "Fuck it, he's a coin dealer."

She burst out laughing. "I'm sorry. I know how to pronounce it, I just wanted you to keep saying it."

He shook his head, smiling wryly. "A wise guy, eh?"

"Why, I oughta …"

The bartender, Kelsey Jackson, stopped by to take Graham's drink order. She was wearing a pink pleated skirt paired with a ratty black tank top. In high school Kelsey had soft, wavy blond hair, but now it was a prickly black helmet. While Graham ordered, Drew studied the autographed ceiling, searching the tiles for his signature.

"You need anything?" Kelsey asked, pointing at Drew's glass. Half-full or half-empty, it was too early to tell.

"I guess so. In a minute."

Kelsey returned to the bar, tapping her tray against one thigh like a tambourine.

"So where's your name?" Drew asked Graham, tipping her head up. "On the ceiling."

"I'm the anomaly. I never signed the tiles." He gave her a sheepish grin.

"I get it," she said, nodding. "Marching to the beat of your own drummer."

"Dude's got terrible rhythm, I'll tell you that."

"Well, at least there aren't bras hanging all over the place in here."

"What?" Graham started laughing.

"You know, there are those bars that encourage the female patrons to remove their bras and leave them hanging around like naughty party favors?" Her cheeks began to warm. "Bras can be so expensive! And you usually have only a few good ones, and really just one you wear most of the time and it's all ratty but so comfy and doesn't make you look all lumpy and why am I going on and on about bras—"

"Gatehouse incident?"

"Oh my God, you heard about that?" She hid her face in her hands.

"I'm sorry," he said, grinning hugely. "I couldn't help it."

She lowered her hands, laughed, and finished her gin and tonic. "Look, this is driving me to drink."

"If it makes you feel better, you're not the first person that's happened to."

"The drinking or going braless at work? I should point out that I put my bra back on almost immediately."

He laughed again. "This is turning into my favorite conversation all week. But speaking of work, how are your students?"

"Well, we're getting into our routine. I'm still trying to figure out the boundaries here. It's not your typical school setting." She rattled the ice cubes in her glass. "There are lots of … parameters. I mean, what's appropriate? I'm not a middle-aged guy. I could get away with the innovative teaching stuff if I didn't have boobs."

"If you were a middle-aged guy, you probably *would* have boobs. We live in Wisconsin, remember? Home of the deep fried cheese curd."

"And now we're talking about boobs."

"Not a bad subject," he said, playfully.

The jukebox kicked out the opening guitar riff from "Rock You Like a Hurricane." Kelsey appeared again with a Jack and Coke for Graham and a fresh drink for Drew. She pulled a ten-dollar bill from her purse, but Graham shook his head. "Put that back. It's on me." He gave Kelsey an affectionate smile. "Add it to my tab?"

"No problem, sweetie," she said, leaning down to plant a kiss on his cheek. Then she cupped Graham's chin in her right hand and pouted, "This is one of my favorite guys," before skipping back behind the bar. Something about their interaction rankled Drew, but she tried not to let it show. She didn't want to be the kind of possessive woman who got jealous when cocktail waitresses flirted with her male friends. Her *platonic* male friends.

"So," Drew said, "did it take you awhile to get used to working there?" She accidentally gulped her gin and tonic and tried not to shudder as the alcohol snaked down her throat and exploded like a hot blossom in her stomach. The drink was much stronger than her first, and her muscles began to unwind.

"Well, it's easier than pronouncing 'numismatist.'"

She laughed. "I'm sorry."

"No, you're not." He flashed a grin, revealing his straight, white teeth. "Seriously, though, the job security is pretty good, but you almost have to be an adrenaline junkie to work there. It's an intense place. Something like being in a war zone, maybe. Relentless boredom and routine, but the second you relax, BOOM! All hell breaks loose and the person next to you is

JESS RILEY

bleeding or washing inmate shit out of their hair." He saw her wince and added, "Sorry."

"That's okay. It's true."

Lost in thought, he took a drink before continuing. "Okay, here it is in a nutshell: I spend my days trying to teach what's normal—how to behave normally, by society's standards—but in a pressure cooker, and to men with severe addictions and warped brain chemistry. And I don't have all the answers. So ultimately, it all feels really abnormal to me. It's not quite the blind leading the blind, but close."

"The sheep leading the wolves?" Drew said. Her eyes flit to the sign posted above the bar, which had hung there for as long as she could remember: *Welcome to Oblivion.* Homage to a similar sign posted above a similar bar in Attica, New York. Another sleepy, picturesque little town home to a sprawling men's prison. Site of the bloodiest prison riot in U.S. history. The sign itself referenced the guards who got off work and "drank themselves into oblivion" in order to relieve some of the stress from working in a powder keg.

He raised an eyebrow. "More like the black sheep."

"So what you're saying is by the time we retire, we might have Post-Traumatic Stress Disorder?"

He grinned. "Good thing I'm a social worker!"

"Is this what you wanted to do in high school? Social work, I mean."

"No." He laughed, but not bitterly. "I was going to major in biology, or natural resource management. I wanted to be a park ranger or something."

"What happened?"

"A girl." There was something a bit too potent about the way Graham was looking at her. Drew felt dim relief when another group of people from work streamed in. She waved at

Janet Sutton, who wiggled her fingers at Drew before making a beeline for the bathroom.

Joe was among the new arrivals. Her insides fluttered at the sight of him. She tried not to watch him laughing at something Kelsey said while snicking the cap from a bottle of Budweiser. She tried to remember the last time she had this visceral a reaction to a man. A man who was all wrong for her—as wrong as she surely was for him.

When Drew was younger, she and her cousins would play a game called "Pet the Bee" in her mother's flower gardens. Whoever got stung last was the winner. Drew knew she wasn't ready for a relationship. She still felt the sting from the last one. But that's what made the game thrilling. You knew you were risking a painful sting or maybe even death by anaphylactic shock, yet you kept coming back for more.

"You ready for another drink?" Graham asked, backing away from the table.

"Okay. But I'll get this round. I owe you, remember?"

He shook his head emphatically. "Forget it. We're still celebrating your new job, so your money stays put tonight. But next week, first round's on you." He winked, then blushed and rolled quickly for the bar. Drew felt a gentle sort of embarrassment for him, because she recognized that forced, semi-flirtatious joviality. She'd done it herself more times than she cared to admit.

She watched him order their drinks and wondered if he was lonely. Surely women found him attractive. He had lively, wide blue eyes with amber speckles; honest eyes that reeled you in, missed nothing, had seen a painful past but were still primed to laugh. He had a strong jaw covered in stubble and a sharp but symmetrical nose. Faint freckles across his cheekbones. A husky, playful voice. She could imagine him leading some underground resistance movement during World War II: quick, clever, quietly brave.

Drew had to admit it. She'd been attracted to Graham in high school. But she'd had a boyfriend back then. She always seemed to have a boyfriend back then. One dud after another. The world's worst fireworks show.

While she rifled through her purse for a tube of lip balm, she heard a familiar voice directly behind her. "Well, well. It's about time you came out after work."

She spun around to face Joe, still wearing his officer blues.

"You look so lonely sitting here all by yourself." He picked up the chair next to her, spun it around, and straddled it to face her. She usually hated when men did things like this—it was too overtly territorial, too clichéd. A pantomime of masculinity. But Joe somehow pulled it off, like he'd invented it. "So what's up?"

"Not much, other than trying to figure out who would intentionally play so much REO Speedwagon on the jukebox." Her heartbeat doubled, and she cursed the surge of hormones surely pinking her cheeks and betraying her emotions. She could never play poker with this man.

"Uh, that was me."

"It was?"

"Hell, no." He smiled coolly. "You need a drink?"

Her eyes darted to the bar, where Graham was chatting with another social worker she didn't know. "No, thanks. I've got one on the way."

Joe casually turned to see what she was looking at. "So, you know Graham?"

From the corner of her eye she caught an unfamiliar woman giving her a dirty look. Her eyes were as black as her ponytail. Drew guessed she was an officer at Lakeside. An officer with some sort of interest in Joe Simon.

"We went to high school together," Drew said.

"Yeah, he told me."

Graham was discussing her with Joe? She tried to discern the meaning of this from Joe's expression, but it was frustratingly unreadable.

"Have you gotten any anonymous love letters yet?"

"From inmates?"

He nodded and took a swig of beer from his bottle, but his eyes remained on her.

"No, but I've learned that the Caesar Millan approach to dog training applies to humans as well."

"There's a story behind that one," he concluded, and she forced herself not to tell it uninvited. He was smiling in a slightly dreamy way. Here was a man with a singular mission: To have sex with a woman who wouldn't ask what he was thinking during the act and who wouldn't want to cuddle afterward. *I could be that woman*, Drew thought. *Just a few more gin and tonics.*

She cleared her throat to break the spell. "So Joe, how long have you been at Lakeside?"

"Four years. I did the academy right after graduating."

"From …?"

His grin grew lopsided. "Same school you went to." He could only mean Laurentide Bay High School. So he was twenty-two. Nearly ten years younger than she was. Not a ridiculous age gap, but he was still so young. She cringed when she recalled how naïve she'd been at twenty-two, and again when she wondered if she'd babysat any of his friends.

Before she could respond, another officer suddenly threw himself into a chair next to Joe. Andy Moffatt, panting and sweaty in a gray T-shirt. "Holy hell. Is it hot in here, or is it you?" he asked her, winking. Andy's face fit together in all the right ways, and the end result was attractive. But he smiled too much and tried too hard. He was the new guy in school every day of his life.

Drew frowned. "Did you run here from Manitowoc?"

"I just came from rugby practice across the street."

"So I smell," Joe said, waving the air in front of his nose. "And since when do you play rugby?"

"I've always played rugby!" Andy craned his neck, trying to locate a cocktail waitress. "Who does Joe's mom gotta blow for a guy to get a drink around here?"

Joe was too cool to even react. Graham suddenly appeared next to Drew, an annoyed look on his face. Kelsey was behind him, balancing drinks on a tray. Gin and tonics for Drew and Graham, and a fresh Budweiser for Joe.

"Thanks, Kelse," Joe said. He handed her his empty bottle and a ten-dollar bill. "Keep the change."

She blew him a kiss and looked at Andy. "Yours is a Bud Light, right?"

Drew stepped outside herself for a second. *Cheers* was a fine show and all, especially since it gave us *Frasier*, but did she really want to be a fixture at a bar where everybody knew her name? And, by association, her business? Andy noticed Graham, as if for the first time, and his eyebrows took a running leap toward his widow's peak. "Hey! I just thought of something."

"Well, don't keep us in suspense," Graham drawled.

"You seen that movie *Murderball*? Those quadriplegics are pretty intense. You should totally play rugby! Find a bunch of guys in chairs, start a team or whatever."

Graham fixed his expression and tone to match Andy's enthusiasm. "Gee whiz, Andy, I've never thought of that! What a great idea! I'll sign up tomorrow!"

Andy scowled. "Do you have to be an asshole all the time?"

"It's in my contract."

"So Drew," Andy said, turning back to Drew. "How do you like Lakeside?"

"I'm still getting used to it," she replied, keenly aware of three sets of eager male eyes on her.

"Where did you work before this?"

She took another too-large gulp of gin and tonic. "A high school in Eau Claire."

As Andy opened his mouth with the next question, Graham interrupted him. "Stop pestering her, Moffatt. This isn't a job interview."

"I'm not pestering her, I'm just making polite conversation!"

"Since when is the third degree polite?"

"Since when do you give such a shit?" Andy's voice had assumed a macho quality that made Drew nervous. Joe watched their exchange with an impish smirk.

"Hey Andy," Graham said evenly, "that hole on your face that's making noise? Shut it."

"Oh, it's okay," Drew interjected, her voice a little too high and nervous. "Don't worry about it." Tired of the tension and testosterone, she excused herself to find Janet and the other teachers.

"But I just got here!" Andy protested. Graham and Joe looked similarly disappointed. There was a time when she'd have been flattered to be the object of such attention. Now, after a full day spent diffusing lascivious stares and inappropriate comments from her students, she was too exhausted to keep her defenses fortified.

She spent the next forty minutes learning about Janet Sutton: her kitchen renovations, her daughter's recent trip to Spain, her husband's inadequacy when it came to both simple home repairs and anniversary gifts, her mother's heartbreaking descent into dementia. An unfortunate musical backdrop, Billy Squier's "The Stroke," played while she narrated how her mother recently partially disrobed at Piggly Wiggly and often confused Janet with her long-dead grandmother.

Later, after Drew slipped out of the smoky bar and unlocked her car door, she heard, "Hey Drew, wait up!" Joe jogged over to her. Drew felt dismayed to realize that she was a sucker for men in uniform jogging casually over to her. "You left without saying goodbye."

"Oh," she said, smiling. "Goodbye." A car pulled into the parking lot, bathing them in a sweep of light—just enough to illuminate his hazel and brown eyes.

"Drew, listen."

She crossed her arms, still smiling. "I'm listening." Crickets chirped in the weeds behind him.

"I was wondering …" he paused to smack a mosquito on his arm. "We should grab dinner sometime." His smile—no, his eyes—held the actual invitation.

"Don't you think I'm a little old for you?"

He pretended to consider this. "No."

"We work together."

He only smiled, his silence implying that it hadn't stopped him before. Logic told her to stay firm in her resolve. Good sense argued that she get in the car and drive home alone. Experience and reason clicked through a PowerPoint presentation with pie charts and flowcharts concluding that nothing good could possibly come from his invitation.

But libido. Ah, libido had kidnapped logic, good sense, experience, and reason and left them gagged and hog-tied in the basement.

Libido didn't mind at all when he stepped toward her, just inches from her, and she could smell the cinnamon gum he was chewing, the secondhand cigarette smoke mingling with the shampoo freshness of his hair. Libido had no problem with the fact that he just lifted her chin in his hand, that he just pressed his lips against hers. Libido didn't care that she liked books and he liked dirt bikes.

In fact, libido would like to submit this question for the consideration of the jury: Ben Who?

13. GRAHAM

There really aren't a lot of guys in wheelchairs in movies or on television. Most people wouldn't notice this kind of thing, but I do, because we tend to look for versions of ourselves reflected in pop culture. *What a relief, someone like me is included as a member of the general public. I'm relatable. I'm normal. I matter.* Most of the characters you might be familiar with are pretty pissed at their situation, at least initially: Lieutenant Dan, Officer Joe Swanson on *Family Guy*, Ron Kovic as played by Tom Cruise in *Born on the Fourth of July*. I get it, because after the accident, I saw red for months. Sometimes it still enrages me, but being angry all the time is so fucking exhausting. Eventually, you get bored with it. You read Richard Russo's new novel, laugh at jokes again, sing along to "Bohemian Rhapsody" on your way to work. You start having Big Picture thoughts, get a little zen during sunsets. The anger relaxes into a weary frustration, or maybe it just hides out, biding its time.

Watching Drew and Joe kissing in the parking lot of Finnegan's, I could feel that familiar, weary frustration begin to warm up in my chest, stretching its hamstrings, doing a few arm circles, getting ready for a sprint. Cockblocked again. I'd been planning on going home too, but after that fun little curveball, I rolled right back into the bar and called Kevin. He was over in ten minutes. Soon we were both slumped in our chairs, nursing warm drinks and listening to the clack of billiard balls over Eddie Money's wheezy braying. Kevin with his trademark Heineken, me with a flat Sam Adams. I felt as sturdy as a sock puppet, but I wasn't drunk. I'd eaten just enough for dinner to effectively neuter every beer I was drinking.

It was a little frustrating, given my current mood. I raise my bottle of lukewarm beer to toast Kevin. "Here's to the repeal of prohibition. God bless liquor."

Kevin clinks his bottle against mine. "Liquor in the front, poker in the rear."

Then, seemingly at random, he begins to unbutton his shirt. "Man, it's hot in here." Kevin recently pierced his left nipple. Now he's constantly inventing reasons to expose himself, waiting for others to comment on it. When Kevin isn't around we imitate him, opening our shirts and saying in deep voices, "Hello, I'm Kevin Lipton. Have you seen my nipple ring? Would you like to touch it?"

I notice Kevin's hair and am shocked to realize it is now two different colors. "Did you ... highlight your hair?"

Kevin smiles and touches his head. "You like that? I needed a new roof for the shithouse." He giggles his maniacal giggle. "So what's up, man?"

I sigh and simply say, "I can't figure women out."

This is an old conversation.

"Yeah, well, join the club. The other day Mandy was laughing and crying, laughing and crying, eating a whole frickin' tub of potato salad while watching some who-the-Christ-knows-what Hallmark movie about Precious Moments and angels and fairy farts." Kevin shakes his head. "Man, chicks got it made. If

I were a good-lookin' woman, there'd be a mattress strapped to my back. I'd put a cash register above my head."

"Yeah, if you were a woman we'd hear you coming down the street. It would sound like this," I purse my lips and blow over the lip of my beer bottle. "Whooooo." Kevin starts giggling and I continue. "If you were a woman, you wouldn't have a vagina, you'd have a ballroom. People would go on a waiting list to host bat mitzvahs there."

Kevin jumps on board, ignoring the easy joke about "ballroom" because his mind is already trained in another direction. "If I were a woman, my vagina would be the size of a stadium. The Packers would play in it."

"No doubt they would," I say, tipping my beer to him.

"Hey," he says, still laughing, "what's a bat mitzvah?"

Kevin, like my friend Trevor, is not one to offer advice on women. Discussing women with Kevin is like going to an all-you-can-eat buffet with a grandmother who lived through both the Great Depression and bariatric surgery: Even if the food sucks and you're full to the point of vomiting, there'll be hell to pay if you leave before getting your money's worth. "Don't sweat it, my brother. You're going to pick up plenty of chicks at this fundraiser we're volunteering at."

I close my eyes and sigh. "I can't believe you signed me up for that."

"You'll thank me later."

Before I can reply I overhear someone behind me saying, "No, dude, I think the medieval times in the eighteen hundreds."

"Try the thirteen hundreds, you numbskull," I mutter.

I am surrounded by idiots. We all are. Look around you right now. I have every faith in humanity's ability to parasitize and completely ruin the planet until all that remains are cockroaches, houseflies, and enough *Now That's What I Call Music!* CD compilations to pave the Everglades.

After we finish our beers and leave, I am not surprised to see the history whiz next to my truck in the parking lot. He's stumbling in place, trying to make sense of his car keys. It's reassuring to know he'll be barreling down the highway in several thousand pounds of steel in a few minutes. When he sees us, he squints at me and blurts, "So what happened to you?"

I blink and something inside me shatters. Let's call it my good cheer. "Funny story, actually. I accosted a disabled guy in a parking lot. Asked what happened to him, if he needed any help getting into his car, whether or not he could still fuck a woman. And wouldn't you know it? He stabbed me in the spine!"

"Hey, asshole—" The guy's eyes narrow into slits and he shambles toward me.

Kevin puffs up his chest and steps in front of me. "Back off, buddy."

Our little history buff holds up his hands in the old "Simmer down, children" style. "Fuckin' relax, dude."

Kevin is still bristling and foaming at the mouth. "Fuckin' relax is right. Now why don't you skip back to your sorority house and change your tampon."

"Jesus, Kevin!" That's me. I turn to the guy and say, "Don't take him seriously, man. We've all had a little too much to drink, let's just move on, forget the whole thing."

My life. One emasculating event after another. I always start out the angry one, and then somehow Kevin hijacks my anger, picking up my sword and shield, and I end up looking like the dickless diplomat who wants to broker a peace accord at Camp fucking David.

History Buff is no diplomat. He's completely uninterested in reaching a peaceful settlement and strides forward to push Kevin in the chest.

"Oh, you wanna start something?" Kevin replies, and I'm troubled to hear joy in his voice. Good bar fights give Kevin a high that no other drug could replicate. He holds his ground and shoves the guy back. Unfortunately, the guy's so drunk he falls flat on his ass, bonking his head on my truck in the process.

At this point, the bouncer, a laid-back guy named Jake, opens the back door of the bar. "What's going on out here?"

Kevin puts on a Boy Scout face. "Nothing at all. A simple disagreement."

"Sure," Jake says, running over to us. "You okay?" he asks the guy on the ground, extending a hand to haul him up.

Once he's up, History Buff rubs the back of his head and scowls. "Asshole pushed me."

"Let's call you a cab," Jake says, herding him back to the bar. Luckily, the guy's too dazed to resist.

I shake my head. "Kevin, one of these days you're going to get yourself in some serious trouble."

"You can count on that. Now let's go eat at Country Plate. I'm fuckin' starving."

I didn't see Drew at work on Friday. I hated myself for looking for her during breaks.

Joe Simon? Really? The guy barely knows his primary colors. So much for her good decision-making skills. My disappointment is so thick you could soundproof an aviary with it.

Kevin and I have just pulled into the gravel parking lot of a private airfield that's been converted into a low-budget midway for the day—the site of a diabetes fundraiser sponsored by

Harley-Davidson Motorcycles of Milwaukee, Wisconsin. "So what do we have to do at this shindig?" I ask, baking in the unforgiving July sun being amplified through the passenger window.

"Sell raffle tickets, I think."

"People actually come to this thing?"

I watch Kevin haul my chair from the bed of the truck and unfold it with a practiced air, locking the side frames in place and positioning it next to me on the ground. "How's that?"

"It sucks." I'm not referring to his wheelchair assembly technique, of course. I'm referring to the fact that I'm in a wheelchair to begin with.

Kevin adopts the tough, no-nonsense tone of a gym teacher. "You aren't going to get all mopey on me now, are you?"

I reach for his shoulder and try not to sulk. "No."

"Good."

I lean on him, sliding into my chair. "But we could have taken my truck. I'm *used* to my truck." What I really mean is that I can much more independently maneuver in and out of my chair from my own truck.

"You drive like an old woman."

"I do not."

Once I'm settled and Kevin's armed his vehicle's anti-theft system, we make our way to the festivities. Warrant's "Cherry Pie" screams from the portable speakers of the KFOX radio booth in the crowded hangar to our right, which has been cordoned off with plastic orange snow fencing. I wouldn't be surprised to learn that the musical playlist was selected by a consortium of local audiologists looking to expand their client base. Biker-types lope around the grounds, buying beer and nachos from the handful of vendors or scoping the gleaming motorcycles on display, many of which will be raffled off later in the day.

Two burly men in sunglasses and black leather chaps are selling tickets at the main entrance. They both have infinite sprays of frizzy brown hair. One has a gray beard almost as long as his hair. "Hey, Chris," Kevin says to him. "Where would you like us?"

"Right where you are. Ticket line begins here." He clears his throat, and it too sounds like a motorcycle being kick-started. He hawks a gob of phlegm to the left of one of my tires. His bearded partner doesn't bother to greet us; he's too busy flirting with a weather-beaten crone in jeans so tight they look painted on. When she's not straddling a hog on one of America's more popular highways, I wonder if she models for *Shrunken Apple Head Quarterly*. "We gotta run one of the bike raffles. You're our relief pitchers. Here," he says, producing two neon blue wristbands. "Put these on. They show you're volunteers."

We dutifully snap the bands on our wrists while he continues, "All's you gotta do is take the money and make sure nobody jumps the fence. Tickets are ten bucks each. You can put the money in this box and turn it in to me at seven tonight." He taps a gray metal footlocker with the tip of one jumbo Kick-You-Back-to-Altamont biker boot.

I snicker a little at the idea of someone jumping the fence to crash a diabetes fundraiser.

"Am I bein' funny?" the guy says, clearly annoyed.

"No, sir."

He crosses his arms and glowers at me through mirrored sunglasses. "I'm a woman, asshole."

This should go quite well.

An hour passes. *Money collected:* $240. *Skin status:* Early stages of possible melanoma. *Hydration:* The Dead Sea. *Vision:* Unable to delineate genders, apparently. *Women interested in me or Kevin:* How do I know they're women?

Two hours pass. *Money collected:* $470. *Skin status:* Barbecued. *Hydration:* The Gobi Desert. *Vision:* Seeing mirages. *Women interested in me or Kevin:* one, but she wanted to sit on my lap and have her picture taken, so I don't really count her as a human being. I'm the only tourist allowed in my life. And I'm only a ride when I authorize it.

Another hour into our shift, the puffy thunderheads perched on the horizon all morning blow in to make a sudden and swift appearance, and it starts to sprinkle. "Hey!" Kevin says. "I brought us some ponchos!"

"You brought ponchos?"

"Always be prepared. Boy Scout motto."

He rummages through the mini-cooler he'd lugged along and pulls out two factory-sealed plastic ponchos, one green and one white. He tosses the green package onto my lap and I tear it open. He's already wearing his white poncho by the time I discover that he hasn't given me a poncho, he's given me a brand new shower curtain. "Uh, dude? This is a shower curtain."

Kevin finishes adjusting his poncho and looks over, astonished. His face breaks into a slow smile. "No way."

"Yep." I shake the fragrant plastic curtain open. "See? You gave me a shower curtain."

He starts to giggle as fat raindrops pelt my forehead. "How'd that happen?" And he's doubled over laughing. "Don't worry, we can fix this. Here." He drapes the curtain over me, and I look like a homeless person.

"I'm not wearing a shower curtain!" I whip it off.

159

"No, wait." He takes the curtain and pulls his Swiss army knife from a back pocket, punching a jagged hole into the center of it. "Now try it." He centers the small, raggedy-ass hole on my head and yanks it down over my face before I have time to protest.

"Would you quit? It's too tight! I'm going to fucking choke to death!"

He's laughing so hard his face turns red while I pop the curtain back over my head, crumple it into a ball, and throw it at him. It unfurls in the wind and drifts off sideways, now useless as a poncho *or* shower curtain. The clouds decide to stop screwing around and get down to business, and the sprinkles become a downpour, even though somehow, the sun is still shining. Bikers scatter, jogging for cover. Kevin fetches the shower curtain and gently lays it over my head. The jagged hole in the middle is just big enough to drench my arm. I sit there, damp and miserable, waiting it out. I don't even care that there's a huge rainbow over one of the hangars. Refracted light can kiss my ass. But I don't have time to stew for long: The clouds are fickle this afternoon and the rain peters out just minutes later.

I pull the curtain from my head. "Great. Now my hair's all fucked up, too."

"It was pretty bad to begin with."

After the sky clears and the sun burns through the post-rain haze, our biker friends return so we can take a break and buy some overpriced refreshments. I profusely apologize (again) to the more androgynous one. "Don't sweat it. Just get your ass to the nacho stand before they run out of brats. On the house for volunteers, so flash your wristbands."

As we dodge the puddles and make our way to the vending area Kevin says, somewhat apologetically, "Jeez, man, I'm really sorry. I thought we'd have better luck meeting chicks than this."

I shake my head. "You owe me, man."

We find a vendor selling gyros and beer and get in line. "Christ, it's hot," Kevin says, beginning to unbutton his shirt.

"Would you leave your shirt on? We're going to be eating."

"What do you mean?" He looks hurt.

At this, the man in line before us turns around. "How is it?" Despite the eye- and lung-melting temperature, he's wearing a black leather jacket festooned with metal: safety pins, nuts and bolts, diamond-tipped rivets, a curtain of jingling chains. His mullet fans out beneath a sweaty American flag-themed handkerchief. He's a bigger guy, pushing four hundred pounds maybe. His gut strains against a Kid Rock concert T-shirt mere inches from my face.

"Fine," I say, irritated. Now KFOX is playing Ratt. "Round and Round." Has no one here escaped from the seedy side of the eighties? It's as if Kurt Cobain never existed. I crane my neck and sadly realize I'm reflexively looking for Drew, or a woman who resembles her.

"You guys see the apehangers on that custom Indian?"

Well, it certainly smells enough like the ape house around here, I think, meanly.

"No, we've been selling tickets at the gate," Kevin says.

"Isn't this a Harley event?" I ask, unable to hide my irritation at the heat, the dust, the bad music, the waste of a perfectly good Saturday, Drew's disappointing choice in men.

"Yeah," the guy says. "They're the main sponsors. But all bikes are welcome. Just check the parking lot!"

While our new pal orders, Kevin tries to keep it light. "Dude, check it out. Hooters booth in hangar nine."

At this point the heavyset biker turns around, looking for the condiment and napkin bar. He's balancing three gyros and a jumbo order of cheese curds in grease-splotched, red and white-checked cardboard boats. "Hey," he says. A fantastic idea has just hit him. "You ever seen that movie *Murderball?* With those guys in wheelchairs who play rugby? You could totally do something like that!"

I nod as if I've never heard this one before. "Hey," I say, smiling brilliantly. "You see that movie *Supersize Me?* You shouldn't have taken it so literally!"

He frowns, his inspired, cheerful expression dissolving into distress. "Excuse me," he mutters, and waddles off to eat his gyros in peace, away from cruel gimps like me. I feel ashamed of myself immediately. I shouldn't have said that.

Kevin gives me a wary look while I move forward to place my order. "Dude, that was kind of uncalled for," he says quietly. But effectively.

I feel microscopic. I feel like a dust bunny under a subatomic-sized couch. "Yeah, well, not much in my life is called-for lately." I know I'm being the Walmart of assholes. My whiny self-pity could block out the sun and hold the world for ransom. But I can't seem to find the OFF switch for these feelings.

"We can leave now, if you're going to be that way."

"Christ, you sound like my mother." I clear my throat and approach the vendor. "Yeah, I'll have the gyro combo basket with onion rings and a Mountain Dew," I say, in an everything's-fine, move-along, nothing-to-see-here voice.

Kevin lowers his voice, adopting the same serious tone my ex-wife used a lot before we divorced. "You're acting like a big baby. Maybe you do need your mommy."

I don't want Kevin pissed at me too, so I take a deep breath and reply, "Sorry, man. I'm just …" But before I can finish, I see someone I did not, under any circumstances, not under threat of torture or death, want to see here today.

Joe Simon. He's laughing at something one of the Hooters girls has just said.

"Shit," I hiss under my breath, my face flooding with heat. "What's he doing here?"

"Who?" Kevin asks, trying to follow my gaze, but I've dropped my eyes and am now staring at my legs. My useless, withered legs.

"That'll be six bucks, even," the guy at the gyro window is saying.

"We're volunteers," Kevin says, flashing his wristband.

The gyro vendor gives us a tight smile and drops my basket on the flip-top counter. "No charge, then."

"Who are you looking at?" Kevin asks again, stepping up to the window to order a corn dog and fries.

"Nobody. Just some jerk I work with."

Kevin looks at Joe, then back at me, adopting a knowing expression. "Oh, I get it now. I know the name of this game."

"What?" I ask, aiming for innocent but hitting petulant instead.

"That girl you like. Chick you work with. You've been friend-zoned, and that guy's in the bone zone."

I just silently chew my onion rings. I suddenly feel the kind of lonely that comes only in bulk and doesn't fit in the pantry.

"Dude, what about that other chick you just went out with? Tabby? Flabby?" He giggles.

"You mean Abby. She has a wandering eye," I absently say, my own eyes wandering back to Joe and the Hooters girls. He appears to be having a great time. And it suddenly hits me why he's here: Joe has diabetes. *Of course*. The prick.

"I hope you of all people won't hold that against her." Kevin takes a giant bite from his corn dog.

"I can't watch you eat something so phallic."

More of the patented Kevin Lipton giggle, this time through a full, chewing mouth.

I'm glaring at Joe, I realize, and for a horrid, lucid moment I'm convinced he sees me too. "Let's leave," I say, urgently. "Let's just get the hell outta here. We're not being paid for this. We don't have to be here."

"We haven't even been here four hours!" Kevin sops up some ketchup with a handful of fries and stuffs them down his gullet.

"Long enough. Tell them I'm not feeling well." Which is correct. Sort of.

He groans, finishes the last of his fries, and brushes the salt from his palms. "You are such a girl, Finch."

I hate when Kevin calls me by my last name. It reminds me of David Spade's nasal character on that awful sitcom *Just Shoot Me*.

Despite Kevin's protests and our incomplete mission (to snag some snatch, in his words), we abandon our posts early. The ride home is bumpy, uncomfortable, and silent. I stare out the window, watching cornfields blip past and thinking about what Kevin said earlier, about needing my mother. The truth is this. I might not need my mother, though she insists on coming over once a week to "help clean my hovel" and "keep me from developing nutritional deficiencies." But I might need someone to take care of me. Someone I can take care of, in return. There's a lot of wiggle room in the phrase "to take care of." It goes along with to have and to hold. For richer, for poorer. In health, and in sickness.

What will become of me when I'm old?

14. DREW

Kissing Joe was unexpected, and it left Drew more confused than ever. She and Ben hadn't kissed until their second date: a trip to a local orchard for caramel apples and pumpkins. Though it had been a warm and brilliant fall day—tailor-made for a trip to an orchard—she'd regretted the suggestion as soon as they arrived at the crowded farm. Late-season wasps buzzed angrily around garbage cans overflowing with used cider cups. The air smelled of goats, which staggered with distended bellies around the dozen rowdy kids throwing ten-cent feed pellets at one another. The line for homemade apple pies and muffins was nearly forty people deep. And all around them, exhausted parents pulled dazed-looking children in wagons with squeaky wheels. It was clearly the place to be that fresh autumn day, but Drew got overwhelmed in crowds. She was starting to feel claustrophobic and clammy, disoriented and panicked. Ben sensed her growing distress and led her to a picnic table under a birch tree. He said, "I'll be right back," and returned a few minutes later with enormous caramel apples dipped in sprinkles.

They spent the next hour people watching, laughing, and telling stories about their student teaching experiences. They were only a few years older than their high school pupils, which provided some entertaining anecdotal fodder. *Grinding at prom? We didn't do that in high school, did we?* and *You won't even believe the note Hayley Kasuboski left on my desk today.* They felt like co-conspirators, members of the same tribe. Ben was solicitous and gentle—a respite after her recent string of dating disasters. She remembered how safe she felt with Ben. How he looked her in the eye when she was talking, how sincere his smile was. This was a man who would never forget his grandmother's birthday, Drew remembered thinking. Who would pull over to assist a stranded motorist. Later, he kissed her with caramel-flavored lips and it felt like a happy glimpse into the rest of her life.

But all of that happened in another lifetime. Today she was in a chilly conference room in Madison, enrolled in an all-day workshop that would yield two continuing education credits. If Drew ever wanted to teach in a public high school again, she needed to stay abreast of educational trends, amassing the advanced credits to prove it. Today's workshop was based on creating classroom community. It was probably better suited for elementary level teachers, but Drew's friend Erin promised she'd be there.

Erin was as different from Brooke as any human could possibly be. Short, solid, and accessible, Erin had been the mischief-maker among Drew's group of college friends, infamous for once inserting a kernel of candy corn in her left nostril and approaching strangers in a bar to ask, "Do I have anything in my teeth?" Her husband of five years was a jovial man named Adam, but his friends called him Elmo because he did a spot-on imitation of the furry red monster, only with a foul mouth and pornographic sensibilities. Before they had their son Liam, they traveled Europe and Asia, sending Drew postcards on which Erin would add random postscripts like, *Congratulations on your ordination into the priesthood!* or *Did you know that "Pinocchio" is Italian for "pinkeye?"* Now Erin taught third grade in Madison, Wisconsin, globetrotting postcards replaced with infrequent texts featuring student antics.

After Drew picked up her nametag and workshop folder, she found Erin standing near a table loaded with pastries and sliced melon, humming a vaguely recognizable jingle. She was wearing a nametag on which she'd scribbled: *Erin Moran*, even though her last name was actually Morgan. This was an arcane reference to both Joanie from *Happy Days* and a picture that had gone viral a few years back, of some mulleted idiot protesting a political event with a sign that read, "Get a brain, Morans!" She hugged Drew and whispered in greeting, "Does my mustache look weird? I tried to bleach it but I don't think it turned out right."

Drew pulled away to scrutinize Erin's upper lip. "I can't see anything."

"Are you kidding me? It looks like I ate a bowl of cellophane noodles Cookie Monster style and didn't use a napkin afterward."

"Well, now that you mention it … that's a really creepy analogy, by the way."

"Better than Italian Albino Santa Claus?"

Drew laughed. "Why don't you just get it waxed like everyone else does?"

"Because I'm DIY, you know that! Also, I'm afraid to."

"Do they still make Nair? Maybe you could just dissolve your mustache next time."

"Yeah, right. Nair on my face. Best-case scenario, it would eat a hole through my upper lip and we'd all have to become supporters of the Smile Train Foundation. Worst case, I'd be overwhelmed from the fumes, pass out, and hit my head on the bathroom counter. Liam would find me and be scarred for life. Don't let Adam marry Stephanie from his office after I die, okay?"

A woman in a long denim skirt and a denim vest bedazzled with embroidered apples and little red schoolhouses suddenly clapped her hands and said, "Okay, everybody, we're going to get started now." The soft din in the room gradually subsided as other workshop attendees sat in the chairs circling the middle of the room. Erin and Drew claimed two blue plastic chairs and slid their purses beneath. Drew scrawled her name on a sticky, peel-off nametag and pressed it on her chest. A diminutive older woman with long gray hair sat in the vacant chair to her left.

"Is this seat taken?"

"Not at all!"

"I'm Sandy Lazarski," she said, extending her hand.

Drew shook it. "Drew Daniels. Nice to meet you."

Sandy popped a shiny nugget of gum from a blister pack, and it skittered onto the floor. "Rats." She tried again, this time successfully. "I teach third grade in Middleton. What district are you from?"

"Lakeside."

She looked confused. "Lakeside. Where's that?"

"The ninth circle of hell."

"What?"

"It's a prison. I teach special ed there."

"Oh!" Sandy chewed her gum thoughtfully, and Drew noticed that something was not quite right with Sandy's left hand. Her middle and index fingers were fused together, as were her ring finger and pinky. The cumulative effect was that of a misshapen claw. Drew got a sudden image of Sandy's students snickering cruelly at her hand behind her back, calling her Crab Hand or Lobster Lady.

The instructor clapped her hands again. "Okay! Everybody settled?" The circle of teachers looked at one another apprehensively. "Great! First we're going to start with an icebreaker. Sort of a get-to-know-you game. How it works is you say your name, and then you do a hand or body motion. The next person repeats your name and motion, and adds their name and a new motion unique to themselves! The third person says the first and second person's name and motion, and adds one for him or herself! And so on and so forth! So the last person has to repeat *everyone's* names and gestures!" She paused and eagerly beamed at her audience, most of whom looked as if they'd found a dirty Band-Aid in their sub sandwich.

Erin groaned and leaned in to whisper, "I'm going to blow my brains out with my index finger. That's my gesture."

"I'm going to flip everyone the bird."

"I'm going to pretend to drink a small cup of Jonestown Kool-Aid and then fall to the floor, writhing in pain."

"I'm going to perform hara-kiri on myself with an invisible samurai sword." Drew furtively mimed disemboweling herself.

The instructor clapped her hands again. "Okay, I'll start." She paused to collect her thoughts and get into character, then shouted, "Yvonne!" She exuberantly pinwheeled her arms, and the circle tittered self-consciously.

She beamed at the unlucky woman to her right. The woman shook her head as if to clear it from this nightmare, but no dice. The nightmare wasn't scheduled to end until three p.m. "Um, okay, I guess I'm next. Ummm … Tina!" She gave a lame thumbs-up à la Fonzie, taking the easy way out.

"Wait, you forgot me!" Yvonne squealed, before the third victim could pull herself from her near-catatonic state of fear to join in the fun.

Tina sighed. "Oh, right. *Yvonne!*" She turned bright red and pinwheeled her arms fast enough to generate electricity.

"Great job, Tina!" Yvonne said, and turned her rabid attention to the next teacher in line. They progressed around the circle, adding jazz hands, a butt wiggle, a few moves from the Hustle and the Chicken Dance, and a weird series of fingersnaps that a sullen man named David contributed. Erin added an intricate popping and locking dance move, and Drew suddenly and malevolently wished she could throw Erin in a box and donate her to charity.

Drew's turn. She ran through the shameful repertoire, rushing through Erin's popping and locking routine, and added, "Drew!" with disco finger points like an extra from *Saturday Night Fever*. As she did, it dawned on her what a nightmare all of this must have been for Sandy. Drew silently berated herself for not simply hopping in place or doing a nice and easy step-ball-change.

But Sandy was a trouper. She completed the entire routine: the jazz hands, the butt wiggle, the dance moves, the finger snaps, the popping and locking, Drew's ode to *Saturday Night Fever*. The rest of the circle suddenly found the floor, or the ceiling, or their own intact hands very interesting.

Afterward, Sandy muttered to Drew, "Well, *that* wasn't awkward."

As the game wrapped up, Yvonne prattled on about building community in the classroom. Some of the attendees whipped out notebooks or iPads and began taking notes. Others paged through the accompanying folder of handouts. Erin leaned toward Drew and whispered, "So how's the new job?" She scrawled tic-tac-toe hash marks in the margin of her notebook and handed her pen to Drew, who drew an O in the center square.

She shrugged. "It's a prison."

Erin drew an X in the bottom left square. "Is it dangerous?"

"Maybe," Drew said, adding another O to the board. "I don't know."

"Come on." X. "Tell me something dangerous."

O. "I didn't wear my seat belt last Tuesday *and* I texted you while driving with my knees."

X. Erin rolled her eyes. "Come on, be serious. Do you work with any hot guys?"

"If this were the sixties, you wouldn't care if any of my coworkers were hot. Instead, you'd want to know if they have anything important to say." Drew had watched a Bob Dylan documentary a few nights earlier, and this was a quote from the film. She drew a final O for the win.

"Are you kidding me?" Erin scowled. "If this were the sixties, I'd be sitting here in my bell bottoms and macramé shawl, *still* wanting to know if any of them were groovy looking."

Drew chuckled, and she was suddenly back in Finnegan's parking lot, tasting Joe's lips. "Well, there is one guy. Very hot. But he's a lot younger than me."

Erin smiled and scribbled their game into oblivion. "Go on."

"... some of the things you can do to build community include capitalizing on each student's unique strengths. When a child successfully accomplishes something he or she is truly good at, they begin to fill what I like to call their 'Reservoir of Resiliency' ... "

"His name is Joe, and he's a correctional officer." Drew felt mild disappointment at her use of the term "correctional officer" instead of "guard," because who was she kidding? But, she supposed, euphemistic language was invented for a reason. And that reason was to make everyone think the garbage picked itself up.

"A guy named Joe's got to be good in the sack. Tell me more." Erin doodled in the margins of a handout.

"Well, there's not much to tell."

"Liar."

"Okay, we made out a little," Drew confessed.

"I miss making out!"

Drew felt a sudden, overwhelming pang of sadness that she and Erin lived so far away from one another. She could never feel this relaxed around Brooke. And once again, she wondered if she'd made the right move. Yes, she was financially strapped. Yes, she needed a sanctuary. But was she doing herself more harm than good in returning to old haunts and habits?

" ... *is just one of the techniques you can include in your toolbox to cultivate a respect for diversity in your classroom ...* "

"You know," Drew said, "I really miss you!"

Erin melted. "Oh sweetie, I miss you too. Move to Madison. You can live in our spare room."

"I'm sure Adam would love that."

"Why not? He always wanted a harem. You can be my sister wife."

Drew affably rolled her eyes.

"Well, Liam would love if Auntie Drew moved in. He's potty trained now, so you wouldn't even have to change a diaper!" Erin fished her phone out of her purse and pulled up a photo of Liam mugging for the camera.

Drew gasped. "Aw, he's getting so big! He's like a real little boy now."

"I know! The other day he said to me, 'Mom, I feel kind of despondent.' When I asked him if he knew what that meant he said, 'It means melancholy; everyone knows that.' Two hours later he threw a barrel of monkeys at my face and balance was restored to the universe."

Suddenly Yvonne clapped her hands briskly, startling everyone. "Ladies!" She was staring at them. "Please refrain from talking. I ask for the same courtesy and respect that you do in your classrooms." Erin and Drew just stared at their folders, though Erin was still grinning. They waited until Yvonne hit cruise control on her lecture before resuming their conversation, this time more quietly.

"So how long will you stay with your folks?" Erin began to draw an unflattering caricature of Yvonne on the pocket of her folder.

"I don't know. They'll let me stay as long as I want, but it already feels so pathetic."

"All the cool kids are moving back in with their parents these days."

"But they're definitely *not* working with their mothers. In prison."

Erin considered this. "Actually? That is kind of cool. It's like if you worked in a tattoo shop together."

"Except the clients can't leave until the state says they've repaid their debt to society."

"I'd totally watch that show." Erin gave Cartoon Yvonne a dominatrix whip and added, hopefully, "Our school district finally has a few new openings. And I happen to know they're looking for special ed teachers."

A tiny bubble of dread popped inside of Drew. She wasn't sure she was ready for something so … *real* yet. She swam around the bait with, "I hung out with Brooke Walters over the fourth of July. Remember her?" Brooke visited Drew frequently in college, especially the first two years. By junior year Drew had grown close to Erin and a few other girls she'd met in her dorm, which gave Drew a new perspective on how dysfunctional her friendship with Brooke really was.

"Wasn't she kind of a bitch to you?" Erin whispered, still sketching. Erin never liked Brooke, not since the time Brooke said to her, "You type really fast for someone with such big fingers!"

"Sometimes."

They fell silent for a minute, but Drew wasn't paying attention to anything Yvonne said. She wondered what Graham was doing. It was a Tuesday; didn't he run two AODA groups on Tuesdays? She wondered who he was eating lunch with. She remembered him blushing when he told her his mother baked the cookies in his lunch, and she smiled. Without preconception, she leaned over and whispered to Erin, "There's another guy at work. Definitely cute. We went to high school together." She paused and added, "But he's in a wheelchair." She felt ashamed that this mattered to her. It shouldn't. She knew that. It wouldn't matter to a better person. A better person would just roll with it, no pun intended.

Erin added two large nipples to her depiction of Yvonne, the soft scratching of her pen strangely reassuring. "So what? Adam's fused to the couch. He's practically paralyzed from the waist down, too."

"You would have still married him if he'd been in a wheelchair? If he had a spinal cord injury?" For the first time it dawned on her that Graham and Joe morphed into the same man would be a really appealing combination.

Erin shrugged. "Probably. He's the only man I've ever met who can put up with me. You know, I can totally see you dating a paraplegic."

"That's the strangest thing anyone's ever said to me, and I work in a prison."

"So tell me more about Cute Wheelchair Guy. I bet he's really good at—"

"Don't even go there!" Drew's cheeks flared with heat.

"Canoeing, I was going to say. But you can't tell me the thought hasn't crossed your mind at least once. Now, what about the other guy. Hot younger man in uniform." She gave a good-humored shiver. "Holy Jesus, I got wet panties just *saying* that."

Drew laughed. "You are so disgusting sometimes. Anyway, hot younger man in uniform is *really* young. We have nothing in common."

"Oh, yes you do. There is one thing you definitely have in common."

"Did I tell you his eyes are two different colors?"

"How fun is that! Are they freaky-looking? Maybe you guys could role-play and he could wear an eye patch! He could be the brown-eyed UPS driver on Tuesday and the blue-eyed furnace repairman on Friday."

Drew rolled her eyes good-naturedly. "I think you and Adam need a vacation to the Sybaris Pool Suites."

"No thanks, I just had a yeast infection. But listen. You'll never be this young, free, or beautiful again. Get out there and get some while the getting's good. And then you should go out with Cute Wheelchair Guy, and tell me all the juicy details. I want to live vicariously through you."

"So your plan is to pimp me out to two of my new co-workers. You're totally thinking like a criminal right now."

Erin chuckled. "Okay, Drew's mom."

Drew knew she wasn't ready for a full-blown relationship. But was she even ready for just a fling? Casual had never really been her style, and it hadn't been Ben's, either. He'd been your classic mensch type, more comfortable with a girlfriend than a one-night stand. He was warm, he was funny, and he was sweet. They fit well together for eight years. They'd shared vacations and family Christmases and job frustrations and all the daily minutiae of a comfortable relationship. The toothbrushes cozily cohabitating in the glass on the bathroom counter. The faded, old T-shirts they each wore to bed, where they'd sometimes grade papers, sometimes read, sometimes have familiar yet satisfying sex. The Thai place where they'd order curry when either was feeling too lazy to cook. She knew that if she took too long primping in the bathroom before an event, he'd yell from the living room, "What's the holdup? Bandits?" She knew that if someone asked about his favorite movie he'd say *Pulp Fiction*, but it was secretly *The Neverending Story*. She knew his mother sometimes hit his father. She knew he'd shopped for an engagement ring two years ago, but he never bought one. She knew, she knew, she knew so very much except one very important thing until it was too late. In the end, the truth didn't so much seep in, finding all the microscopic cracks in the door. Instead, it hit her like a bullet train, and she'd been sleeping on the tracks for months.

When the facts about what he'd done began to take shape, she could barely breathe. It was as if someone had sliced open her chest and poured something searing over all of the soft, essential pieces inside: a sizzling flow of lava that dissolved everything good in its path, carbonizing her happy memories of Ben into charcoal.

She'd endured painful breakups before, yes—there had been a particularly brutal one her sophomore year in college when she was dumped on her birthday by a charismatic hockey player named Wyatt, who'd introduced her to sushi, *A Clockwork Orange*, and his parents. In retrospect, she'd seen that one coming; she'd felt Wyatt pulling away for weeks. But she'd never known a relationship could end in so spectacularly *public* a fashion, nearly without warning, leaving her psyche riddled with shame and self-doubt. She was now part of a select club of women whose common sense was routinely and disdainfully questioned after the smoke cleared: *How could she not have known? How could she be so dense?*

So. She was leery at the prospect of making herself emotionally vulnerable again. And the old question she'd pondered since losing her virginity to Troy Whittaker was once again front and center in her mind: Was it possible to have sex without engaging your emotions? Before Ben, she would have said no. She'd heard of those fabled women who claimed to be able to separate sex from love, enjoying uncomplicated affairs without getting tangled in the many emotions that always seemed to trip everyone else up, but she'd never met one. They seemed like a fabrication by *Men's Health*. The legendary woman with the emotional and sexual wiring of the average man. Possibly damaged, but brassy and real and raw.

But now, after Ben, Drew wasn't so quick to say no to this question. Her emotions, especially those having anything to do with the romantic side of things, seemed to have been put in a deep freeze. She was beginning to fear they'd never thaw—and if they did, they would be nothing but dehydrated relics, crusty with ice crystals. However, the physical parts of her that woke up during puberty had inexplicably developed a new, reckless appetite. It wasn't healthy, she knew that, but it felt like a logical step in whatever trajectory she now traveled.

She felt like a broken bone that hadn't been set properly, healing in a crooked, imperfect pattern. What she glossed over while Yvonne motioned for the group to take a break was the vague, discomfiting notion that in order to regain full function, someone would need to break that bone all over again.

15. GRAHAM

Sometimes it feels like my life was scripted to give the guy upstairs a giant laugh. I've been in a funk since last week, when I saw Drew and Joe kissing in the parking lot. This is the foundation of my little house of misery, so to speak. *Next we have the framing:* At my latest doctor appointment this past Tuesday, they discovered I had a bladder infection and put me on antibiotics. *Here come the walls:* Which gave me a red, raw rash all over my face and body. *The insulation and siding:* My mother's over right now, cleaning my kitchen, stocking my fridge with barely edible casseroles and giving helpful dating advice. *The plumbing and electrical hookups:* I've been getting too much attitude lately from an inmate named William Delfranklin, a litigious jerk whose favorite pastime is suing the State of Wisconsin for a host of perceived infractions including—but not limited to—the quality of ventilation in the NEXUS program unit, alleged mail tampering, and the (unacceptable) amount of protein in his diet. *And finally, the roof that tucks everything in, keeping the rain out and the carpet fumes in:* Oh, and have I mentioned I'll never walk again? Hee-haw!

"Graham, are you listening to a word I'm saying?" My mother is kneeling on my kitchen counter, her head buried deep in one of the higher cupboards. "My god, this macaroni and cheese is nearly six years old!" Her voice is a muffled echo.

"So throw it away." I'm on the couch in the living room, flipping around on my Xbox Live main menu. Trevor's logged in, playing *Gears of War 3*. One room away, I hear the ancient box of macaroni hit my garbage can. When I bought that box, I could walk. I tucked it away on that top shelf myself.

"All I'm saying," my mother continues as she empties my cupboards, "is that you shouldn't be so hostile to the idea of meeting a nice girl, settling down. I won't live forever, and who will bring you healthy meals when I'm gone?"

"Hopefully nobody."

"Oh, stop. You won't meet a nice girl to take care of you with that kind of attitude, mister." My mother is from the era where women still lived at home or worked as secretaries until they found a husband. Then they got married, experimented with gelatin molds, and had half a dozen kids.

"Ma, I already tried settling down with a nice girl, remember? That worked out well, didn't it?"

"How about meeting someone with that nice eHarmony service? They have attractive commercials." My mother has no idea I've been dating girls I've met on various online dating sites for the past few months. She is also highly susceptible to advertising, and is one of those people who actually do so when the voice in the prescription drug commercial suggests, "Ask your doctor about" whatever magic little pill they're pushing.

"I know," I say with false jocularity, "maybe I could put an ad in the paper. *Wanted: subservient girl who enjoys cooking, cleaning, and washing piss-soaked sheets. Lesbians welcome. No nymphos.*"

"Graham, I didn't raise you to have such a filthy mouth."

"Sorry," I shout tonelessly, not meaning it. *Piss, lesbians,* and *nymphos* are not part of my mother's lexicon. I shut off my Xbox and channel surf. HBO is airing a Bob Saget stand-up comedy special, and I turn down the volume so my mother doesn't hear a bad word and fall off the countertop after a massive stroke.

There's the crisp sound of contact paper being clipped from a roll. "Oh, did I tell you? Your cousin Samantha wants to organize a family trip to Disney World in Florida. For the whole family!"

As opposed to Disney World in Rhode Island. "I'm not going," I say flatly.

"I don't blame you. I'm not so sure your father and I want to go, either. The Walt Disney Company supports the gays, you know."

"For Christ's sake, Ma. Walt Disney was a Nazi sympathizer. Isn't that enough for you?"

"Listen, mister, your mother is not a Nazi!"

I can't help it. I burst out laughing.

At this point she comes out of the kitchen, rubber glove-clad fists on her hips, scowling. "What's so funny?"

I know I'm lucky. Many people with spinal cord injuries need at least part-time in-home assistance. I can manage fine by myself most of the time, but my mother drops in weekly to vacuum and scrub things down. She usually brings a noodle and hamburger casserole or soup I can freeze for the week. The bad part is that I have to listen to her mounting bewilderment at the assault on traditional family values in today's cultural cesspool. Violent video games? Evolution? Hillary Clinton's cleavage? Get thee behind me, Satan! But the most offensive new development to her is the fact that "the gays" are not crouched behind a pair of old boots in the closet. Well, I may be exaggerating some, but not by much. I've learned long ago to avoid topics like immigration, flag burning, and stem-cell research at my parents' house. I only wish they could do the same in mine.

Still, we're family. And as much as I despise many of my mom's views (as much as she despises mine), she raised me to respect my elders, treat animals and children kindly, never litter, and revere education—not to attend and successfully graduate from the best college to take me was never an option with her. Which was probably the largest contributing factor to our now-opposing viewpoints, but she'd never concede the point or downplay the value of a solid education, and I'd never bring it up anyway.

I smile at her. "Ma, I appreciate you helping to clean my kitchen. But if you don't tuck in that bottom lip, a bird's going to poop on it."

"I told you that when you were little," she says complacently, and her frown does indeed turn upside down. "And what's this about helping? Last I checked, I'm the only one doing all the cleaning!"

"Ma," I say, trying not to roll my eyes. "You don't have to do this."

Her expression grows suddenly somber, and she begins pulling her gloves off, finger by finger, while she walks into the living room. "Graham, I have to tell you something." She perches hesitantly on the edge of the couch, near my feet.

"Oh Christ. You and Dad are getting divorced."

She makes a vacant face, as if her brain simply can't make sense of such an impossible notion. "No, no," she says. "And don't say 'Christ.' It's just … now, don't get upset, but I broke your shredder."

I laugh, unexpectedly and so loudly it startles us both. "Wait. What are you doing using my shredder?"

"I was shredding your junk mail."

"Why?"

"You don't want anyone to steal your identity, do you?"

"It's not the worst thing that could happen."

"It was that darn March of Dimes."

"What are you talking about?" My bemusement is shifting into irritation.

"They tape nickels in their junk mail so you open it, and I forgot to take it out before I shredded it."

"Just to be clear, you broke my shredder with a nickel from the March of Dimes."

"Really, they should rethink that tactic. I bet lots of people break their shredders on those nickels. And then they use the money they might have donated to the March of Dimes to buy a new shredder." She stands and brushes an invisible speck of dust from the arm of my wheelchair, which is parked nearby. "So do you want to come with me?"

"Where?" I ask, exasperated.

"To buy you a new shredder. I have to run a few other errands, but now we can add it to the list."

I cross my arms and give her a look. "Are you making left turns yet?"

My mother scowls at me in reply.

"Then I'm not going with you." A few years ago she was nearly T-boned while trying to turn left at a busy intersection, so now my mother only makes right turns in the city. As a result, a simple trip for a gallon of milk now takes twice as long and gives you vertigo.

"I don't want to run errands, and I don't want you shredding my mail."

"Fine, but don't come crying to me when every last cent in your bank account winds up in Nigeria. Now. Should we do a few quick standing exercises?" She extends a hand to me and patiently waits. "You need to keep up with your physical therapy."

I give her hand a dirty look, willing her to withdraw it. But after a moment, I take it.

The following Saturday night I am at a crowded, brightly lit convention center in downtown Laurentide Bay. I am attending a beer- and wine-tasting fundraiser in support of the local Humane Society. And I am with Abby.

She called three nights after our dinner at Roots—the very night I'd been considering calling her. I still haven't decided how I feel about her. In a way, she reminds me of my family holiday get-togethers. I look forward to the event the week before it transpires, and the event itself is stocked with all the ingredients of a good time: a banquet of delicious food and comforting scents, reunion with people I share fond memories with, and decent conversation that can be made more interesting with a bevy of alcoholic beverages. Unfortunately, an hour or two into the day, I'm tugging at my collar, staring at a random football game on TV, exchanging the occasional grunt with the new boyfriend of a cousin ten years younger than me, and watching the clock like an atheist at mass.

So in theory, Abby's great. In person, she's also great. But probably not for me, because she feels more like a compromise than the love of my life.

Abby volunteers at the Bay Area Humane Society and Animal Shelter and had two free tickets to the fundraiser. I insisted on paying for mine, though. It's for a good cause. I also insisted on driving, and I believe my reasons for such were made abundantly clear during the last fundraiser I attended with Kevin. "Wow, you've got quite a system here," Abby says while she watches me park and exit my truck and smoothly retrieve and enter my chair. I used to feel uncomfortable under such scrutiny, but I've grown used to it. You can get used to almost anything.

"A system born of necessity," I say as we make our way from the parking ramp to the convention center. The night is balmy and still, and the air smells of algae. The glare from orange arc sodium streetlights makes our fellow pedestrians look like relatives of George Hamilton. Downtown traffic cruises by, the hoods of cars gleaming like black beetles.

Abby catches my eye and smiles demurely. "I'm really impressed, Graham. I don't know how you feel about people saying these kinds of things to you, and I apologize if this sounds strange or rude, but I'm humbled by your self-sufficiency."

"It's okay," I answer, oddly touched by her sincerity. "You do what you have to do. Can't stop living just because I can't walk." Though I sound comfortable with my situation, I dislike directly acknowledging this obvious and annoying fact. And what am I going to do, put myself in a group home and eat applesauce all day?

"Of course," she says, blushing even more deeply. When we reach the convention center, I punch the silver plate-sized button that mechanically opens the pneumatic glass doors. There is, of course, a blue wheelchair-bound stick figure engraved on the button. Since the accident, I've become quite attuned to the language and symbols of accessibility. "After you," I say.

"Oh! Are you sure? Okay. Thanks!"

Abby dances awkwardly in, casting a worried glance back lest the automatic door swing shut and slice me in half before I make it through. Either she's the most insecure woman on the planet, or she's harboring some serious maternal feelings for me. Some women are like that with guys in chairs—they want to take care of you. Which sounds dandy at first, until you realize there is usually some kind of price to pay for the caregiving. Maybe they expect blind devotion, above-average listening skills, superhuman patience, who knows.

But listen—just because a dude's in a chair doesn't mean he's not capable of screwing around behind his girlfriend's back. If you don't believe me, I'm more than happy to tell you the tale of Shawn McKeown, a quad who wouldn't commit to oxygen if he didn't have to.

Once inside, we check in at the main table and pick up our swag bags, which contain iced cookies shaped like dog bones, a book of coupons for local goods and services, and small commemorative glasses etched with the date and name of the event: *The 8th annual Dog Gone Good Time Brewfest.* "You can use the glasses when you visit the tasting tables," Abby says, beaming. Both of her eyes stay put the way good, obedient little sensory organs should.

But her answer erases any doubts I may have held about this being a serious tasting event for sophisticated wine aficionados. It's clearly an excuse to bid on chintzy raffle items, clog your arteries with fried finger foods, and get hammered on cheap booze by way of oversized shot glass. The ballroom is packed with maybe five hundred people, and the doors have opened only twenty minutes ago. I am ass-level with everyone, which is always annoying as I'll probably have a stiff neck later from looking up all night. Not to mention the reduced air quality at this altitude. I'm pleased to note clear paths running through the maze of vendors; everyone seems to be gravitating toward four tables in particular: Capital Brewery, Harbor City Brewing Company, Cold Springs Winery, and the Door County Distillery. There are dozens more, but these four have the best name recognition, the most elaborate displays, and female bartenders with great smiles and amazing tits. I'm sure most women would find the male bartenders attractive as well, if they could actually see them through the cloud of Axe body spray.

"Want to check out what Central Waters Brewing has to offer?" Abby suggests. Her tentative body language and darting eyes tell me she's still feeling awkward around me—about as comfortable as Michael Vick guest-hosting the Westminster Kennel Club Dog Show. I wish I could say this is a rare phenomenon, but it isn't. A few hours together is usually all it takes to clear up the gaudy attentiveness of a new acquaintance, at which point they nearly stop seeing me in the chair and start seeing just me. I'm hoping Abby is no exception.

"Central Waters it is," I say, smiling with a flourish. Minutes later, after sampling a malty Oktoberfest, the oatmeal chocolate stout, the foamy Mud Puppy Porter, and a golden Happy Heron Pale Ale, I'm a bit more cheerful. I don't even feel guilty that I didn't sniff or swish before swallowing. Soon, there is little to distinguish individual weisses and wheats and lagers and ryes. Malted barley, hops, yeast … the basic components, plus a few spices or adjuncts … individually sampled, perhaps in a candlelit bar walled with oak casks, the subtle aromas and flavors could be noted and savored. But in this sterile, noisy, packed arena, where you're slamming each variety so the man in the long line behind you will stop tapping his toe and rolling his eyes because you dared to take the time to breathe between gulps, everything begins to taste like a rerun. You simply can't detect gamey or raisiny complexities in a Cabernet Sauvignon when you're pounding it in the middle of what feels like a parade of homes showcase at the county expo center.

Abby's cheeks are pink, her eyes wide and bright. If she isn't modestly inebriated, she will be shortly. "Want to try some wines?"

How does the saying go? Beer before liquor, never been sicker? Liquor before beer, have no fear? Oh well, it's all tumbling about in the ethos now.

"So Abby," I say, pretending to admire the buttery backbone of a generic merlot from a local winery, "how did you get involved in volunteering at the Humane Society?"

"About two years ago I wanted a Yorkie. I found an ad in the paper: *Puppies for sale, first shots, dewclaws removed, dewormed, health guaranteed, yadda-yadda.* So I called, reserved one of the girls from a new litter, made a down payment, everything. When I got there, I was shocked at how dirty the place was. But I took my new puppy home, went on with things. Two months later, she died of kidney failure."

Her eyes, mercifully focused on the same point above my left shoulder, glisten with emotion. "Looking back, I mean, if I know then ... wait." She blinks for two solid seconds, determined to get the words right. Her voice is getting that mechanical quality that tells me her blood cells are performing a Technicolor synchronized swim tribute to barley and hops. "If I knew then," she says, enunciating carefully, "what I know now, I would never have gotten Oreo from those people. It was a puppy mill, is what it was."

"And the experience was all it took to make an activist out of you," I finish, mildly impressed that she's the kind of girl who will take a broken heart and elevate it into something graceful and selfless. Although the argument could be made that even altruistic acts are selfish, but let's leave that deconstruction to the creepy philosophy majors tonight.

"Right," she says, smiling gently. "So now I stop in at the shelter twice a week to clean kennels and walk dogs people don't want anymore."

It might be the Cherry Bourbon Stout, but I suddenly want to rescue all of those dogs people don't want anymore. All the pit bulls and lab mixes and part-beagles and scruffy spaniels with funky-smelling ears. Bring them all home so we can pile on the couch and watch old Steve McQueen movies together, go for rides to the dog park where I'd throw the tennis ball again and again, maybe I'd dress the smaller ones in funny little Halloween costumes they'd hate, but just for an hour until I could take a few pictures. I'm shocked to realize that getting a dog has never occurred to me before now.

And just as I'm imagining dressing my future retriever like Mayor McCheese, I spot Drew. With Brooke. Laughing together as they sample cherry-infused vodka from the Door County Distillery.

They haven't seen me. Probably because I'm tucked so neatly into the crowd. Drew, as usual, looks heartbreaking in jeans and a crisp white cotton shirt. Brooke just looks like a bitchy Chlamydia vector in pretty much the same outfit. What is the deal with girls dressing alike? I remember Caitlin calling her friends before social events, whispering into the phone, "What are you wearing?" The pretense of course being that she didn't want to show up in heels and a little black dress if it was a chinos and flip-flops affair. And then they'd coordinate their outfits and everyone at the party would look like a personality-devoid clone of everyone else. I find it hard to believe that Drew conspired with Brooke on their wardrobe for tonight's festivities, but I also find it hard to believe Drew would kiss a walking herpes sore like Joe Simon, and that actually happened.

A small voice inside of me, one that sounds an awful lot like Kevin, says, *Knock off the self-pity and lighten up; you're on a date with a nice girl who seems to like you. Straighten up and fly right.* I am on a date with a pleasant young woman who doesn't deserve to spend the evening with a sniveling, peevish baby. "Would you like to try some wine?" Abby is asking me. Her eyes are eager to please.

Drew likes Joe. She will never like you.

My brain gives my face a direct order: *Smile, goddammit.* And like a hot knife through an ice cream cake, my lips slip into a smile that feels easier than it really is. It's a phony, denture cream smile: *Fix it and forget it.*

"Let's do it," I say, uncomfortably aware of just how lame I sound.

And at that very moment I hear a surprised, "Graham? Is that you?"

Given that there are perhaps fifteen wheelchair-bound individuals in all of Laurentide Bay and I'm the only one below the age of forty, the question is, at best, rhetorical. At worst, indication of a vision problem.

Ah, Drew. Let me Drew you a picture. I spin around and my already plastic smile morphs into something even more make-believe. A parody of a smile. I probably look like a serial killer.

"Hi, Drew," I say.

"What are you doing here?" she asks, and she seems genuinely delighted to see me. Brooke just stands there grinning like a weasel.

"Drinking, people-watching, raising money for a good cause." Abby smiles patiently next to me, and I add, "Drew, this is Abby. And Brooke." The girls shake hands, which strikes me as weird. It always seems like such a masculine thing to do. But what are they going to do, hug someone they just met?

"Nice to meet you, Abby," Drew says, and do I detect a slight change in the atmosphere? A miniscule stiffening of the brow and smile? Maybe. Or maybe I'm developing my own vision problem.

"I didn't know you'd be here," I say, carefully.

"I didn't either until a few hours ago. Brooke had an extra ticket and called out of the blue, so …" Drew's smile seems wistful, or maybe that's just wistful thinking on my part.

"I'm actually here for a more mercenary reason," Brooke says. "I'm scoping the competition for the Roots brewpub."

"I didn't know Roots had a brewpub," Abby says, and she reminds me of an eager, goofy puppy, blissfully galumphing through a minefield.

"Oh, we don't. Not yet." Brooke swirls the merlot in her commemorative tasting glass. "It's in the preliminary design stages."

"You work at Roots?" Abby asks.

Brooke offers what could be construed as a benevolent smile, but in my head I see Cartoon Brooke with a giant mouth and rows of shark teeth, opening wide to chomp Abby's head off. "My husband and I own it."

"Oh, wow! I love Roots," Abby says, delighted. "It's the best place to eat in Laurentide Bay. I bet all your customers would agree."

I doubt Brooke would even want the words "customers" or "eat" associated with her restaurant, preferring instead that her "guests" "luxuriate in the seductive textures and flavors of cutting-edge American cuisine." She closes her eyes for a too-long blink and offers a smug, icy smile. "Thank you."

My instinct is to pull Abby away from this jackal. Drew seems to sense my discomfort and adds a bright, "So Abby, how do you know Graham?" Her smile is open and warm.

"We met online, actually."

"That's probably the best place these days," Drew says. I can't tell if she means it.

At that very moment, an interruption—a jostling, a bumpy collision with my chair. And a tall man who reeks of body odor and menthol spills a large, cold splash of beer on my head. I feel myself reflexively recoil while it trickles down my back. "Oh shit, sorry, buddy! Didn't see you down there."

Abby's face slides from happy to horrified in a millisecond, and she and Drew scramble to the nearest vendor for napkins. Brooke gasps. And it's like a scene in a movie, where time grinds to a near-halt, all the talking winds down to ten RPM and giant, blurry faces zoom in with huge, concerned eyes while the room spins round and round. I close my eyes, leaning forward and forcing a smile, and time resumes its normal speed.

I look up and say, "Don't worry about it. Happens all the time." I wish this were a lie. I don't think the damage is too bad, but I stopped feeling the cold liquid near my tailbone.

Abby returns with a bar towel and frantically begins dabbing at my back. "Here," she says, gently blotting.

"I'm fine," I say, dying a little inside.

Brooke just stands there with her arms crossed, looking irritated and disgusted. Drew arrives on the scene with napkins and a concerned expression. In the grand scheme of things, having beer spilled on you is uncomfortable, but usually not cause for such mortified concern. Having beer spilled on you when you're little more than a piece of furniture to the spillee ... well, that's another chapter entirely.

"Hey, buddy, I'm really sorry." The tall, pungent man awkwardly grasps the handles of my chair, unsure what to do.

"Don't sweat it," I say, my tone sharp. When people grab my chair, it feels like they're grabbing me.

He wisely backs away. "Can I get you something?"

How about the ability to walk again? Can you pour a cup of that down my back?

"Do you need a beer?" The guy won't shut up. "Anything?"

Yeah, I think. I need people like you to stop treating me like a child. I need to feel my toes in dewy grass. To feel the itch of a mosquito bite on my knee. I need to be able to ride a mountain bike again through the undulating, forested hills of Kettle Moraine State Park. I need women to look at me the way they used to. I need to know that when I wake up, I can swing both feet independently onto the floor, feel them wriggle into warm slippers while the aroma of the coffee my wife has made drifts upstairs—heady and comforting, a promise of the day to come.

Mostly, I just need to wake up whole and loved again.

16. DREW

The next Friday night Drew found herself at a party with Joe. It was a typical backyard bonfire, with red Solo cups of cheap, sloshing beer, people with loud mouths and suspicious-looking tans, the fire giving everyone the smell of smoked sausage. As soon as they entered the overflowing split-level house, Joe was mobbed by coworkers and friends, exchanging hugs and back pounds. Drew smiled behind him, patiently watching, peripherally aware of a man in a Milwaukee Brewers baseball cap materializing at her side. He stood next to her, tipped his head toward a group of people chatting in the corner, and said in a low voice, "Can you believe those two got back together after all the shit that went down between them?"

Drew frowned, confused. Had he mistaken her for someone else? "Uh, I'm sorry? Who are you talking about?"

"Your butt cheeks!" He winked and walked away, leaving her flustered and embarrassed. She'd been there thirty seconds and already she felt out of place and old. The only person in the room who remembered when the Berlin Wall fell, the only girl to have worn scrunchies without irony. Joe went to high school with this crowd. How many of them were home from college for the summer? She wanted to warn all of the hopeful-looking girls: *Be careful, even the nice ones can fail you.*

Brooke had called earlier in the evening, wondering if she'd like to drop by Roots to help taste-test a few new appetizers Mark was considering adding to the menu. When Drew told her that she'd already agreed to go out with Joe, Brooke gasped melodramatically. "Is that the hot guy you work with? The one you told me about?"

"The one and only," Drew said, immediately thinking, *well, not the* ONLY. "What kind of appetizers?" she added.

"A fig jam, walnut and blue cheese flatbread, garlic-seared mushrooms, and …" She lowered the phone to yell into the distance. "Honey, what's the third appetizer?"

There was a muffled reply.

"Tortilla-wrapped queso blanco, deep fried, with fresh tomatillo salsa."

"You're killing me."

"Sweetpea, bring him with! You can both try them."

As tempting as the invitation was, Drew wasn't yet ready to introduce any of her dates to her friends. Not to mention she still hadn't determined if she was really dating Joe, or if Brooke was really her friend. "I'd love to," Drew said, "but I think I'm going to take a rain check."

So here she was, watching her younger date prime a half-barrel to dispense her beverage, the rim of his own empty cup clamped between his lips. My, he was attractive. He probably never had an ugly day in his life. He would even look good with a mullet and a cold sore. As she thought this, Joe looked up and caught her eye to smile around his cup, pumping away on the tapper. The overall effect was fairly titillating. While she watched, the man in the Brewers cap returned. "I'm going outside to make out," he said. "Care to join me?" He winked again and left.

Joe handed her a foamy cup of beer, smiling thoughtfully. It was a smile that could sell an oil slick to a member of the Sierra Club. Ice cream to the lactose intolerant. "He must like you. His usual line involves going halfsies on a bastard child. Once he asked a girl when she was going to let him 'get all up in those guts.'"

"Gross," Drew said, delighted.

Joe rested a hand on her forearm. "We don't have to stay long. I just wanted to drop by to say hi."

She barely registered what he was saying; her entire focus was on the touch of his hand, the warmth now radiating through her body from that remote juncture of limbs.

Joe introduced her around, though Drew felt like she'd met them all before. Ten years ago. The guys had the optimistic faces of people working part-time gigs before something more permanent came along. Adulthood, for example. In their snug tops and frayed denim skirts, the girls looked uncomplicated and fresh from the wrapper. Drew's age and checking account both demanded that her wardrobe be based on classic, high-quality separates that would never go out of style. So she had the linen and cashmere and wool, but usually in tan or black or white. Outfits that read more "trainee at H&R Block" than "carefree co-ed." Tonight she wore a green silk halter top with white cotton pants she'd picked up on sale last fall at Banana Republic. A decent look for someone in her early thirties, but too age-appropriate to blend in with the natives.

After Joe was dragged away into another conversation with a friend, Drew found herself alone on the back deck, swatting at mosquitoes. A girl with moody, brown eyes and strong, well-defined cheekbones spun around next to Drew and extended a manicured hand. "I'm Anna," she said, segueing into an innocent question that nearly sounded like a demand. "So how long have you known Joe?" Anna smelled like peonies and campfire. Drew shook her hand, which was heavy with rings on nearly every ice-cold finger.

"Not long. A month, maybe?"

Anna's unrelenting scrutiny gave Drew the feeling of being cased before a burglary. "We went to high school together."

Immediately, this reminded Drew of Graham. She was pleasantly surprised to run into him at the fundraiser last weekend. But not quite so pleased to see him with that girl ... Abby. *She seems nice,* Drew thought, giving herself a fake pep talk. Graham deserved to be happy. Why would she be even remotely envious of his finding it with someone?

"Hel-*lo?*" Anna was asking her.

"Um, sorry?" Drew snapped out of it, feeling heat flood her cheeks.

She rolled her eyes and sighed heavily. "I was asking where you got your shoes. They're totally cute."

Drew looked down at her strappy sandals. "DSW?"

"I *love* DSW." She took a sip of beer. "So you met Joe at work? Are you a guard, too?"

"No, I'm a teacher."

"Really. What do you teach?"

"Interrogation tactics," Drew shouted over the din of the party. "You get an A."

Anna smiled and furrowed her brow, trying to make sense of this. She tilted her head and repeated, "What?"

Drew sighed. "I teach special education."

Anna wrinkled her nose. "In prison? There are retarded people in prison?"

What was taking Joe so long? "You'd be surprised," Drew said, crossing her arms, still glancing over her shoulder for Joe. For anyone, really. Even a troupe of mimes. Unfortunately,

Anna interpreted her desperate distraction as an invitation for further badgering.

"So what kinds of things do retarded people do to wind up in prison?"

Drew didn't want to argue semantics with such an insensitive idiot, so she decided to be blunt. "Rape, murder, armed robbery, burglary, aggravated assault, you name it."

Anna continued her suspicious stare. "Huh. That is, like, so messed up." Behind her, the fire crackled as the flames suddenly leapt into the air. The crowd howled in appreciation.

"You don't know the half of it," Drew said, thinking of Ricardo Mariano winking at her during a spelling test earlier in the day, then pretending to have something in his eye.

Just then she sensed someone behind her. Joe, her fabled life preserver in very anatomically correct male form. "I see you made a friend," he said.

Emboldened by the fact that she'd probably never see this woman again, Drew pointed to Anna's spectacularly displayed cleavage and clarified, "*Three* friends, actually!"

Anna's face registered first confusion, then flustered pique. "Nice meeting you," she mumbled and disappeared back into the crowd. She never even asked Drew's name, but since Joe's pants likely had less a zip-fly and more a turnstile, Drew didn't think she would have asked, either.

"Hey, want to get out of here?" Joe asked, pressing a hand against her lower back. "I'm kind of hungry. How about you?"

Back in his Jeep, Drew watched Joe prick his finger and measure his blood sugar level with a glucose monitor. It beeped, and he recorded some numbers in a small notebook he pulled out of the glove compartment. "I'm a little high," he announced. "Gotta get my Lispro freak on." Drew watched, fascinated, while he stuck the syringe of insulin in his arm. Blindness, amputation, stroke, and impotence, she remembered from high school health. The price of screwy blood sugar levels and a disobedient pancreas, if you didn't look out.

"I'm the only person I know who's on a first-name basis with his doctor," he said, tossing his paraphernalia back into the glove box. "It's pretty much an all-around pain in the ass."

"Does it hurt?" Luckily, she stopped herself before adding, *when you prick yourself?*

He shrugged. "Not anymore. It did when I was little."

"How old were you when you found out? That you had it."

"Six."

"What happens if you're high?"

"I get the munchies and laugh at everything."

"No, I mean your numbers. When they're high."

"I suppose they do the same thing." He grinned.

"You don't do it a lot, do you?"

"Do what?"

"Get high."

"God, no. Piss tests and all. Between work and my doctor, I'm pretty much on a fun-free diet."

"I find that hard to believe."

"Hey," Joe said, switching conversational gears, "sorry about Anna."

Drew carefully chose her words and tone, going with the neutral but banal, "She was interesting."

"Yeah. We used to go out, a long time ago." He didn't follow this up with further explanation, and Drew didn't ask.

They drove to Sam's Drive-In, a local frozen custard joint that still had carhops. Joe parked in an empty space, and they studied the backlit marquee menu for a moment. "Know what you want?"

Drew nodded. Of course she knew what she wanted. Whether she'd pursue it was another topic entirely.

He turned his headlights on for service. A girl in a pink skirt bounced over, pen and pad in hand. Her braces glimmered as she slipped a plastic number under the windshield wiper.

"I think we know what we want. Drew?" He caught her eye, a slight smile playing on his lips. You'd have to be a shrub to miss the real meaning of that statement.

"Uh, I'll have a caramel cashew sundae."

"And I'll have a chocolate malt."

"Are you supposed to eat that?"

"Come on, Ma, just one. It's small!"

Drew smiled. "Okay, but don't come crying to me when your legs fall off."

He turned the key forward one click in the ignition, and the dash began to glow a soft red. Iron Butterfly's "In-A-Gadda-Da-Vida" was playing on WLKE, as it did every night at nine p.m. sharp on this particular station. "I have this theory," Drew began, "that until WLKE stops playing Iron Butterfly every night, Laurentide Bay will never get a Montessori preschool."

Joe gave her a crooked smile that told her he had no idea what a Montessori preschool was. They sat in silence for a while, watching other customers eat ice cream in their cars. A woman in a neighboring minivan was frantically wiping spilled malt from her lap while she shouted at two kids strapped into the back seat. Drew decided to shift to a more traditional conversation topic before reality reasserted itself and she lost her nerve. "So tell me how you decided to work at Lakeside."

"Well, I didn't want to work construction. They were hiring. Decent pay, decent bennies, decent coworkers. And I'll always have a job if I want it—criminals aren't exactly in short supply." He shrugged and said nothing about college. He was the opposite of Ben, and right now that was everything she wanted. Their carhop suddenly appeared, balancing a dented tray with their order. She hung it on Joe's window, and he passed her the sundae. "I don't think anyone really grows up wanting to work at Lakeside. It's not like it was my life dream anyway."

"It's been an interesting transition for me." She popped the maraschino cherry into her mouth. "I mean, my former students might have joked there wasn't much difference between public school and prison, but I'd have to disagree. Especially when you're the one up at the chalkboard."

"Well, you're a woman. That's usually the case." She glanced at him, trying to read his expression. Where was he going with this? He continued, "Some people say women shouldn't be allowed to work in a men's prison."

So this was how he did it. Seduction by irritation. "Well, some people have very interesting opinions about women."

"I think women are wonderful," Joe said slyly, tapping his straw from its paper sheath.

"So do you think women shouldn't work at Lakeside?"

"Maybe. But I wouldn't have met you if that were the case."

"There it is."

He seemed amused by this. "There what is? Anyway, how do you like working with the dregs of society?"

"What do you think, people like us could never go to prison?"

"Basically. You have to *work* to do serious time. These guys have rap sheets longer than I-94." He paused to taste his malt.

"Well, I'm sure most of them grew up in less-than-perfect homes."

"If you changed the bios of all the guys in prison now so that they would have been raised by happy families in the suburbs, ninety percent of them would *still* end up in prison.

And do you know why?" He pointed to her nose. "Genetics. It's as simple as that. There's a criminal gene."

"That's a pretty simple way of looking at it."

"All I'm saying is wait and see. Just read some of the files. You'll be shocked at how many guys come from a long line of criminals. It's the family business."

She could feel her blood pressure rising and narrowed her eyes at him. "What kind of life do you think you'd live if your mother left you with a pedophile uncle while she went off to smoke crack?"

"Please!" He smirked. "Listen, sweetheart. Excuses are like Toyotas. Everybody's got one."

"I don't have a Toyota."

"Oh, relax." He chewed on his straw, still giving her that go-to-hell smile. "I'm just messing with you."

"Remind me never to discuss religion with you."

"You know, you're very high-strung."

"So I've been told. How's your malt?"

"Pretty good. How's your sundae? Can I have a taste?"

She passed him her dish and watched her spoon slide into his mouth. Lucky spoon.

Joe turned the radio down. "So tell me about your family. I can't believe Sara's your mom! Did she ever leave you with a pedophile uncle to go smoke crack?"

"All the time," Drew said. "It was our Friday routine."

He grinned. "Okay, sorry. I'll be serious. What about the rest of your family?"

She stirred the melted remains of her sundae. "I have a younger brother, Nick, and a younger sister, Wendy ... we're pretty typical." She suddenly missed her siblings fiercely.

"My parents are divorced," Joe said, matter-of-factly. "But after my brother died, they started sleeping together again. Isn't that weird?"

She didn't know what to say. He had diabetes, divorced parents, and a dead brother. Next he was going to tell her he read to an elderly blind woman named Bernice on Tuesday afternoons. If he did, she would definitely sleep with him. But what if she got pregnant? They might get married. They would serve greasy chicken and canned green beans at their wedding, buffet-style. They'd have one of those relationships where you have lots of animal sex, but your children constantly have runny noses and act unruly in public. He would never want to watch *60 Minutes* with her. They would drift apart, and she'd meet a sensitive, wounded man who wore glasses and enjoyed sea kayaking. There would be an affair. The divorce would be brutal. Their daughter's grades would suffer, and she would become promiscuous at an early age. Later, her parents would start sleeping together again out of loneliness or that original animal attraction, who could say. She would tell this to a boy while out on a date and add, "Isn't that weird?" And it would be.

Drew shook her head and cleared her throat. "I'm so sorry."

"Car accident a few years ago. Left a wife and my nephew, Jake. He's four now."

"Oh, God … that's awful." No one close to her had ever died. She tried to imagine Nick or Wendy dying and shivered. It was an alien, horrible thought. But when she imagined Ben dying, it felt like her heart had walked into an empty stadium. There was simply nothing there except echoes and a few old ticket stubs stuck to the cement.

He shrugged. "Hey, it's okay. I'm really all right about it. I got a little crazy for a while, but life goes on, you know?"

She looked at him, still concerned. "Where does your dad live?"

He set his malt glass on the tray. "Milwaukee. But he spends every holiday with us, carving the turkey at the head of the table like nothing ever happened." He turned the headlights on again to summon the carhop. "But it could have been worse. I know someone who sewed anchovies into the curtains before she got divorced. Her ex and his new girlfriend couldn't figure out where the smell was coming from, so they had to move."

She decided to change the subject to something a little lighter. "So. Laurentide Bay High School. I bet you played football."

"You got me. Linebacker. Number seventy-four."

"I knew it." She imagined how he must have looked in his uniform, running across the well-lit field on a Friday night. All the cheerleaders probably fought to decorate his locker before games and get in his pants afterward. "Prom king?"

His smile widened. "And homecoming."

"Aw, aren't you All-American! Were you in the Boy Scouts, too?" She couldn't suppress her laughter. "Did you take the Waves to state?"

He cringed, still smiling. "God, you're making me sound like some asshole on a CW show."

She wondered how many people he'd slept with. She waited for the expected little ping of jealousy, but … it never arrived. She took an emotional inventory and came up with: curious, indifferent, lonely, and aroused. A confusing and combustible mix she hadn't felt in years, if ever. *He's a younger coworker*, she reminded herself. *One who's probably slept with half of Laurentide Bay*. She waited for the self-reproach to kick in, for her conscience to take control, but nothing changed. She felt nothing but the steady drumbeat of irresponsible want.

"I was a complete dork in high school," he continued.

"You were not."

"I was! I didn't have a girlfriend till senior year."

"And it's been a revolving door ever since," she added cheekily.

"You're so mean," he said, chuckling. Their eyes met, and something unspoken flashed between them. An acknowledgment that this was all merely a prelude to the main event, which may or may not take place later that evening.

She opened her mouth to address this somehow, to make her decision final, and closed it again. Joe saw this and smiled. "What?" he chided, his right hand finding a companionable resting spot on her left thigh. "You want to say something, so let's hear it."

Her eyes dropped to his hand on her leg, which had sent a ripple of heat waves up to the parts that really mattered. When she looked up again the words had already left her lips: "Take me back to your place." She could barely breathe. Her heart pounded. Who was this new girl that spoke so bluntly? And more importantly, how long would she be sticking around?

He immediately tapped the horn and waved their waitress over. "Here," he said, fumbling with his wallet and handing her a twenty. "Keep the change."

Joe lived in an old Victorian rental near the lake with two other guys who both happened to be out. Pizza boxes and dirty glasses littered the kitchen, and wires snaked all over the living room, connecting the stereo and Xbox and plasma TV to four speakers, one in each corner. All of the furniture was secondhand, but the driveway and garage were stuffed with parked toys: Jet Skis, snowmobiles, a boat on a trailer, a four-wheeler.

Priorities, Drew thought. She remembered the apartment she shared with Ben. They did have a complicated entertainment center with more applications and buttons than a cockpit, but their place had also been homey. There were original paintings on the walls, cushy throw pillows on the red couch, scented candles in the bathroom, stained glass panels hanging in the kitchen window, framed photos of their life together propped on nearly every available surface: Ben and Drew on a ski trip with friends, at Thanksgiving with his family, hugging on a sailboat at sunset, the two of them clustered with smiling, tipsy friends at a Minnesota Twins game.

There were no cushy pillows in Joe's living room, no original paintings on the walls; there were two neon beer signs casting a faint red and blue glow, and that was fine with Drew.

"You want something to drink?" he asked, flipping on the television and padding barefoot into the kitchen. "We've got beer, rum and Coke, vodka, lemonade …"

"Coffee, tea, or me," she said, settling into the couch and kicking off her sandals. She knew that once this high faded she'd experience less an afterglow and more a sugar crash. But like anyone on the verge of a binge, the realization did nothing to deter her.

He poked his head around the door frame. "What'd you say?"

She smiled. "I said, 'I'll have whatever you're having.'"

He returned to the living room with two bottles of Budweiser, one of which he handed to her. They grinned at one another and clinked their bottles together because it seemed like the thing to do. They stared awkwardly at the television for a few seconds, drinking beer. *This is why people get drunk before casual sex,* Drew thought. But she was grateful that he'd grown reticent and nearly shy. It was unexpected and sweet. But now that she thought about it, it was also very smart. *Let her think it was all her idea. Maybe that's his angle.*

Before completely losing her nerve, she asked, "Do I get a tour of the rest of the place?" She'd come this far. It felt like a cheap and seedy question, but they were adults. Some of them had been one for a longer period of time, but what could you do. She had needs, he had needs, they weren't there to play Scrabble.

He gave her a lazy smile, stood, and extended a hand to help her up.

He slowly followed her up the stairs, which felt like a curious mating ritual itself. His bedroom was neat. Sparsely furnished and clean, with a dresser, a chair, a television set, and a nightstand with a small metal lamp. There was no bookcase, but there was a bed with a blue comforter, and this was good enough for Drew. Joe sat on his bed and leaned back, propping himself up on his elbows. She could feel him staring at her while she wandered over to his dresser to look at a framed photo: two boys in baseball uniforms, squinting into the camera, posing with their gloves. They both had brown, shaggy hair, and the smaller boy had one hazel—

"Turn around," he said. They'd been teasing and flirting just moments before, but his voice had cooled.

She turned and looked at him nakedly. When she saw the look on his face—self-possessed and serious—something clicked in her mind like the tumbler of a lock, and a door swung open. *So this is how it will be*, she thought.

"Take off your shirt."

Drew could imagine this same scene playing out dozens of times in this same room, with different girls who giggled and protested. She hadn't been one of those girls in a long time. She pulled her halter top over her head, let it drop to the floor behind her, and stood in the low light. She held her arms at her sides and stared back at him in a way that felt not quite defiant, not quite deferential.

"Now your pants," he said in a practiced, detached tone. With another man, it could have turned into a joke; she might have rolled her eyes or laughed. Instead she slowly untied the knot at the waistband of her white cotton pants. They slid to the floor and puddled around her ankles, and she carefully stepped out of them, now clad only in a pair of white panties.

Goosebumps marched across her exposed skin, her nipples hardening in the cool breeze spilling through the open window, but she kept her arms still. "Should I take—"

"Not yet." He pushed himself off the bed and walked over to her. He ran a finger down her jawline, tracing a hypnotic pattern on her neck, her chest, which was starting to rise and fall more quickly. He slid that hand around the back of her head, the other around the nape of her neck, and pulled her forward, into a blue sliver of moonlight.

She closed her eyes when he pressed his soft lips against her mouth, parting her lips with his tongue. She eased into the kiss like a warm bath. Tentatively at first, then more decisively. It was the kind of dark, determined kissing that could get you high, make you forget your birthday, even your own name. Had anyone ever kissed her like that? He read every tremble, every sigh, every heartbeat, adjusting his intensity on cue, as if her response to him was unfolding on sheet music. He was completely absorbed in her, his breathing ragged and his body tense with excitement, but she found his skill, and the fact that his mouth *still* tasted of mint, as if he'd figured out a way to hide his gum in a pocket behind his molars, mildly unsettling all the same.

But she hadn't come here to feel settled.

He paused to pull his shirt over his head, exposing a well-muscled torso, a soft, vertical line of hair above his waistband, a jagged constellation of three pink scars, each maybe an inch long, on his side. Instinctively, she reached out to touch them.

"I got stabbed at work," he said, like it was no big deal, everyone gets stabbed at work from time to time, just ask your accountant or the barista at Starbucks.

"Jesus," she said, lifting her eyes to read his expression.

"Don't worry about it," he said, kissing her chin. "I don't," he said, kissing down her neck, down her collarbone. "There are more interesting things happening," he said, deftly slipping two fingers below the lace trim of her panties, tugging them down her thighs. He cradled her cheek with his left hand, watching her face while he dropped his right hand between her legs. He held her gaze for a few breaths, wearing an expression that might pass for bored or drunk in any other situation. She closed her eyes to escape his strange scrutiny.

"Open your eyes," he said.

She shook her head, drawing a sharp breath as his touch grew suddenly rough. She opened her eyes and his fingers relaxed again. As her breath began to hitch in her throat, he once more lowered his mouth to hers. She melted into the kiss.

Drew was shocked to find that she felt remarkably unself-conscious, despite her obvious arousal. Relaxed enough to enjoy everything he was doing to her, her mind uncluttered with To-Do lists or commercial jingles or paranoia about whether she had a double chin from that angle, nothing distracting or unpleasant. Was that the secret to good sex? Not really caring? But more important even than the fact that he was making her feel exceptionally good, and he clearly enjoyed doing so—Joe made her feel anonymous. He knew nothing about Ben or her life before Lakeside. She was a blank slate in his eyes. And that, his seeing her as a near tabula rasa, was almost enough to convince her that she was. That she could be anything, even a person with no history. A person who wasn't interviewed by the police in her old apartment, fielding questions she had no answers for. A person who hadn't seen her future led away in handcuffs.

Stop. There were more interesting things happening here. *There is no Ben,* she thought. Soon enough, the last year would be a distant memory. Soon enough, Joe would be the optimist in her.

She was faintly aware that he'd unbuckled his belt, tugging it through the loops in his shorts. He folded it, flexed it for a few thoughtful beats, dragged it gently across her stomach before snapping it around her hips with a casual flick of his wrist. He caught the other end and pulled her down to the floor. *A bruise tomorrow,* she dimly registered when her knees hit the hardwood, not caring.

Finally they reached the point where she'd have to ask the question she hadn't had to ask in more than seven years. "Do you have a condom?" Her voice shaky, disoriented.

He bit her inner thigh, hard enough to make her gasp. *Another mark.* "Don't move." He sat up and pulled open a drawer in his nightstand.

Even though she'd been celibate for over a year, she was still on the pill.

But she wasn't sleeping with a virgin.

And that turned out to be a very good thing.

17. GRAHAM

Hostage negotiation skills. They're probably not something you learned in school. Well, unless you grew up in Detroit. I admit, this is just the kind of adrenaline-fueled professional development that keeps me from quitting and rolling off into the sunset. We're receiving the training in rounds, and it just so happens that Drew is in my cadre. As soon as she sees me parked behind the back table, she gives a little wave and heads over.

My heart, oh, my heart. Will it ever stop hiccupping when I see her?

"Hey, Graham, how are you?" Even under these unflattering fluorescent lights, her face could win the Super Bowl.

"I'm good, and you?"

She arranges herself in the chair next to me before fixing me with that award-winning smile. "Excellent."

She's content, even buoyant—but I find something disturbing in her smile. I know, I've heard the rumors that she and Joe Simon are—if not an item, then an article, a piece, maybe even a bit. They're certainly something, and I don't have to tell you how disappointed I am about this turn of events. I'm so disappointed that I decide to put it out there, just serve the shit up rare and bloody.

"So I hear you and Joe Simon …" I say, forcing a rubbery and painful smile.

The good mood slides off her face and she blanches. "Who told you?"

So it's true. Lakeside is incredibly incestuous, and it can't keep a secret. There's a better chance that a first-grader would keep mum about discovering a money-shitting Pegasus in her closet than anyone on the Lakeside payroll would sit on the news that Employee A is screwing Employee B. This doesn't even begin to touch the can of maggots that gets opened if the inmates find out about such interoffice (or is it interpenal?) romances. Bottom line, dating one's colleagues isn't against prison regulations, but it's enough to earn a stern and candid discussion with administration.

"Well," I say, "word gets around pretty fast in here." I'm discouraged, but my heart isn't broken. Not really. It's just sitting on the bench watching the game, waiting for the coach to put it in, but the clock's winding down.

Her face has gone crimson. "We only went out once."

I laugh in a too-harsh way. "Well, that's all it takes here."

At this point, when my face is hard and my mood is pissed, Sergeant Kleinman strolls in with the last of this session's attendees. Sergeant Kleinman, as one who emerged from the South Bend riot with four scars, broken ribs, and enough horrific anecdotes to keep family dinners interesting for five lifetimes, is the only person in the room who can honestly list both "hostage" and "hostage negotiation skills instructor" on his resume. Unless one is a hostage to polyester, tastelessness, and dandruff, because then my celebrated colleague Jerry Lang would certainly qualify as a Master in all respects.

"Good morning, ladies and gentlemen," Sergeant Kleinman says after everyone has found a seat. "Today I'm going to tell you a story. It's a story that could save your life, so pay attention."

Thirty sets of eyes and ears are trained on nothing but him. *Shhh* ... was that a pin drop?

Sergeant Kleinman tells us about the South Bend prison riot of 1993. He was a fresh-faced officer with just two months of employment under his belt. Stationed in the yard during his unit's recreation hour, he ordered a patdown of a suspicious-acting inmate with a long history of gang activity. During the search, he discovered a shank made from a chunk of metal bedspring; the inmate grabbed Kleinman's wrist, a scuffle ensued, but Kleinman managed to pin the offender to the ground. Unfortunately, a dozen of the inmate's fellow gang members rushed to his aid with fists, feet, and homemade weapons of their own. A frenzied dog pile, other officers racing in to help, a blur of kicking and punching and choking and stabbing.

Half an hour later word was out and the entire prison had crumbled into chaos as institutional tribes seized the opportunity to take retribution for unresolved conflicts with other inmates as well as grudges against staff. Under a cloud of tear gas, the Hispanics went after the blacks, the blacks went after the neo-Nazis, the neo-Nazis grabbed control of the school, and everybody else either hunkered down or contributed their own little individual rampages to the larger stampede of anarchy.

With help from the riot squad, every unit was returned to lockdown and order except the recreation yard, and Sergeant Kleinman became one of five hostages in a twenty-eight-hour standoff that culminated in the riot squad rushing the unit with a sharpshooter, stun guns, and more tear gas. Ultimately, after triage and medical treatment as warranted, the hostages returned home to their weeping families. Only one correctional officer quit. The rest were back on the job within three weeks. The body count? Just one. An inmate named Damon Pouncey who was stabbed to death in the yard.

"That count would have been even higher had we not been trained to think before opening our pieholes, to treat every inmate with humanity and fairness even if what you think he deserves is a castration. You are not judge or jury. You are not God. You are not here to make friends. You are here to do a job professionally so you can return home at the end of the day to kiss your husband or wife and tuck your kids into bed."

He pauses to let this sink in before going on to tell us that he never thought he'd come out of the situation alive. His captors tormented each hostage with the constant threat of death, kicking walls near heads, poking groins with the sharp end of a busted mop handle, screaming obscenities in their faces. I glance around the conference room at my semi-terrified coworkers staring at Sergeant Kleinman. We're in the mosh pit of training activities. This is exactly the kind of discussion I'm in the mood for today.

We need to consider escape routes, says Sergeant Kleinman. If push comes to shove, what would we do? Where would we go? We shouldn't lose our heads, or we could lose our lives. "Even something as simple as standing on a desk to lift a ceiling tile, crawling up and hiding behind the ductwork could keep you from ending up in a pine box," he says.

"I doubt the ductwork is handicap-accessible," I whisper to Drew.

Though her face is still pale, she smiles. Not because my joke was even remotely related to funny, but just out of polite acknowledgement of my efforts. *She's too nice,* I think, suddenly and irrationally furious. *Save the polite, patronizing shit for the counter guy at Quiznos.*

"Always know where your exits are, both marked and unmarked," Sergeant Kleinman suggests, the most masculine flight attendant in history.

I wisely choose this moment to lean in to Drew and ask, "You didn't sleep with him, did you?"

She furrows her brow and scribbles tight circles on a notepad. "That's none of your business!"

I've gone too far. Too late now. Can't seem to stop. "Oh no," I say, adopting a bemused tone while I watch her cheeks flush. I want to stab things with my smile. "You didn't, right? Don't tell me you did!" And I make that face—the face the junior high bully made when he's teasing you but you're not quite sure of it. Honest to God, making that face hurts like hell.

"Graham," she hisses, "I really don't want to talk about this now."

It is a crying shame to have such a difference of opinion on that subject. "Drew, you do realize ..." I let my sentence hang open-ended while I think of a tactful ending. "You do realize he's got a bit of a reputation around here."

She presses her lips together and stares straight ahead. I look at those lips, the same soft lips I've imagined kissing a hundred times, and get a sudden mental image of Drew on her knees in front of Joe, a stupid, dreamy smile on his face while he thrusts into her mouth, her small hands wrapped around his stupid, skinny ass. A bomb of jealousy explodes inside of me and I have to grip the desk to steady myself. Everything in my field of vision vibrates with the shockwave. My heart feels as if it's exchanged blood for acid. My ears are burning, my skin cold, my jaw clenched. Joe Fucking Simon. How could she not know his personal goal in life is to give more rides on the baloney pony than a petting zoo sponsored by Oscar Mayer? She's *got* to know it. Or worse, what if she does know, but doesn't care?

"You do know that, right?" I continue. "I'm only saying this because I don't want to see you get hurt." Half-bullshit, half-truth. "This is the kind of thing that people love to talk about, and you don't want them talking about it here. Trust me."

"Well, it's good to know you've got my best interests at heart," she says in a chilly voice.

I really see her now, as if for the first time. She looks angry, but also frightened. Vulnerable. I feel my own jealous anger recede a bit. *Shit.* I want to rewind the last fifteen minutes and keep my mouth shut on the key points of contention. "I'm not trying to be a jerk," I say. "But be careful. Seriously."

I reflect for a fraction of a second on how deeply and blithely I've become a case study in Wanting What You Can't Have. I should take my own advice.

A booming voice intrudes, squashing our little conversation flat. Sergeant Kleinman. "Children, it might be a good idea to pay attention." He nods in my direction. "Especially you." I stare at the table. My hands are tingling. "What would you do if the shit hit the fan?" he asks me. "What's your escape plan, buddy?"

I wish I knew.

At noon I make a phone call. "Abby?"

She hesitates, but when she recognizes me her voice is refreshing and pleasant. Alka-Seltzer for my emotional hangover. "Graham, is that you?" I hear children laughing and babbling in the background. It's like listening to the family you always wanted. If I shake my head just right, like a finger flicked

215

against the brain, I could even pretend I'm calling home during my lunch hour. To see how the wife and kids are doing.

"Hi, yeah, it's me. Listen, I'm sorry to bother you at work, but I was wondering …" I rub my forehead. "If you aren't busy tonight, would you like to get together?"

"I'd love to!" I can almost see her smile through the phone. "What do you have in mind?"

I laugh—it's not really appropriate to her question, but it feels like she's lifted the lid on my bad mood, and my relief looked around at its options and decided, *Let's go with the laugh.* "You know," I say, "I have no idea!"

She pauses. "I could cook you dinner. Do you like enchiladas? Or we could go out."

Immediately I wonder about the wheelchair accessibility of her house. What a ceaseless pain in the ass. If I could feel my ass. I decide, as I usually do in these kinds of situations, to just tackle the issue head-on. "I would love to try your enchiladas." The innuendo! It's back in the saddle. This can only be a good sign. "So how's your place as far as maneuverability?"

"Oh!" I can hear a little girl singing the *Itsy Bitsy Spider* song, faintly. "I think it should be okay. I live in an apartment complex. On the first floor."

"My kind of floor."

We make a date for seven o'clock. It's as good an escape plan as any.

18. DREW

Five more inmates had been assigned to her classes. The busloads of new arrivals kept chugging into the parking lot. The prison had been operating above capacity for months, but every state prison was bursting at the seams that summer. Talk began to circulate (spurred mainly by Lisa Crane) that the Department of Corrections, in an attempt to alleviate the overcrowding, would contract with private prisons in Tennessee, Oklahoma, and Texas and start shipping inmates south by late summer. And somebody was making a sweet pile of cash on inmate transfers to these overstuffed, understaffed stables.

Everyone's stomach tightened a little with the news. The inmates began to talk loudly about hunger strikes and quietly about riots. Most of their families could barely afford gas money to visit them now; plane tickets to Oklahoma or Texas were completely out of the question. Even prison staff whispered about the out-of-state shipment in hushed, tight voices, as if it were a feral dog that had to be handled gently or it would bite.

Drew continued to work with Howard Bell and Leroy Johnson, and by Thursday morning, Howard felt ready to tackle the first book she'd offered. It was a story about a teeny-tiny woman who kept hearing a ghostly voice calling, "Give me my bone!" from her basement.

Howard Bell labored over the book, a composer obsessed with the right transitional bridge. He sounded out every letter carefully with only a little help from her, and managed to get through three pages on his own. After finishing each page, he insisted on re-reading every word until he didn't stutter over the material. Then he copied each sentence in his notebook in scrawling, jittery penmanship. When they finished, Drew felt as if she'd run a marathon in moon boots.

Leroy Johnson asked for help after every practice GED test he completed. Drew explained his errors as best she could, helplessly aware that he forgot everything the minute he returned to his desk. It made her crazy. She read his file during one of her free periods. He was sentenced to fifteen years for shooting his sister's boyfriend in the arm. Watching Leroy hunched over a test sheet with the earnest concentration of Ralphie decoding a message from Li'l Orphan Annie, she couldn't believe it. He was so polite and shy. Yesterday they played hangman with words like GLORIOUS and FABRICATE. And he had almost murdered someone.

A few of the inmates started saying unusual things to her. Like Jim Nabors, no relation to the actor. He'd begun lingering after class, telling her she was going straight to hell if she didn't accept Jesus Christ as her Lord and Savior. Jesus came to him in his dreams, he said. Then one day, Mr. Nabors tried to hang himself with an old sock. He was better than the guy she sometimes passed in the hall who liked to verbally accost her when the mood struck, shouting: "Oppression! Economic devastation! Freedom is a gun! Revolution or death!"

Drew asked Graham to meet for lunch on Wednesday; he said he was sorry, but he had too much paperwork to catch up on. He seemed disappointed, but it was the kind of disappointment you're looking at through the wrong end of a telescope: doll-sized and distant. Drew knew Graham wasn't happy that she had a ... what? A fling? With Joe. His behavior during their Monday training session made that abundantly clear. It also served to clarify her suspicions that Graham might see her as more than a friend. She wondered again if he was dating Abby, beginning to fear she'd be weirdly and inappropriately obsessed with their relationship, if one developed.

And what of Joe? Today was Friday. She hadn't seen or heard from him in almost a week, since she quietly slipped from his bedroom before dawn on Sunday. She tried to distract herself with filing and organizing, drafting lesson plans she probably wouldn't use. She participated in an IEP meeting with the visiting school psychologist and one of her new inmate charges—Colossian Cronin, who had the perfect name for a Marvel supervillain. Later that night on the phone, she told her friend Erin about him.

"What would your supervillain name be?" Erin asked her.

Drew didn't even need to think about it. "Disillusioned Doris."

Life was loudest at work, but there were quiet nooks and crannies in the day that gave her too much time to think. And finally, all over again, the uninvited encore presentation, she found herself straining to remember evidence of Ben's unhappiness before everything changed. The thing she kept returning to was the fact that during their last three months together, he was watching an awful lot of MTV. Like a voyeur, living vicariously through the spray-tanned, shiny, and wrinkle-free. Like he was trying to re-absorb youth by osmosis. Turned out osmosis had nothing to do with it.

Drew agreed to play hangman again with Leroy Johnson at her desk because he said he needed a break from studying. The rest of the class was sleepwalking through independent study for their own upcoming GED tests, flipping through books, or clicking through math drills on one of the classroom computers. Leroy chose the word INFALLIBLE.

"Mr. Johnson, that was an awesome word!"

Leroy shifted in his chair, smiling shyly. "I read it in a book." It was cold and drizzly that afternoon. Raindrops beaded the windows, snaking south in erratic trails. "I know you not supposed to tell me, but was college hard?" He said this to his hands in a polite, soft voice.

Drew paused before answering, "Yes, it could be challenging. But it was worth it."

"What did you major in?"

"Education."

"To be a teacher, right?"

"Yep."

"You get scholarships?"

"Are you thinking of applying?" Drew asked brightly.

"Maybe. I want to go back to school for business or something."

She smiled and tapped the pad of paper before them, though it bore little relation to what they were discussing. "There's no doubt in my mind that you could do that, Mr. Johnson. But first we've got to get you through the rest of your HSED tests."

"Hey, I heard a joke today in my unit."

At that point Drew noticed two of her students, Leslie Parks and Jamal Spinks, arguing in low, tight voices in the back of the room. She cleared her throat. "Everything okay back there, Mr. Spinks?"

Neither inmate responded. Instead, they stared hard at their desks. Leslie began slashing angry lines through something on his notebook. When she was convinced their argument had burned itself out, she turned back to Leroy, forcing a pleasant expression. "So. Your joke. Is it clean?"

He nodded brightly.

"Okay then, let's hear it!"

"All right. Where does a king keep his armies?"

"Where?"

"Up his sleevies."

She laughed, genuinely touched by the joke's innocence. "That's cute." Leroy beamed bashfully at his notebook. She'd never seen him so animated. She wanted to ask him why he was there. She'd already read his file, but she wanted to hear his version. She'd say it like a concerned big sister: "Leroy, what on earth are you doing here?"

He picked up his pencil and began to twirl it. "My mom and sister, they coming up on the bus to visit tonight."

"That's great, Mr. Johnson."

"Your mom's a real nice lady," he said.

Drew froze, anxious about where this conversation was headed. She sensed Leroy was harmless, but her intuition wasn't the most reliable these days.

And at that moment Leslie lunged for Jamal. A sucker punch from left field. Before she could react they were down on the floor punching and grappling, grunting. Jamal's foot kicked his desk, which squawked and tilted back, threatening to topple completely. Desk chairs scraped across the floor as her students stood to get a better view of the action.

"It's on! It's on, motherfucker!" someone gleefully shouted.

"Stay in your seats!" Drew shouted. "No, no, oh God no," she heard herself saying. Her heart vaulted into her throat and lodged there. "Stop it! Stop it right now!" They continued swinging their fists at one another while the rest of her students yelled and cheered them on, forming a ring around the brawl. Drew stumbled for the call button on rubbery legs, pressed it frantically. "Send an officer. There's a fight in my room. Hurry!"

She turned to the fighting inmates, nearly strangled by fear. *Oh God, what if one of them has a weapon?* Her heart was beating so fast it felt like one singular, keening note. "Stop fighting!" She wasn't even aware she'd said this except on some primal level. Her voice sounded a thousand miles away. Her class devolved into the coliseum, the plebes cheering the gladiators. Teams had been chosen, alliances forged, desks tipped over. Papers littered the floor. Jamal's elbow pumped the air with every strike, most of which landed on Leslie's face with sickening smacks. Complete, shouting chaos. She'd lost control. She never felt more unprepared and frightened in her life.

One of her students yelled, "Here come the poh-lice!"

She barely had time to synthesize the fact that Joe and Officer Nguyen were sprinting in, heading directly for the fighting inmates. "It's your boy," an inmate shouted. *My boy.* My boy. *Joe.* Panic squeezed her heart when she saw the bright sprays of blood on the tile floor. *Oh Jesus, Oh Jesus.*

Joe reached for the flailing arms of Leslie and earned a wild blow to the face. "Goddammit!" he shouted, whipping his head to the left, trying to get Leslie under control. Nguyen got Jamal in a headlock and pulled him away. His feet kicked out at desks as he was gracelessly hauled to the side of the room. Two other officers materialized in a blur of blue shirts and jingling keys—a little late.

Leslie went kicking and shouting obscenities, blood streaming from his nose. "Police brutality! This shit's police brutality!" Joe didn't even catch her eye as he helped Nguyen zip-tie plastic handcuffs on Jamal.

Her legs had turned to jelly. "Sit down, all of you," she said in a reedy voice. No one listened. "SIT DOWN!" she screamed, her voice stretched thin and tight, and fifteen sets of eyes turned to her. Grudgingly, they sat. She scanned the room. Which student shouted *"It's your boy!"?* Everyone craned their necks to watch Jamal being frog-marched out in cuffs, their eyes bright, hopped up on adrenaline. And Joe was gone.

"Show's over, guys," the last officer to arrive said. She didn't know him. His nametag read *Westphal.*

"I don't know what happened," Drew said, her pulse still racing.

"Don't worry about it," Officer Westphal said, out of breath. "But lucky you. You get an appointment with Baumann." He called for a spill kit on his radio, to clean up the bloody floor. Will Baumann, one of Lakeside's Security Captains, wore a *What Would Jesus Do?* bracelet and rode a motorcycle to work on warm, sunny days. She'd heard that one of his sons had been in and out of jail four times before his twenty-third birthday. When you were the cop's son or the preacher's daughter, that was, she supposed, the obvious way to rebel.

She glanced back at Leroy, still slumped in his chair next to her desk, staring down at his notebook with murky, worried eyes.

The bell finally rang. She watched the inmates file out, whooping and peacocking about the fight. After they left she closed her door, locked it, and looked at her hands. They were still shaking slightly. She returned to her desk, sucked in a deep breath of sour air, and fell into her chair. She stared at the room in a daze for a second, before catching a glimpse of Leroy's

JESS RILEY

notebook from the corner of her eye. She reached over and cautiously picked it up.

Peace Out, Ms. D was written in the corner.

"Sweetpea, you need a drink," Brooke said on the phone when Drew told her about her day. "Come over here immediately. We'll take good care of you."

She was too worn to resist. When Drew arrived at Roots, it was almost ten, the dining room nearly empty, but about a dozen customers—summer people, by the look of their outfits—still drinking at the bar. They were all tan and relaxed, the way enough money in the bank and enough love at home let you appear to be. Mark stood behind the bar shaking a martini over his shoulder, nonchalantly, like a bartender in a film. He saw Drew and smiled. "Just in time," he said, whisking a chilled martini glass onto the bar and disconnecting the shaker to pour what looked like a dirty martini into it. He plopped in a fat, skewered olive and set the drink before her with a flourish. "On the house."

"Thank you. You have no idea how much I needed this." She took a deep, grateful sip, savoring the way the alcohol warmed its way down to her stomach where it blossomed like a boozy, hothouse orchid. "Mark," Drew said, "you probably make the best martinis in the world."

He chuckled, his cheeks forming deep dimples. "I guess you really do need to get out more." At that point Brooke swirled in from the dining room in a black wrap shirt, her hair pulled back into an efficient and elegant ponytail. She was far too sexy for Laurentide Bay, Drew decided. Brooke belonged in Chicago, with a gangster or a venture capitalist for a husband. Someone dangerous who wouldn't always come home for dinner when he said he would.

"Darling," she said to Mark, kissing his cheek. "Darling," she said to Drew, leaning over the bar to kiss her cheek. "Ooh, I like your sundress. Very cute. Now tell me all about your big, bad, scary day." Brooke claimed the stool to Drew's left and mouthed *Thank you* to Mark when he poured her a glass of Malbec.

Drew told Brooke, who nodded thoughtfully. "That is scary."

Drew took the last sip of her martini, only slightly alarmed at how quickly it had found its way into her bloodstream. "One more?" Mark asked as he shelved the last of the glasses he was washing. *He looks so domesticated,* Drew thought. He belonged in a Volvo commercial. He would never balk at wearing sunscreen, a seat belt, or a condom. She pictured him wearing an apron, and her heart nearly broke.

"Yes, one more please," Brooke answered for her. "Drew, are you sure that *prison* is the best place for you?"

"You make prison sound like it's a bad thing," Drew joked, halfheartedly. She sighed and added, "I'm not sure of anything anymore." It was the truest thing she'd said in weeks, and giving voice to her trepidation shone a light on something in her heart that she'd rather keep in the dark.

Brooke checked her watch and glanced back into the dining room. The last server was anxiously watching the clock, hoping to telegraph to his lingering two-top that the kitchen was closed and he had places to go, people to see. The couple got the message, left a stack of bills on the table, and prepared to leave. Brooke waved as they departed—the woman was pregnant and glowing, her husband smiling benevolently. "Thanks, guys! Have a great night!"

They waved back and walked into the night together holding hands. They were going to listen to something mellow and fresh on the way home—The Middle East or Greg Laswell, maybe. They would laugh about the way their waiter looked like a grown-up Macaulay Culkin and she would feel the baby kick and place his hand on her stomach. They would glance at each other with a happy little thrill. It would be a moment they'd each remember until the day they died, and at that moment, Drew would have given anything to be one of them. Something acid twisted in her stomach for a second, and then it was gone.

Brooke faced her, smiled kindly, and clasped Drew's hands in her own. A soft gesture, the sort of thing that made you fall in love with her just a little bit. "Common Courtesy is playing tonight at LakeFest. Do you want to go? Forget about life for a while, as the song goes?"

Common Courtesy had made the rounds among the summer resort towns in southern Wisconsin for as long as Drew could remember. They wrote their own stuff, but when they played the local bars, they stuck to the crowd-pleasing covers that the drunks would whoop and bonelessly dance to.

The lead singer, a redhead with a voice that could fill a canyon, wore pigtails and leather pants tonight, smacking a tambourine against her thigh as she skipped from one side of the stage to the other. The band was grinding through their version of "You Oughta Know," and the Friday night outdoor crowd, half tourist/half local, was rowdy, drinking until the walls were low enough to clamber over into a land of grittier possibilities. Brooke danced in, clapping along with the audience, hip-shaking her way to the bar. Men turned to watch her, their keen eyes bouncing over to Drew, then back to Brooke. Drew immediately wanted to be drunk. For the next twenty years.

And they set sail in that general direction right away. Drew felt reckless. Like everything was rushing past her, right through her fingers ... but everything was so unrecognizable to her now, she wasn't sure she wanted to hold on to it anyway.

They passed an hour this way: dancing a little, drinking a lot, holding brief, shouted conversations that went nowhere because it was nearly impossible to hear what was being said over the Joan Jett and the Chrissie Hynde and the Pat Benatar. As Drew watched her friend shimmy her hips and sip her drink, lost in her own world, it hit her again. How funny Brooke had been acting on the few occasions they'd gone out together since Drew had returned. Offhand comments, a stray wistful glance here and there, fragile gestures other people might miss entirely. But Drew knew Brooke. At least she thought she did. "Brooke," she shouted between songs, and Brooke leaned in, pulling her hair away from her ear to hear better. "What's going on with you?"

"Mmm?" Her face betrayed no emotional change in the weather.

"Everything okay with you? You seem a little ... I don't know, like you've got something on your mind." Like a miscarriage. Or money problems. Or cancer. Or ...

She looked at Drew, nearly blank. And then she blurted, "I've fallen in love with someone."

"What?" Drew leaned in, and this time she was the one cupping her ear to hear better.

Brooke didn't repeat herself; she simply stared at Drew with wide eyes, her mouth agape. She looked horrified. Betrayed by her own mouth. She seemed terrified of what might come out of it next. *I throw rocks at the elderly,* maybe, or *I laugh when babies get ear infections.*

Drew frowned, still puzzling out what Brooke had said. But gradually the words found their way down her ear canal, into her brain, and the tiny word processors synthesizing information in their little cerebellum cubicles cracked the code and messengered the memo to Drew's heart: *I've fallen in love with someone.* You didn't need an Ivy League degree to decode this riddle. Brooke had fallen in love with someone other than her husband. She was having an affair.

Without hesitating, Drew turned and marched a hundred and eighty degrees in the opposite direction, the sea of people parting before her. She didn't even know where she was going. *Away from Brooke* hummed through her mind like a mantra. *Away from Brooke.*

"Drew, wait," Brooke shouted. "Where are you going?" Drew stopped, her back to Brooke, breathing a little too fiercely. She turned to find Brooke beside her, her face a mixture of worry and fear. "Drew, please."

She thought of Mark, staring wistfully at Brooke across a crowded room. A wash of hot anger let loose inside of her, mixed with pity for Mark, and a definite lack of surprise. "What the hell, Brooke," Drew said. She turned her head again and stared at the band, hostile. "With whom?"

Brooke smiled weakly. "You're always so grammatically correct."

"Who gives a hot shit about grammar! Who are you screwing around with?" Drew felt a powerful urge to shove Brooke, hard.

Brooke winced. "You don't know him. He's ... older."

Drew looked up at the cloudy, starless night sky. Where were the helicopters extending rope ladders when you needed one? "How long?" She started piecing the other man together in her mind. *Also married. Silver hair at the temples. Tan. Plays tennis. Owns lakefront property.*

"Since winter. Does it matter?"

"Why even tell me? I don't want to know this!"

"I wasn't planning on saying anything, but you asked, and it just came out—"

"Right, I asked for it," Drew said bitterly. "You know, Mark is my friend, too."

"I'm sorry," Brooke shouted over the din, suddenly pulling Drew into a hug. "I'm so sorry." Drew stiffened reflexively and imagined herself in a scene from a movie, yelling, "How could you? Mark loves you so much!" Or maybe something like, "Wouldn't it have been simpler to just get some Botox and take up scrapbooking?"

But instead of yelling or quipping or recoiling in disgust, Drew endured Brooke's hug sadly, arms at her sides. "I don't want to hear it." She stepped out of Brooke's arms and shook her head. "I'm not going to tell you what to do. You already know what you should do." *You stupid, miserable woman. Throwing everything good in your life away with both hands.*

Brooke lowered her eyes.

"I'm too tired to deal with this right now. Just don't—" Drew nearly said, *Don't do anything stupid*, but it was a little late. She let her sentence evaporate, feeling bereft of words and heart. She thought of Mark, and the spark of anger ignited again in her stomach: a low, steady blue flame. She wanted to smuggle him off to Tuscany and be his Lowenstein. Feed him grapes and nurse him back to emotional health.

These things always had a way of blowing up in faces. You can't keep a lid on secrets. And Drew suspected that Mark felt he might be in for such a ride. He knew Brooke, knew what she was capable of, knew what she needed in such a small town. Fidelity wasn't really one of those things.

Drew was suddenly startled by a pair of warm, strong hands dropping over her eyes, a cagey "Guess who?" whispered in her ear. She jumped. Side effect of her new job, she supposed.

Drew pried the hands off and spun around, composing herself and manufacturing a smile. "Hi, Joe." She was both thrilled and deflated to see him. Her mind offered this: *You would have had a snappy comeback if those hands belonged to Graham. But Graham would never have been able to sneak up on you like that anyway.*

But her body offered: *It's HIM! Strike up the band! Arrange the flaming baton-twirlers!*

It's only physical, she reminded herself. *Just lust. Some kind of twisted, mutual escape valve.* And those physical things, with no love or respect or loyalty to bind and preserve them, had a short shelf life. They were limited-time offers. Three months, tops.

"What a day, huh?" Joe said. "Bet you were glad to leave."

Still. Those would be quite the three months.

Drew wondered if Brooke's affair was really only physical. She might be on the tail end of it already. And she could return to her life with Mark as if nothing had happened. Drew was made slightly wobbly by the fresh anger this unleashed in her.

"You okay?" Joe asked, steadying her arm. *Anger only harms the vessel in which it is carried,* her mother always said. So Drew tried to diffuse her rage, stamp it down, swallow it whole. She took a breath and focused on his handsome face. *Right eye, left eye. Brown eye, hazel.* She remembered the sound he made as he entered her, and she suddenly wanted to hear it again. *To see if it would be the same,* she told herself. She felt a peculiar mix of shame, desire, relief, and melancholy, but mostly desire—and imagined a heroin addict feeling the same way before filling the syringe, tying off, and shooting up "just one more time."

Ben's shadow passed over a primitive part of her brain, and she shuddered.

Joe was still looking at her with concern. "One too many of these, I guess," she finally said, flashing a sharp grin and toasting him with her empty plastic cup of ice. Brooke watched them apprehensively.

Drew shouted introductions as the band leapt into "So What" by Pink. Brooke and Joe shook hands, and Drew had to fight the urge to slap Brooke's away. All of the anger still pulsing through her like a bitter, black ink would probably give her heartburn. Maybe lower back pain. A physical manifestation of an emotional issue.

"Your cup's empty," Joe observed.

"Yeah." She handed him her cup. "Surprise me."

He returned a wicked smile. "You can pay me back later."

I'm drinking a lot lately, she thought, somewhat remotely. She watched him disappear into the crowd to fetch her drink and decided that under the circumstances, alcohol was one of the better coping mechanisms in her arsenal. Looking around at the crowd now, it seemed a rather popular one, too. She heard Ben's voice in her head: *Honey, be careful. You barely know this guy. What if he slips something in your drink?*

Let him, she would have replied, if Ben were here.

"Is that the guy?" Brooke asked, turning to Drew. "Joe? The one you're seeing, but not really?" She looked hopeful and conciliatory.

"I don't know what I'd call it."

Brooke gave a cautious smile, brows raised in earnest optimism. "This is a good thing, right?"

It was an awkward role reversal for Brooke, manufactured and even wheedling. Drew was surprised to discover that it made her embarrassed on Brooke's behalf. "Probably not."

A group of younger women in skimpy tops and short skirts migrated nearby. One of them looked like a Malibu Barbie doll belonging to a crazy preschooler, with frizzled, wild hair, visible tan lines, and a bright red bra beneath her tight white tank top. She studied Drew with heavy, blue-lidded eyes. "That guy you were just talking to. Are you with him?"

"Yeah, she's with him," Brooke said, prickly and loud. "She's his girlfriend. He's totally in fucking *love* with her." She crossed her arms and glared at the girl, who made a sour face in answer and turned around, facing the stage again.

Drew started to laugh. "Go, you! Champion of fidelity superstar! Woo-hoo!" She laughed and laughed until she got the hiccups and tears streamed from her eyes.

Just then, a guy Drew and Brooke had gone to high school with—Kevin something, and wasn't he a third-shifter at Lakeside?—race-walked past on a mission to the Porta-Potties. He spotted the deeply tanned, frizzled blond girl and announced brightly, "Hey, Bret Michaels, lead singer of Poison!" He pointed a finger at her before disappearing into the crowd. "Ladies and gentlemen, Bret Michaels from Poison!"

Later. Behind the bar. Joe was holding Drew up against the wall, near the dumpsters. Thrusting into her, bruising her. The bricks scraping her back, but she didn't care.

After all, everything in life was a limited-time offer.

Even pain.

19. GRAHAM

I love me some Monty Python. Anytime the dogs of depression start barking again, I think of the song, "Always Look on the Bright Side of Life" from *The Life of Brian*. Because all things considered, trying to date with a catheter and being unable to feel your orgasms isn't the worst thing in the world. I still have full use of my mind and two of my four limbs. I can still see, smell, touch, taste, and hear the world around me. My family is loyal, tolerable, and often surprisingly enjoyable. I have amusing friends. I am dating (Yes! I'm Sort Of Dating!) a woman who enjoys cooking and the company of small children. I am holding a rifle in my hands.

Indeed, I am holding a rifle in my hands—.223-caliber semi-automatic, aiming at the bullseye at the Lakeside rifle range. I lock the target in my sights. I squeeze the trigger. The .223 explodes, the stock slamming against my right shoulder with a rewarding thump. The acrid scent of gunpowder briefly lingers in the air before drifting away on an invisible current. I have made a small black hole in the paper target just centimeters from my mark.

It's incredibly satisfying. I reload the chamber and fire again. *BANG!* My shoulder absorbs the kickback, welcoming the abuse. This time I hit my target dead-on. Bullseye.

I may be a commie-pinko liberal, but damn, do I like to fire a gun. Go ahead, make the obvious metaphoric connections. I don't mind, because you'd be right. *Tell them what they've won, Bob.*

"Nice shootin', Tex," Sergeant Wilson says to me. He's a jaded lifer, a year away from early retirement. A classic gun nut, but as far as gun nuts go, he's my favorite kind—just crazy enough in an entertaining sort of way to tolerate on a near-daily basis. Sergeant Wilson is, as you may have guessed, an avid hunter, the walls of his home plastered with the mounted heads of trophy game. He once told me a story that will probably stick with me forever, about the first time he took his adolescent son hunting. How his son shot a buck four times, and it wouldn't die, and he ended up wrestling with it, trying to snap its neck, covered in blood and hair and openly sobbing because it simply refused to die, which would have also ended the nightmarish screaming coming from its mouth. Wilson chuckled while he told me this, but I left the break room shivering.

I lift my earmuffs and grin. "What?"

"Nice work!"

"Thanks." Qualifying on the institution rifle range is required for all security and upper management. For me and all other non-security staff, however, it's optional. And with .223-caliber bullets in shorter supply for those of us on the public payroll (much is being diverted to our national adventures in drier climates), my time at the range is somewhat limited, though I think I have my chair to thank for security's leniency on that issue.

Later tonight I'll be meeting Kevin at the gym. I try to get there at least twice a week, and I shoot at the range maybe once a month. When I cram both activities into one day, I can hardly stand the excitement. Just thinking about it makes me want to order a rare steak, inject some steroids, and attend a December Packers game shirtless and drunk.

But now I aim at a paper target and take out my frustrations. I re-masculate myself a little by engaging in an activity that gladdens my father's heart and reassures him that all is not lost as far as his oldest son is concerned. It gladdens my own heart too, just for a little while.

Abby has decided to take me dog shopping. Well, not so much "dog shopping" as "dog adopting" at the Bay Area Humane Society. Incessant barking ricochets down the concrete kennel run, and I can feel a headache materializing behind my forehead. The air smells of urine, wet dog, and cheap dry kibble. "Did you grow up with a family dog?" Abby asks hopefully as we make our way to the kennels.

"My parents were cat people," I shout over the din. "We had this big fluffy thing named Fat Ass Charlie. He loved to eat, bite, and puke on throw rugs."

"Hey, I was going to ask you—does Lakeside have a service dog program? You know, where inmates work with shelter dogs to become service dogs for people with disabilities, or vets with PTSD." She's looking at me—no, *studying* me—intently. I feel her gauging my own candidacy for service dog ownership.

"No, but I know what you're talking about. I saw a documentary about it."

She nods vigorously. "Oh, it's a wonderful program. I wonder how we'd go about starting something like that where you work."

"I could talk to the warden, see if it's even possible."

"Oh, would you? That would be so great!"

For some reason, the conversation leaves me feeling vaguely annoyed. Even though the idea of a sweet-eyed, constant canine companion who could pick up dropped pens and flip light switches for me is appealing, *I* want to be the one to arrive at that kind of decision. Or maybe I'm irritated with myself; why hadn't I thought of this earlier?

We stop at the first kennel on the left. "Okay. This one's a lab/beagle mix. Female, about three years old." The dog begins to whine and leap at the cage door, tail wagging violently. "Her name's Ricky."

"Hey, Ricky, don't lose that number," I say, extending my right fingers toward her muzzle. She's wagging her tail so enthusiastically that her entire body flaps back and forth. "Aw, you're pretty friendly, huh!" A puddle forms between Ricky's back legs. "Uh-oh, and a submissive pisser, too."

"Yeah," Abby says in that soothing monotone of hers. "Ricky's a bit excitable."

Next up is Sprout, a male Chihuahua/terrier mix. "Sprout's about four years old, neutered, heartworm negative, and knows many of the obedience commands already," Abby announces while Sprout races back and forth across the kennel floor, then spins in circles, then back and forth again. "Unfortunately, he's also got a little bit of food aggression, but we're working on that."

She waves at the dog the way you might wave at a small pre-verbal child. "Isn't that right, little guy?" she adds in a baby voice. "You don't like to share so much?" Sprout responds with a pinched yap, which takes the training wheels right off my headache.

We investigate all of the dogs in this manner. I'm investigating Abby a little further, as well. I'm trying to find the cracks, is what I'm really doing. And therapists across the nation would back me up on this: Our best matches are those who are not going to rescue us, not going to be rescued by us, but those who more closely mirror our own wounds, bruise for bruise, scar for emotional scar. We need to begin on the same starting line, or at least similar starting lines, and let's face it: My starting line isn't even on the same track as Abby's. I could try to be happy with her; she'd certainly try to make any partner happy, because this is what she does. She's a people pleaser. A cookie baker, a sender of flowers, a reliable volunteer when volunteers are called for. And in the beginning, it would be nice. But I'd have to play a lot of catch-up to reach her level of thoughtfulness and reliability. Am I up for a relationship with the Fred Rogers of girlfriends when I feel like the Moe Szyslak of boyfriends? Could I come through the other end of the tunnel to find some measure of contentment in daily life, or would I end up resenting Abby for having that kind of contentment all along?

"And here we have Avis," she says, crouching next to a small and scruffy terrier mix. The dog is sitting right behind the cage door, gazing at us with brown, soulful eyes, her tail flipping back and forth with barely controlled excitement.

"Why is she named after a car rental company?"

"Well, someone here wanted to call her D'nisha Avonda Ba Nai-nai Jackson, but she responds to Avis. She's a four-year-old terrier mix. Already spayed, just a bit of a skin allergy. She's on a special diet to help with that, but it's not expensive." Abby giggles as Avis begins to play-bow and dance, eager to be freed. "I think she likes you." Without turning to face me, she adds softly, "Almost as much as I like you." Her earlobes have blushed a deep pink.

I nearly stop breathing. Forget everything I was just thinking. *She likes me.* I bask in that warm, comforting fact for a few seconds. "I like her, too," I finally answer, smiling. My meaning is clear—at least I hope it is, and she looks at me with both eyes and her own gentle smile. She seems to understand perfectly.

"She's all yours. If you want her."

20. DREW

The prison began shipments of inmates out of state the third week in August. Thirty left on the first bus to Oklahoma. Three of the guys sobbed wildly the night before the bus arrived. One had to be dragged, kicking and shouting and crying, onto the bus. Another inmate got out of the trip by slitting his wrists with a dull knife somebody smuggled from the kitchen unit, and he now festered in solitary confinement under a suicide watch. They said he'd be shipped to the Winnebago Mental Health Institute in a week or two.

The inmates were growing more restless. One day in third hour, Victor Hansen exploded, refusing to work on any GED practice tests. Drew threatened to write him up for disobeying orders, but he didn't seem to care. He mouthed off. "What makes you think you can help me? You think you better than me or something?"

She considered tossing him out of class, but instead she said, "Nobody thinks they're better than anybody. I can help you because I actually give a—I actually care what happens to you. And you're not going to find too many people who feel like that in this world, Mr. Hansen."

He spent the rest of the hour sulking and pretending to read a book.

In sixth hour, Riley Stevenson threw a tantrum, refusing to work on a GED practice test and ratcheting up the tension in the classroom for the rest of the hour. After the outburst he flapped angrily through a book, ripping some of the pages where they met the spine. Riley Stevenson made Drew impossibly nervous. He told her one day in a smooth voice that he knew people who could get her noticed, if she caught his drift.

"You should be paying more attention to your own welfare," she replied, trying not to laugh. Get her noticed! What, did he want to be her pimp? Every time he beckoned her over for help with a math problem, she felt helpless and sadly angry, knowing it was only an excuse to ogle her body. She never walked directly away from him. She wasn't giving him any material for the stream of pornography running through his head.

Inmates like Riley Stevenson keep Drew in baggy blouses and loose-fitting slacks every day. Unfortunately, her wardrobe choices did little to deter the oglers. Every time she stood hallway duty between classes, inmates stared. Sometimes she stared back, mouthing a challenging, *What!?* to a particularly obnoxious one. Most times, however, she ignored the looks, helplessly feeling their eyes crawling over her body. Saying anything to deter them would only exacerbate the problem. Like when someone says, *Don't think of Donald Trump in a track suit.*

Now try to think of anything else.

The ringing bell after sixth hour drained everyone from her classroom. Riley Stevenson sauntered out, flashing her a final baleful look. She turned to Leroy before he left. "You did great on the reading practice test. I think you're ready to take the actual test."

He beamed.

"I'll write you out a slip with your practice test score, and you just take it to the guidance counselor, Mr. Bishop. He'll sign you up for the next test."

"All right." His smile lit up his entire face. Drew pulled a slip of paper from her top drawer and scrawled his name and the score he'd earned on his practice test. She looked up at him when she came to the next blank.

"What's your number?"

"354978."

"Which unit?"

"Seven."

Joe's unit for the past few weeks. She hadn't seen or heard from him since LakeFest. She cocked her head and waited for the bruise from this realization to sink its teeth into her heart … but it didn't. She wondered again if she should send a search party for the Normal Feelings. The ones most girls might be having right now.

She was glad to have a prep period during seventh hour. No more sentence structures to diagram or false smiles to wear. She walked back to one of the computers, abandoned by a student mid-game. The screen posed the question, *Do you want to continue? Press Y or N.* She sat before the monitor, considering the question. Did she want to continue? Depends on what she'd be continuing. If it was the gear her life seemed to be stuck in, she'd have to say N. She played with the mouse, watching the arrow dance around the screen. She clicked N.

After work, she strolled past the picnic tables full of inmates talking with their families and friends. A group of children shouted at one another in the playground area, riding the metal dinosaurs and rabbits on steel springs. One girl who couldn't be more than five sat alone in the sandbox, tracing lethargic patterns in the sand. She was wearing overalls with a picture of Minnie Mouse on the bib. Drew wondered which inmate was her father. Given the option, she might click N, too.

Brooke said she had someone she wanted Drew to meet.

"It's not a guy, is it?" Drew asked, suspicious. She had no interest in being set up with one of Mark's single friends, nor was she eager to meet The Other Man. The Country Club Homewrecker.

"Nope," she said. Her voice had a golden glow Drew hadn't heard in a while.

The following Saturday, they met at a coffee shop near Laurentide Bay's picturesque harbor, long since gentrified from grubby docks to charming shops and cafés. The gray, weather-beaten clapboard siding still wrapped the buildings, but now the weather-beaten part was carefully sculpted and factory-made, like new jeans with that already-lived-in look. The air usually smelled pretty fishy near the harbor, which made it difficult for the cafés to entice people to eat outdoors. But today the air just smelled fresh and green, with a hint of iodine. Like a clean seaweed wrap—one you might get at an upscale spa.

Brooke was sitting at a table outside the coffee shop under a red umbrella. There was a girl with her, maybe eleven or twelve years old, her hair in a messy brown ponytail. They were both wearing sunglasses and studying menus. When Brooke saw Drew, she gave a cheerful wave and stood up. They hugged in greeting, Brooke's young companion watching from her chair. "Drew, this is Chloe. She's my Little Sister."

Little sister. *Little sister.* Brooke didn't have a little sister— not by birth, anyway. After a few beats, Drew made the connection. *She's mentoring this young girl?* "Nice to meet you, Chloe," she said, extending a hand. Chloe shook it, but didn't say anything in return.

Drew pulled up a chair. Brooke was still smiling, her wedding band glinting in the sunlight. "We were thinking of having some peach iced tea and cookies. They make the best cookies here. Soft and warm and gooey in the middle."

Drew wondered if Brooke brought Chloe to serve as a buffer between them and a conversation about The Affair. "I didn't know you were a Big Sister," Drew said lightly. "How long have you known each other?"

"Since winter," Brooke said, beaming at Chloe. Chloe just kicked her feet back and forth and stared at her menu.

As long as Brooke's been having the affair, Drew realized. At that point a waitress approached to take their order. They requested the peach iced tea and cookies. Chocolate chip.

"So Chloe, what grade are you in?"

"Second." So she was off a few years in her age estimate. She'd always been terrible at interacting with kids. Some people had a knack for it. Her friend Erin, for example. How else could she get through day after day surrounded by high-octane miniature adults keen on bathroom humor? She was a pro. But Drew? Despite once being in second grade, she had no idea how to interact with a small human in that demographic now. She felt acutely aware of her adult status. What were second-graders into? An idea came to mind: *why not just ask?*

Drew turned to Chloe and asked, "What are the second-graders into these days?" *I sound sixty-eight. I sound like a sixty-eight-year-old just released from decades of institutional living on another planet.*

"I dunno," Chloe said, smiling for the first time.

Inspiration struck. "Cheese? Do you guys like limburger cheese?"

She scowled, giggling. "No-oh!"

"I know! I bet you're into small engine repair." Hey, this was fun!

"No!"

Brooke smiled tightly, watching their exchange. "Chloe likes to draw."

"Oh, I get it! You like to *draw* small engines."

Chloe shook her head and gave an exasperated snort, smiling in that goofy tween way. The last time Drew had spent any significant time with another person Chloe's age had been nearly two years ago, with Ben's nine-year-old nephew, Tyler. They'd played Guitar Hero, and Tyler had specifically requested "War Pigs" by Black Sabbath, the choice and performance of which had her cracking up for days after. Maybe she wasn't giving tweens enough credit.

Their server returned with tea and cookies. Drew cleared her throat and got serious, taking a sip of tea. "Okay, what do you like to draw?"

Chloe shrugged, blushing and kicking her feet again. Seagulls flapped and squealed above, waiting for crumbs to fall.

"It's okay," Brooke said to Chloe. Her voice was high and encouraging. "You like to draw horses, right? And landscapes? Like the beach?" Brooke directed her next statement to Drew. "She's a very talented artist."

It almost felt like Brooke was trying to prove her own decency. Yes, I'm having an affair, but *Look!* I'm mentoring a troubled child! Interpreting on her behalf, no less. You could feel the battle raging beneath her skin between Being Good and Being Brooke.

Chloe leaned in and whispered something to Brooke, who glanced at Drew and smiled.

"Hey, no secrets!" Drew playfully admonished. At this, Brooke whispered exaggeratedly in Chloe's ear. They teased Drew by stage whispering nothing back and forth, giggling.

They shared a pleasant hour together; tea and cookies followed by a little browsing in the shops, acting silly and smelling scented candles. At one point Brooke leaned in to tell Drew what Chloe had whispered in her ear: *"I like her."* It made Drew smile. What a better, less complicated world it would be if we could be all so forthcoming about our feelings!

The only time they flirted with meaningful conversation was when Drew lightly asked, "How's Mark?" And Brooke tossed back an equally breezy, "Great!" After which the wind changed direction, blowing all evidence of Brooke's marital problems out over the expansive, twinkling blue lake.

It was a subtle but agreeable day, with lots of brilliant sunshine, no schedules to follow. Even the temperature was a cooperative and polite seventy-four degrees. There simply weren't enough of these kinds of days. Drew watched Brooke and Chloe try on funny hats at one of the shops and became suddenly and truly aware that she was having a nice time. Brooke wasn't the Big Bad Wolf, not really. She was actually a bit like Gretel, more lost in the woods than she'd ever admit. They'd never have much in common, but that was okay. Drew could still try to be her friend. And friendship, in whatever form it took, could be a soothing balm for wounds to the heart.

Howard Bell had finished three children's books and was reading a new one. *Green Eggs and Ham.* He twirled a pencil. "So I only got a week left, and they releasing me to minimum at Racine."

"That's great, Mr. Bell! Are you excited?"

He nodded, smiling. "The first thing I'm gonna do is get me some of them chili cheese fries. And a big-ass blue Icee."

"Yuck," Drew said, wrinkling her nose and grinning. She considered telling him blue food coloring was banned in Finland, Norway, and France, but what would be the point? Concern for such things was relative. There was a sliding scale. A hierarchy of needs. Just ask Maslow. He'd tell you that all of the guys here were trapped at the bottom of the pyramid.

"I wish I could take these here books along, so I can read them to my kids." He pulled a handful of wallet-size photos out of his back pocket, and Drew sat very still. Howard Bell never talked about his children. Other than her first college roommate, Drew had never known someone so private. "This here's Timothy, this here's Shantell—" He shuffled them, almost dropping them. "And Reggie, and Marcus. I don't have a picture of Kimmy yet."

"They're beautiful." Drew felt an indistinct sadness, wondering what fate had in store for these children. *Life was hard enough without* … "You know, they have a library in the Racine facility, and once you're released, you could always check out the books at the public library." She wanted to press this. If he didn't keep reading, he might forget everything they'd worked so hard for.

"Yeah, I know."

"Why don't you take these two books with you. I formally approve it."

"For reals?"

"For real." She hesitated before asking the next question. "Do you talk to your children often?"

He brightened. "At least once a week on the phone. Reggie and Shantell coming to visit this weekend. Taking the bus up with they moms."

"That's great," she said, and they continued to read.

After class she felt a mix of pride and despair. It wasn't what she expected, really, working in a prison. But helping people more broken than she was right now might be exactly what she needed. It might also be the only thing she was capable of until she hauled herself back onto dry ground.

Time ticked on. Riley Stevenson continued to ask too-personal questions, and she continued to evade them. He'd recently started carrying on about how his case was going back to court, and he would be released by Christmas because he was innocent. When some of the other inmates heard, they started laughing. "We *all* innocent," said one.

Sometimes when she heard inmates griping about the system, she agreed. They couldn't buy their freedom in the courtroom, so here they were. Unwanted, uneducated, unskilled. One day in class a new student started crying because his father had never built him a tree house. She thought the issue was larger than that, really—it was the realization that there were actually fathers out there who did such things with their sons. But then she read about their offenses. How could she feel sorry for someone who raped a fourth-grader or shot a fifteen-year-old kid in the face over a vial of crack? Thinking about it too much gave her a headache. She wanted to save all of them and none of them.

So she helped the ones she could. Leroy Johnson, for example. He'd passed his reading test and was taking practice social studies tests and feeling pretty damn good about it. They had to go over his incorrect answers again and again, but he was making progress. Completion of his high school equivalency diploma didn't mean a law degree or an energy-efficient home with tastefully colored siding, but it was a step in a positive direction. Drew would be thrilled to see him setting employee attendance records at the Piggly Wiggly and renting an apartment with covered parking.

Drew was standing outside her classroom door at the end of the day, bags on her shoulder, keys jingling as she locked the door behind her. Janet Sutton exited her classroom at the exact same moment, locking her own door. "Hey, I'll walk with you," she said. "Christ almighty, what a day. Four years till retirement and counting."

"Really? You don't look nearly old enough to retire."

"Ha! Honey, you need to get your eyes examined."

"Oh, stop," Drew said, grinning a little. "You can't be a day over forty."

She patted Drew's back. "Aren't you a sweetheart. Blind as a bat, but sweet."

They saw another teacher, Greg Lansing, locking his door and heading down the hallway to the office. As they walked behind him, Drew watched the sole of his right shoe slide off. He kept walking, unaware of his crumbling footwear. "Hey Greg," Janet shouted, "part of your shoe fell off."

He backtracked to pick up his sole, exasperated. "I just glued this on at lunchtime."

"Oh, that's so sad," Drew said, laughing. "Time for some new shoes, maybe?"

Janet adjusted her shoulder bags and said, "Between your need for an eye doctor, my need for new knees, and Greg's need for a shoe cobbler, I think we're all kind of a mess."

"Janet, did you actually use the word 'cobbler?'"

"That's what they are, right? Shoe cobblers. They cobble shoes."

"Janet," Drew said again. "Are you secretly an elf? Are you a time traveler from ye olde Denmark?" She laughed as they rounded the corner at the end of the hallway. Drew turned to her, about to make a joke about Hans Christian Andersen, when she ran into a tall inmate in standard-issue greens. "Oh! Excuse me," she said, taking a step back, and then she looked up. Her smile evaporated. Her next words died in her throat. Her skin went numb. The inmate looked at her. She looked at him. They locked eyes. They stood there, frozen. When Drew could breathe again, she broke the silence in a voice that sounded foreign and wrecked, with a single word that slipped out before she could stop it.

"Ben?"

21. GRAHAM

"I just can't decide," Kevin says, his arms folded across his chest while he watches Avis bound around my back yard with a knotted rope toy in her mouth. Every few feet she stops to savagely shake it back and forth. "Is it a speed bump or a dust mop?"

"It is actually a highly complex food compacting system. A vast array of edible and non-edible items go in the front end, and through some intricate and mysterious feat of science, these materials are miraculously transformed into an amazing number of foul-smelling brown logs that exit the back end."

"I don't know. Looks like a dust mop to me." He does The Giggle, but at least his next statement is something a normal person might ask. "So Abby picked this mutt out for you?"

I nod.

"What, are you getting serious with this girl? You bang her yet, or no?"

"Leave it to you to wax poetic on the romantic side of life."

More of the Kevin Lipton laugh. Avis gallops toward us with the rope clamped in her mouth and hurls it at Kevin's kneecaps. He picks it up and tosses it for her, and she tears off after it. "So, did you?"

I sigh. "No. She's a nice girl, Kevin. You've heard of nice girls, haven't you?"

"I've heard rumors of their existence, yes."

"I'm sure Mandy would appreciate hearing your opinions on this subject."

"She's too busy planning her wedding."

I raise an eyebrow. "What wedding? I haven't missed something here, have I?"

"No, it's the same wedding she's been planning since birth."

Avis romps back without her toy, panting, and lies down next to me. "You mean the one where she marries an actual human being who cares about her?"

"Yeah, that's the one! Poor kid, mixed up with a guy like me."

I just smile and shake my head. Kevin was actually quite the romantic in high school, but having his heart crushed under the heeled boot of girl after girl—plus witnessing the marriages of several of his friends implode *plus* being a little too attractive to the opposite sex for his own good—has turned him into a jaded and sometimes opportunistic bastard.

"All right, for real now. Do you like this girl?"

I shrug. "Yes and no. And the simple fact that I have to give you that kind of an answer indicates that this probably doesn't have a future, right? Or is everyone this ambivalent when they meet a nice girl who wants to settle down?"

"Whoa, whoa, whoa." Kevin flashes a palm: the universal gesture for *Slow down, you're not making any sense and about to make a very piss-poor decision.* "She actually told you that after a few dates? She wants to settle down with you?"

I frown dismissively. "No, not exactly. It's more in the way she looks at me." The way I look at Drew, I suddenly realize. "Why does this have to be so damn complicated? I mean, you know, right? You know when you've found the one, right?"

"I only have one qualifying question. Do you spit or swallow? Answer that correctly, and you get me for life."

I shake my head. "You are one disturbed individual."

"The best ones always are."

After Kevin leaves, I'm restless. It's a gorgeous Saturday afternoon, and I have nothing to fill it that doesn't involve a screen of some sort, so I decide to take Avis to Laurentide Bay's only dog park. She perches on the passenger seat of my truck, watching the world fly past, panting in a way that looks like a smile. Halfway there I take a detour past Drew's parents' house. I've been feeling guilty for distancing myself from her, and especially for being such a jerk to her about the whole Joe business. Drew and I are not going to happen, we're not going to hold hands at the movies or kiss goodnight or buy one another sentimental birthday cards, so I just need to grow up and move on.

Somewhere in the back of my mind I entertain the idea of stopping in to say hello, of apologizing for being so moody lately, but I know I'll probably just drive by. Maybe I'll see her dad mowing the lawn. So I'm surprised that before I even reach her house I see her running on the side of the road, her ponytail bouncing left and right with each step. My heart burbles a little at the sight of her long, firm legs, and I will it to behave.

As I slowly pull up next to her, I'm surprised to see she's crying; her cheeks are wet with tears, her face drawn in an expression of pain, ear buds connecting her to an iPod but disconnecting her from the outside world. I power the passenger-side window down and tap the horn lightly. She turns her head and sees me, eyes widening in surprise. She lets out a small shriek and stumbles on the asphalt.

"Oh, hey, sorry!" I shout. "I didn't mean to scare you. I just saw you here on the side of the road, thought I'd say hi." When she doesn't say anything for a few seconds I add, "Are you okay?"

She pulls her ear buds out and tries to hastily compose herself, sniffing and wiping her cheeks and eyes with the palms of her hands. "Yeah, I ... I was just jogging, listening to some Joni Mitchell." Her voice is nasal and heartbreaking. She's blushing, not making eye contact.

"Well, I can see how that would make anyone cry."

A grateful, surprised laugh escapes her lips in one brief note. Avis is whining, leaning out the window toward Drew, tail flapping frantically back and forth, ears splayed back submissively. "She's cute. Is she yours?" Drew reaches over to scratch beneath Avis's muzzle; Avis licks her fingers eagerly, prancing at the open window.

"Yeah. I just got her."

"Aww," Drew says. There's nothing like a friendly dog to put a smile on the face of the brokenhearted. "She's really sweet." She leans in and lets Avis lick her cheek.

"Hey, you want to go to the dog park with us?"

She looks down the winding road, and I can see her mind working at how to answer this invitation.

"Just a thought. I mean, if you have nothing better to do today. Her name's Avis, by the way. "

"Like the car rental place?"

I sigh. "Yeah."

Thirty minutes later we're sitting at a picnic table in the dog park. We've both thrown Avis's tennis ball a dozen times until she finally tired of the game, wandering off to sniff shrubbery and urinate everywhere another dog already has. This has been another of the surprises of dog ownership: that female dogs mark territory, too. I could extrapolate on that fact and connect it to a larger universal truth about gender no matter the species, but who has that kind of time. Also, I'm out of pot.

"Thank you, Graham. For asking me to come with you."

"I thought it might make you feel better."

She smiles a watery but grateful smile. "I do feel better."

I catch her eye. "Can you tell me what's wrong?"

After a moment's hesitation, she blurts, "Brooke's having an affair."

"Oh." I sit back and nod thoughtfully. "That is kind of depressing. Not surprising, but certainly depressing."

She laughs a ridiculous, exhausted laugh. In addition to my recent discovery (or rediscovery, more likely) of female territoriality, I'm also beginning to discover (or rediscover, once again) the many variations and pitches tucked into a woman's laugh. So many more nuances than a man's laugh. "No, I don't know why I just told you that. That's not why I was crying." She twists her sporty digital watch or heart rate monitor, whatever it is, around her wrist, and for the longest moment I'm not sure she's going to follow up with an explanation. But then she breaks the silence with, "My ex was transferred to Lakeside this week."

"Oh." *Holy shit!*

"I know you've probably heard everything about what happened already. Everyone has."

I shake my head. "No, umm..." I feel my own face growing warm, because I *had* heard most of the sordid details. Drew and her ex were both teachers, and he had been caught in a far too intimate position with a fifteen-year-old student. I also know he's been sentenced to six years for this ill-advised indiscretion. What a flipping idiot. On so many levels, really.

"It's okay. It's fine if you have. I mean, he's not … he's not a real criminal, I guess. It was … I mean, it's not like he's a pedophile." Her eyes go wide, as if she can't believe what she's saying. "Well, yes, yes he is, actually!" She releases a wild and unhappy laugh. "He'll be a registered sex offender when he gets out. He won't be able to live near schools or playgrounds. He'll never teach again. He'll … people will …" Her voice hitches, and her eyes have filled with tears again.

Hesitantly, I reach over to touch her arm. "Drew, I'm so sorry. I don't know what to say. I'm sorry you had to go through that." I know from personal experience that people always say insincere shit when tragedy strikes, like, *Oh, I can't even imagine what you must be feeling*, or the inane and meaningless favorite, *Everything happens for a reason!* or the one that makes me want to light my own face on fire, *It's all part of God's larger plan for you!* But here? I don't even want to try to imagine. This didn't happen for a reason. And it was certainly no part of God's master plan. To watch your boyfriend sentenced to prison for basically molesting a kid? Man. Who comes through the other end of that experience without some serious internal damage?

The title of a song by 311 floats through my mind. "Beautiful Disaster." Like Phuket after the Christmas tsunami. She's still paradise to me, but there'll be a lot of cleanup needed to recover from this not-so-natural disaster. Kevin is fond of saying that the beautiful ones are always the most messed up. It's like there's a penalty to pay for such a birthright—perhaps to make up for the inherent advantages of being born with a pretty face. Like life is nothing but a giant bully trying to throw black paint on the most pristine of landscapes. To smash the best, most clever papier-mâché art project in class and then later on the bus, to throw the crumpled remains out an open window. Not that the latter ever happened to me, but you get my point.

She suddenly finds her voice and pulls her hands back, about to gesture violently with them. "It was horrible. I mean, I have friends who have been two-timed, and look at Brooke, cheating on her husband—the nicest man you'll ever meet. God, are there any relationships that haven't been affected by infidelity? Is *anyone* faithful anymore?"

I think for a minute. "My parents, I'm pretty sure. But donut pillows, constant nagging, and compression socks aren't the biggest turn-ons, so I think that might have something to do with it." My parents are "older" parents, having married in their late thirties. My mom was the only gray-haired mother at my younger sister's kindergarten parent-teacher conferences, and my dad could have written the book on hands-off, couchbound parenting. At this point in their lives, they're just happy when the Packers win or the Buick starts on the first turn on a subzero January morning. Nothing like three wild children born within five years to pummel you into a weary, fine-tuned appreciation for the simple pleasures in life.

She smiles gratefully, but just for a second. "I think I always knew, on some level. The signs were all there. He bought all these new clothes, started whitening his teeth. He lost weight. And he seemed much more enthusiastic about coaching cross country—something he *hated* doing. At least, he hated it before …" Her voice drifts off, but then it's back again, with authority. "We both went above and beyond for our kids, coming in early or staying late to tutor once in a while, writing letters of recommendation, chaperoning at dances. I just never … there were rumors near the end, but there are always those kinds of rumors in high school. You laugh it off—just some dopey teasing, a kid with a crush. And you're so busy living life, so busy trusting and doing your own thing, so self-absorbed you miss every clue. And the girl. That poor girl. And you know? He was a good teacher, too! Until ..." She shakes her head and softly adds, "What a waste."

She grows silent, rubbing her forehead. Suddenly she looks at the sky and yells, "I'm so stupid!" She balls her hands into fists and pounds her thighs.

I don't answer right away, out of respect for her anger and grief. There are no more tears; instead she takes a deep breath, blows it out slowly. Finally I say, "Drew, you're not stupid. You just wanted to believe him. To believe you would only be with someone capable of good things," I offer. We watch Avis and a black lab sniff one another.

She plucks a long blade of grass and begins twisting it into various shapes. "I guess we all believe what we want to believe."

"Don't take this the wrong way, but ... did you think this might happen when you got a job at Lakeside? I mean, that he might be transferred there?" I almost didn't ask, because I wasn't sure I wanted to know the answer.

"I don't know. I guess it might have crossed my mind, but it ... I don't know. I mostly just wanted to run back home, go back in time to a place where I didn't have anything real to worry about. I wanted to feel safe and whole and not so ... *lost* all the time. To be with people who loved me." She smiles feebly and adds, "I wanted to escape, and what better place to do that than prison?"

"I know *all* about that," I say ruefully.

She suddenly looks at me, blushes, and shakes her head. "God, I'm sorry, Graham. My problems are ... they're so minor. I didn't mean—"

"Hey, no worries." I still have too many questions for Drew, and I try to think of a decent enough segue to lead to the next one. As I ponder this, a crow hops out of the sky and begins picking at a piece of road kill beyond the dog park fence. "I hate crows," I say, scowling.

Drew sighs and says, somewhat wistfully, "Oh, not me. The American Crow … they get a bad rap. Crows were hit really hard by the West Nile Virus a few years back."

"Yeah, I read something about that."

"Did you know that when a crow loses his mate or offspring, he returns home to find comfort from his parents?" Her eyes are dreamy, focused on that godawful ugly bird.

I frown. "Really?"

"Yeah," she says, turning to me, eyebrows earnestly raised. "They really do." We both watch the crow pick at the smashed squirrel a bit longer. If the crow is metaphor for Drew (and you'd have to be sniffing glue to miss that one), then the mangled squirrel it picks at must be my heart. *I hate you, Drew,* I suddenly think. It bubbles up from the margins of my subconscious, no warning, no hint at all. The fury and speed with which it flies through my body startles me. Then, this: *There is a fine line between love and hate.* Then, depressed resignation. Acceptance, even.

Finally, I break the silence as gently as I can with the first of many questions I still want to ask. "Have you told anyone he's here? Does your mom know?"

Drew nods. "She knows."

"Did you tell security yet?" I pause before adding, "He'll probably be transferred again." The rule is simple. If you, a prison employee, learn that an inmate with whom you've had a prior relationship has been transferred to Lakeside, you must report this knowledge to security immediately. In nearly all cases, that inmate is shortly transferred elsewhere to avoid any possible security hazards. It actually happens more often than you think. Your sister's abusive, alcoholic ex-husband, the firebug kid you went to high school with, your neighbor's sticky-fingered grandson ... though you may have exchanged ten words with any of them in your life, these inmates know you—they know personal details about you—and that could pose a problem should a riot or hostage situation ensue. Especially if you're the hostage.

She looks at her hands. "I read his file. And I know the criteria for being transferred to Oklahoma or Texas or Tennessee." She sighs and says softly, "He meets all of the benchmarks. Non-violent, no special health needs, already finished his ... his sex offender treatment in Oshkosh." A woman pulls up, two huskies panting out the open back window. They see the crow and start barking, spooking it into flight.

We watch it flap languidly away, as if it's swimming through the air. After a moment Drew quietly adds, "A transfer to one of those private prisons would kill him." It sounds as if it physically hurt her to actually say those words.

She could be right. The inmates in general pop have never been fond of pedophiles (diaper snipers) or rapists (tree jumpers), so they're common targets of inmate violence. Not to mention that the private prisons to which he'd be transferred are crowded and violent hellholes staffed by undertrained, underpaid, underequipped people. I heard the starting wage for officers in Tennessee was something like nine bucks an hour. That's around eighteen grand a year to risk your life and take abuse on a daily basis. What's the incentive to do a good job? I bet the turnover rate is astounding. I bet attacks on staff are three times the rate here. So, no thanks—I'll take my officers well-paid, well-trained, and unionized, if you please.

I watch Avis run up to a fluffy collie, play-bow, and take off. The collie gives chase. I've never met Drew's ex, and I hate him. I hate him for molesting a kid, I hate him for hurting my friend, and I hate him for shoring up the belief commonly held by too many wounded women that all men think with the wrong head. Which leaves those women hostile, suspicious, and stingy with affection. Which makes their men frustrated, cynical, and slightly sex-crazed, sneaking off to spank it in the family room at two in the morning to some kind of freaky German porn. So the wheel goes round and round, its own little sad, unbalanced, unending gyroscope. And who wins in all of this? The diamond industry, that's who. Florists. Watercolor greeting card peddlers.

At this point, a panting but happy Avis returns to us and pointedly pokes her nose into Drew's right calf. "Well, hello there! Are you feeling neglected?" Drew rubs Avis's ears, sending her into a state of dog bliss. Her tail thumps on the ground and Drew looks up at me. "I'm sorry, Graham. Blah! Enough of that. Tell me something happy. Something nice. Are you still seeing Abby?"

"Yeah, I guess so." I unwrap a stick of gum and pop it in my mouth. I offer a piece to Drew, but she declines. "I always feel funny with the labels, you know? 'Dating,' or 'seeing,' or whatever. Remember when we were kids and you asked someone to 'go out' with you, and then all you'd do is talk on the phone or pass notes in the hall? Where were we going? We never went anywhere! And everyone would ask, 'So how long have you and Sally been going out?' And you celebrate your anniversaries by the week, so you'd say, 'Oh, we've been going out for three weeks.' And as a three-week anniversary present, you'd exchange those ugly fake gold broken heart necklaces. The whole thing was asinine."

Drew smiles. "Ah, simpler times."

"Hey," I say gently, capitalizing on the lighter turn the conversation has taken, "I want to apologize for being such a jerk with the whole Joe thing. It's none of my business who you spend your time with."

She frowns, as if I've said something confusing. "Nothing was … there's nothing going on with us. It's not like we were 'going out.'" She pauses before smiling in a small, dispirited way. "Are you actually sorry?"

"Yes, I'm actually sorry."

"What?"

"I'm sorry."

"Say it again." Her smile is wider now, but there's an edge to it.

"I'm sorry," I repeat carefully. "It was rude of me, it was none of my business, I was being a jerk." *Get in and get out. Like a surgical strike.*

"I almost believe you."

I open my mouth, pausing before I speak, because what comes out next—what I really want to say—could change everything. *I'm terrified to reveal how badly I want you, how much you make my heart pound when I so much as catch a goddam glimpse of you. How I'm both disturbed and thrilled by the hope you've reawakened in me—hope for things I'd nearly given up on. I'm scared you'll reject me, I'm scared I'll lose even your friendship, so I pretend I'm fine with being just your friend. It makes me sick to see you pick the other guy, the absolutely wrong guy, but I get it. Because if I were you? I probably would have done the same thing.*

In the end, I simply look at my hands and say, "I was jealous." I hold my breath, waiting to see how she interprets this.

"You were jealous?" she asks softly.

"Look at me, Drew." I motion to my chair, which is a cop-out. I can imply I'm envious of *anyone* able to walk down the beach hand-in-hand with the person they love, anyone who can have even routine, vanilla sex before falling asleep, and I'm still making peace with how much this has changed for me. But

Drew's smart, so of course she knows what I'm really jealous about. Now she knows my heart.

"I am looking at you," she says, her voice a blend of defiance, sympathy, and ... discovery? My cheeks begin to burn under her gaze, an awful naked feeling crawling into my chest and lodging there, like a stuck vitamin. She takes mercy on my growing discomfort and breaks the spell with, "It's getting late. And Avis looks pretty tuckered out." She reaches down again to pet my dog, who sticks out her tongue to smile and pant, completely unfazed by the human drama unfolding around her.

"Wouldn't it be great to be a dog?" I ask.

Drew gives me a sardonic grin. "Depends on your owner."

We follow this down the conversational path a bit longer and change subjects again on the ride home, to family camping trips from our youth: S'mores, pudgy pies, deflating air mattresses, and more six-year-olds shitting in the woods than all the bears in Yellowstone. Later, I'll reflect on how effortless that shift felt. I'll think about how easy it is to talk to Drew. I'll start comparing her to Abby again. The delicate, nearly fragile curves of her features. Her laugh. The way she sneezes like a cartoon character with a high-pitched, *Ah-chirp!* The way she raises one amused, skeptical eyebrow when she doesn't quite believe something I'm saying.

The way we both pretended we weren't stealing glances at one another on the drive home.

I'll convince myself that I'm the one who can make her trust men again, that I'm the only one who can make her smile every day for the rest of her life. I'll convince myself that I could be happily married again. That divorce is only something you see on TV. I might even convince myself I'll walk again. Why not?

And suddenly, your surgical strike nicks an artery and things end up a whole lot messier than you intended.

22. DREW

You are a teacher. You live with a man you love, a man who loves you in return. He gives excellent back rubs, and you wonder if that's how it all started. He is also a teacher, in the same school as you. In fact, his classroom is just down the hall. All of the students adore you both, of course.

Unfortunately, one of them—she's blond, overdeveloped for her age, her locker is pasted with poetry and cross country photos—adores the man you love a bit too much.

Doubly unfortunate, the man you love ends up adoring her a bit too much as well.

When your love of eight years cheats on you with an adolescent—a girl you were responsible for teaching, for guiding into adulthood really—you break in places you can't even define, of course. That's the obvious. But though you were only one idiot victim in the whole sordid mess, you will also be alienated from your colleagues, your students, from some of your friends, some of your family, and even certain facets of pop culture. They were the unanticipated stumbling blocks in daily life, popping up without warning when you were just trying to order a mocha latte and make your way to work. Lolita? Drew couldn't stomach references to it. "Don't Stand So Close to Me" by The Police was an auto-change on the radio. And there were two simple reasons she'd never seen *Beautiful Girls* in its entirety when it made the rounds on the movie channels: Timothy Hutton and Natalie Portman.

You begin to suspect all young girls in skimpy tops, and all men who seem a little too restless, a little too uncomfortable in their presence. You begin to suspect them of things that may have never even entered their minds, and you're the one who ends up feeling filthy when you lay your head on the pillow after the sun sets.

Why did he do it? There were a thousand answers to that question. Part reclamation of youth, maybe. Some kind of last-ditch effort to stave off aging. Ego. Attention. The thrill of the forbidden, the taboo, the secret. But maybe it was also just sex. Maybe—maybe he even thought it was love. That was the best explanation she could give.

So now Drew was working in the prison that incarcerated him. And simply the knowledge that he was institutionalized with her—that he could be just dozens of yards from her at a given time—kept her body humming with adrenaline. She felt like a riot could break out inside her without notice. When she really considered what it meant—her being there, working in Lakeside—it hit her like a hard rubber slap: Every decision she'd made since Ben's arrest had led her to this very place. She didn't really want to work in another public high school, not really. The cellar of her mind had orchestrated her move here, hoping on some subconscious level for one more confrontation, for closure, for half-baked revenge of some undetermined sort, for final proof that it had actually even happened.

If she needed final proof, there it was in prison greens. There it was with bloodshot eyes, a bruised expression, and those familiar long eyelashes that now looked more like a lunatic fringe. There it was in the hallway, saying to her over and over and over, "Oh God, Drew. Oh God."

After an accident, you sometimes hear reporters referring to the walking wounded. "There were no fatalities, but we've got a number of walking wounded." Drew felt like one of the walking wounded. She kept walking around, waiting for the wounds to heal ... waiting to feel *normal* again, whatever normal was. Emerging relatively whole after several other heartbreaks in college, she knew it was possible to return to that place of balance, after a while. Healing would come with time—as regular and anticipated as a holiday or a birthday. But this time it simply ... didn't. She kept watching the clock, waiting for it, but it never arrived.

And the girl? Her name was Colby. Drew had advised her student council group. Colby was pretty and shy, one of the sweetest girls Drew had ever met. Her family moved to Minneapolis after the trial, and that was the last Drew heard of her.

On the way home from work that day, the day she ran right into Ben in a school hallway quite different from the one in which they used to meet between classes, she was quiet.

Her mother was quiet for a long while as well. "You need to tell Frank Bailey," she finally said.

Drew just nodded.

She would make that happen. She would do whatever she had to do. She would sever her emotions from the parts of her brain that allowed her to function on a daily basis. It would be a clean but vicious divorce. She would arrange no visitation, no alimony, no contact whatsoever. In fact, if she wanted to stay vertical the next few days, it would be a good thing if she took a restraining order out on her emotions altogether.

Suppress. Deny. Forget. Harden.

Or fail.

Here was the thing. She wanted closure.

She wanted to see him punished.

She wanted to see him one last time.

Because part of her still loved him.

Two days later Ben was already transferred out of state. It happened so quickly, with a speed both rude and brutal, like a bandage ripped off before the wound had closed. His assigned location made him unavailable to Drew, but even if she invented an errand or sweet-talked an officer to gain proximity to him, she wasn't sure she wanted one final confrontation. What could she say that hadn't already been said?

She saw him the next afternoon, as he slowly followed the white line to the records office, shoulders slumped. Drew knew it was him immediately, and she'd have known it was him even if she closed her left eye and he faded into little more than a green blur. It was raining, but he made no effort to cover himself from the downpour while other inmates splashed through puddles around him, holding folders over their heads as they jogged to class or work or the health services unit. She was in the school office making copies and listening to Lisa Crane talking about a baby shower she'd been planning. At just the right moment Drew glanced out the bank of windows across the rec field. And there he was.

Two feelings—grief and longing—tore through her heart simultaneously. They ripped through her, hot and sour, and she stood there, absorbing all of it. She had to stand perfectly still so she wouldn't race outside into the rain after him and grab his arm, beg him to tell her they were just having a nightmare and would wake up very soon. So powerful was this pang, this fiery urge to run after him and beg for a do-over, for some sort of explanation that would make it all go away, that she rocked on her heels a little and had to close her eyes until it passed.

Lisa joined her at the window and asked, softly, "That's him, isn't it?"

Drew managed a nod.

"You did the right thing," she added, referring to the fact that Drew told security of their relationship. Hearing this made Drew feel like a snitch. Like she had betrayed *him*. Like it was stamped on her forehead that she may have considered, even for a moment, to keep it all a secret. But secrets were what got them into this mess to begin with.

Oh, Ben. My funny, generous, weak Ben. Remember when you broke your ankle trying to impress me on your cousin's skateboard? Remember how we camped at Copper Falls and the raccoons stole our hamburger buns? Remember the time you smuggled a kitten into my apartment to cheer me up after I had my wisdom teeth pulled? Other memories began to flood her heart, bottlenecking painfully at the valves: the smell of his shirts (sporty shower gel and spicy dryer sheets) ... his battles with the Tupperware drawer ... his panicky denial when she confronted him ... the looks of horror on her students' faces... watching a police officer help him into the backseat of a squad car, his wrists handcuffed behind his back, his face pale and blank. Running to vomit in the staff bathroom.

Lisa was still staring out the window, watching and frowning. "You know what? Forget him. He got exactly what he deserved."

Drew didn't answer, at least in any way that she was aware of. But she was grateful for Lisa's concern, even if it was only there for the sake of appearance. Drew watched Ben disappear into the administration building through the rain-streaked window. It would be the last time, she was certain, that she'd ever see him. She waited for goosebumps, for the familiar chill to spread through the hollow parts of her chest, for a clap of thunder even. Something to mark the magnitude of this moment. But there was nothing left. Nothing at all.

"Happy hour tonight?"

It was an abrupt and strange question to ask, but somehow perfect in what it offered. Drew felt herself nodding, more at the concept of an hour that might be happy than anything else. "Yeah. Sure."

Right now, she was trying to hold it together with whatever glue she could find. Yes, her current batch of adhesives had toxic fumes, but one of these days she'd find a window to open. Air the place out. She kept hoping, anyway.

There was one bright spot in the midst of it all. Howard Bell was being transferred to minimum—the final stop before release. He finished reading the phonics list and turned to her. "Miss Daniels, I want to thank you for everything you done for me."

She smiled honestly for the first time in a while. "Well, that's what I'm here for."

"My transfer is today," he said proudly. "Then just a month till I'm released for good."

He'd been talking about his transfer for weeks, and here it was. She was oddly sad to see him go, but she reminded herself it was a good kind of loss. "So we're not going to see you here again."

"I hope not!" he said, laughing. She was filled with a quiet hope and the familiar gentle pride she used to feel when her students graduated and set off for the big, wide world. *I helped,* she would think. *I'm doing something meaningful.* But she wondered how Howard would support himself or his children once he was back on the streets. You couldn't climb too many rungs of the corporate ladder with a criminal record and a first-grade reading level. Social Security disability payments would help, she supposed.

He shook her hand, and she watched him walk out of the classroom for the last time, unusually emotional over it. What came to mind was slightly warped and not quite appropriate: *My little chick, leaving the nest.* But this was quickly followed by something a bit more true.

Please God, let him make it.

23. GRAHAM

It's a Wednesday evening after work and I'm sitting in a picnic pavilion at Kohler Andrae State Park eating a burger and talking with Janet Sutton. Well, not so much "talking with" as "being bored nutless by." I have so unplugged myself from the conversation that all I really know about it is the subject: her niece's smart mouth.

"Well, that's a teenager for you," I say distractedly. It's filler, really—the verbal equivalent of the cotton batting stuffed in pill bottles, but it's all that Janet lets me punctuate her filibuster with. What I need here is the Dave Chappelle "Wrap That Shit Up" box.

I scan the crowd for an out. We're here to celebrate another social worker's retirement, and though nobody's said it yet (give us time), we're all thrilled that John Moody is leaving. He's exactly what his last name implies: moody as fuck. Every workplace has an Eeyore, and John Moody's been ours since forever. A font of depressing statistics, happy to rain on any parade even in the planning stages, ready to kick any positive development in the shins.

All of the social workers are here, most of the whiteshirts from security, the majority of office staff in the admin building, and many of the teachers, having carpooled together, are just arriving. Drew is among them, I'm pleased to note. She sees me and a genuine smile lights up her features as she heads my way. She leans down to hug me and the neckline of her shirt dips to give me a heart-stopping, perfect glimpse of cleavage.

"Hey, are you hungry?" I ask when I find my voice. "The hamburgers look a little sad, but Kelly Wagner baked cupcakes. She said there's a tiny hacksaw in one of them."

Three hours later the party has thinned, and a loud, combative volleyball game is being played under the blinding white field lights. Drew and I are talking about work at a picnic table on the edge of the festivities. I wish to God there was something other than prison or high school that connected us. "I had a pretty crap day today actually," I admit, nursing a flat Coke. "I had to tell an inmate his mother died of stomach cancer."

Drew sighs heavily. "That's horrible. Can he go to the funeral?"

"Yeah, under guard. But still. The guy took it pretty hard."

"I didn't know you had to do those kinds of things."

"Yeah. Telling convicted felons when beloved family members die. Doesn't that sound like a job scraped from the folds of Larry King's scrotum?"

This makes her laugh and scold me. "Graham!" I don't even bother to hide my glee.

"On a lighter note, this morning Randy Smith called me 'Mr. Willett,' and when I corrected him he joked, 'Oh, you white people all look alike.'"

She smiles at this. "Is Randy Smith the guy who killed his wife with a bowling ball?"

"No, that's Larry Kirkland. Randy's in for armed robbery."

By then the second-shift guards have pulled into the parking lot. Including Joe. Looking very cozy with a female officer who'd recently transferred from Dodge. I catch Drew watching their entrance.

"Well," I say.

"Well," she echoes, "it was only a matter of time."

"I'm sorry, Drew."

"Don't be. Like I said, we were never really 'going out.'" She attempts to add a smile, but it misfires and looks more like a grimace.

Joe whispers something to his female companion and heads toward us. When he arrives he says, "Hey, what's up?"

Drew and I glance coolly at one another before I respond. "Not much. You?"

He sits, still chewing on a cocktail straw from a drink most likely consumed in a bar on the way here. "You guys hear what happened tonight?"

We both shake our heads.

"An inmate in my unit got shanked in the showers."

I perk up. "Who was it?"

"Leroy something."

The color drains from Drew's face. "Leroy who?"

"Shit, I'm totally blanking on his last name right now. Does it matter?"

"Is he okay?"

"No, why?" He looks at me, then back at Drew, confused.

"He died?" Drew asks, softly.

Joe nods.

"Leroy Johnson?"

He nods again, glad to have the gap in his memory plugged. "Yeah, that's it."

"Oh my God." She abruptly stands, banging a knee on the underside of the picnic table. "I have to …" She careens toward the parking lot.

"What the hell?" Joe asks.

"That was one of her students," I explain. "Which you might have known if you actually gave a fuck about any of the women you put your dick in."

Joe flicks his chewed-up straw at my face. "She didn't seem to mind."

Rage shoots through me, and I crumple my soda can and hurl it at him before I know what I'm doing. It bounces off his chest, and a few brown drops of cola stipple his shirt. There's a dangerous beat while his face turns purple. "If you weren't in that chair…"

"You'd be in the hospital by now," I finish for him. I'm already headed for Drew before he has a chance to respond. I don't give two shits about the waste of carbon behind me, but what is clear is exactly how I feel about Drew. I love her. It pulses through me, alive and tenacious. I am deeply, hopelessly, effortlessly in love with her, even if she will never feel that way about me. But I don't even care. I just want to give her what she needs, and right now, what she needs more than anything is a good friend.

I find her crying quietly, sitting curled up on the asphalt next to her car, arms wrapped around her shins, head resting on her knees. She speaks softly without looking up. "He just passed the reading and social studies tests for his High School Equivalency Degree. He was going to take the math exam next week. After just a few more practice tests."

"I'm sorry, Drew."

I park next to her and she stands, leaning against her car and wiping her eyes. "I didn't bargain for this when I took the job."

"Nobody does."

"Leroy was a good kid."

I try not to smile at that, both Drew's naïveté and the idea that any of the inmates are "good kids." Maybe I'm more jaded than I thought. "You got attached to him."

She nods and finally makes eye contact. "I guess I did, a little."

"It happens."

"I'm going to write a letter to his mother tomorrow."

I just nod.

"You think you're getting better, things are starting to feel normal again, and it's like life slaps you in the face and says, 'Ha! That's what *you* think, sucker!'"

"Kicks you while you're down."

"Why does that happen?" She looks plaintively at me for explanation.

"You know how people always say that you don't start to get better until you hit rock bottom?"

"Yeah?"

"Those people sit too close to microwaves."

She releases a nasal laugh. "All I seem to do around you lately is cry."

"I knew I shouldn't have gotten this haircut."

She offers a watery smile. The next thing I know she's grabbing my face in her hands and kissing me hard on the lips—trying to, anyway. My mouth is in a state of shock. My eyes fly wide open. She quickly realizes that I'm not quite participating (*Drew is kissing me! Drew is kissing me! Lips, wake up! Tongue, what the hell is wrong with you?*) and pulls back. "Oh God. I'm sorry, I'm so sorry." Her voice is soaked in embarrassment. She hides her eyes with one hand, peeking out at me between her slender fingers. "I don't know why I just did that."

I wish to God that kiss had come from a place of real passion and feeling for me. But I know exactly what it was. It was an SOS from a sinking ship. "Don't worry about it," I say, and I can feel the sheepish heat flooding my face. But in between, there's this: *What does this mean? Will this mean more?* I want it to mean more so badly it feels like a second heart sitting heavy in my ribcage, beating desperately next to the one that normally gets broken in times like these.

She leans against her car again and crosses her arms. "Graham, I really am sorry. I don't know what got into me." Even in the dark, her face glows. "You know what, I think I'm going to head home. It's been a long day."

"Okay." And then because I don't want her to leave, "Are you sure?"

"Yeah. I just need to be alone right now."

"Talk to you tomorrow?" Already I miss her, can feel her slipping through my fingers. *So damn close, yet so far...*

She nods and quickly climbs into her car. While I watch her pull away, I say, to no one in particular, "I think I've figured out why we work at Lakeside. It's not because we love to be paid little for verbal abuse. It's because we're broken. And maybe broken people work there to remember that there's always a rung beneath them on the ladder to hell."

I'm startled by some lazy clapping and a slurring voice behind me: "And the Oscar for Best Supporting Actor in a Dramatic Role goes to ... Graham Finch!" Andy Moffatt is lying on the grass to my left, almost underneath a picnic table, twirling an empty beer bottle and chuckling. "And the crowd goes wild!" He does a hushed roar and rolls away, covered in grass clippings, still laughing.

Figures I make one heartfelt soliloquy in my life and this douche has to ruin it.

24. DREW

There was a lockdown after Leroy's death. They even brought in dogs to sniff for drugs. There wasn't much room in the hole, but they managed to find space for three known gang leaders suspected in Leroy's death. Seg would be their final way station before shipment to max, once the paperwork went through.

"Think they'll have it on the news? I mean Leroy's death," Drew said to Janet, who had wandered into Drew's empty classroom that morning to deconstruct what happened. Everything was chilly and empty today: the school hallways, the classroom, Leroy's desk. Drew.

"Probably, but nothing in-depth. I lost two my first year. Breaks your heart, but it happens."

It happens. Drew felt like a raft someone had punctured. Only fate had allowed her to grow up in a good neighborhood while Leroy Johnson had probably been afraid to take the garbage out in his own. But now he was dead, and what difference would it make to anyone but his family and her?

Janet glanced at the clock. "Oh hey, I have to make a phone call." Before she left, she clumsily patted Drew's arm. "Plenty more Leroys just waiting for your help."

She thought of Howard Bell thanking her, shaking her hand, walking out of the prison gates on a sunny day. She didn't see him leave, but when she pictured it in her mind, it was always a sunny day. It didn't seem right to make a fresh start when it was raining.

Some of us might make it, she thought. And faith in that outcome had to be enough.

Once Janet was gone, Drew pulled out a pad of stationery and began to write. There were a few false starts, but after the third *Dear Mrs. Johnson*, it began to flow.

Twenty minutes later she sealed the envelope and addressed it. She surveyed her classroom again. Though it never really did feel like *hers*. And wasn't it always easier to let go of something that never felt like yours to begin with?

That Friday, Brooke invited Drew out on her boat. They cruised through the balmy early September night over the lake, to one of the quieter bays. There were four other boats anchored there, bobbing on the black waves, lit only by their navigation lights. When the breeze was right, you could hear laughter on those boats, small but surprisingly clear.

Drew tied her cold, windblown hair into a ponytail. "Ben's at Lakeside," she finally said. "Not for long, though."

Brooke stared at her, trying to read Drew's emotional state, while Drew did everything she could to contain it. "Are you all right?" she asked sincerely.

"Maybe. I'm drinking too much. Kissing the wrong people at the wrong time. My students are dying. You know, I may need to rethink my whole recovery strategy."

"Kissing the wrong people?"

Of course Brooke would prioritize the kissing over the dying. Drew shook her head, disappointed despite herself. "Forget it."

Mercifully, Brooke did. They sat in contemplative silence for a bit, drinking gin and tonics and listening to a conversation drift over from one of the neighboring boats. It sounded like a couple onboard was celebrating an anniversary. "Here's to love—you guys figured it out," a dark silhouette announced grandly, and Drew could see him lifting a glass in the moonlight. And then everyone on the boat chimed in. "Hear, hear," silly and tipsy and happy. Something about overhearing this unleashed every emotion Drew had been suppressing. She turned to Brooke, hot with sudden fury.

"I lied," she said. "I am going to tell you what to do."

Brooke froze.

"You're going to pull your head out of your ass and stop seeing this other man."

Brooke stared at her drink.

"You think you're soul mates, right? Well, news flash! All you're feeling is dopamine. You're addicted to him, to the excitement of sneaking around. Do you think that would last in the day-to-day? If you got divorced and ended up with him, picked up his dirty socks and smelled his morning breath every day and got a chance to get sick of his stupid habits?" She sucked in a ragged breath. "And what about Mark? This would destroy him. I don't know a thing about this other guy, but I can guarantee Mark loves you more. And if you lost him, you would regret it for the rest of your life. By the way, this other guy? He's married too, isn't he?"

"Yes." Quietly, nearly a whisper.

"Kids?"

Brooke continued to stare at her drink.

"I'll take that as another 'yes.'" Drew shook her head. "This guy will never leave his family for you. I don't care what he's told you. Brooke, you haven't fallen in love with this guy. You've fallen in love with the *idea* of him, with the fact that he's probably filling a gap in you that really only *you* can fill. Brooke, you need to get out. Now. Before people get hurt. Before you lose your business, your husband, your self-respect."

"My self-respect's already long gone." She stabbed her drink into a nearby cup holder and buried her face in her hands. "I don't know how it even started. I love Mark, he's my best friend, we're partners in everything, and I *know* he knows me best and loves me more than anything. But the idea of touching him began to repulse me at some point ... I don't know why ... and I just ... Mark would *die* if he knew just how much I don't deserve him. *I* want to die." Tears began to rain in dark, deliberate drops onto the deck beneath her face.

Drew softened. She didn't feel like lecturing anymore. The old Brooke would have shot back a snippy *"This isn't about you and Ben."* The Brooke in front of her now was turned inside-out. But if Brooke had made that reply, she would have been partially right. These were actually all the savage, heartsick things Drew wanted to say to Ben, with a few substitutions of detail. But it was much too late for closure with him.

"Brooke," she said gently, "what would you tell me if I were you right now?"

At first Drew didn't think she'd answer, but finally Brooke began to speak. "That if he really loved you, he'd get a divorce. And if you really loved him, and yourself, so would you." She straightened, and the rest poured out. "That you and Mark should go to counseling. That no marriage is perfect. That you're being selfish. That nothing good comes out of nothing but lies. That love isn't supposed to hurt so bad. That real love *never* hurts this bad."

"Well," Drew said wryly, "I don't know about that last bit." She stood, steadied herself as the boat rocked against the soft waves, and sat down next to her friend, trying to think of a happy memory to distract them. Something brighter to hold on to. "Remember when our parents took us on that tour of model homes when we were in second grade?"

Brooke stopped crying, and the corners of her mouth twitched, flirting with a smile. "And we tried washing our hands in the bidet."

"Yeah. I was like, 'Oh look at this neat little sink for kids!'"

"And everyone laughed, and we couldn't figure out what was so funny."

"Who takes their kids on a tour of a model home?"

"The same mother who says she hopes you choke and die when you won't share your Halloween candy with her," Brooke said.

"The same parents who feel each other up on the beach while you're building a sand castle twenty feet away," Drew added.

They smiled together, their oddball memories the perfect temporary emotional patch. It was too late for closure with Ben, but it wasn't too late to forgive him by proxy. For the first time, it seemed possible to make peace with ghosts.

After they ran out of things to say, Brooke started the engine and pulled anchor. She steered them back to shore. Drew watched the other boats grow smaller and smaller in their wake, until their lights disappeared completely.

The next morning Drew found her parents outside, weeding together. "Need help?" she asked, hoping they didn't.

"Sure," her father said. "Want to mow the lawn?"

She shaded her eyes with a hand and surveyed the yard. Ten acres intermittently dappled in the shade of oaks, maples, birches, and poplars, marked by a privacy screen of Colorado blue spruce, peppered with her mother's themed gardens: the cutting garden, the moon garden (comprised solely of night-blooming and white flowers), the meditation garden, the butterfly garden, the herb garden, the rose garden, and the potager, bursting with rampant squash vines and fat eggplants and ripening tomatoes and glossy peppers nearly ready to harvest. Sprinkled between the gardens were birdhouses (including a colony of white gourds on a telescoping pole), birdbaths, bird feeding stations, a pond, and a greenhouse stuffed with all of the tools one might need to maintain such a serious addiction to backyard living. Altogether, quite the obstacle course.

Did she want to mow the lawn?

"Not really," she finally said, like she'd even considered it. "Why don't I make dinner tonight instead?"

"You're not going to make one of those weird ethnic dishes."

"How about barbecued chicken, corn on the cob, and tomato sandwiches?"

"Done," he shouted, and stopped weeding to pick up the pellet gun that he always kept handy when working outside. He hoisted it to his shoulder, aimed, and fired at the flock of starlings chattering and screeching in the spruces. One fell to the ground and the rest scattered. He popped another shot at the cloud of departing birds, but missed.

When she was younger she'd weep over her father's ruthless approach to bird population management. He tried to simplify it for her. "Honey, you like the Purple Martins and bluebirds better, right?"

She'd sniffle and nod while he wiped away her tears. *Progne Subis. Sialia Sialis.*

"Then this is what we have to do."

European Starlings and English House Sparrows were brought over by well-meaning immigrants. Just a few hundred birds more than a hundred years ago. Invasive species with a talent for viciously outcompeting native cavity nesters, delivering a major blow to bluebird and martin populations. So her father used traps and guns to give the home team underdogs a chance to bounce back from the damage done by what he called the "trash birds." It wasn't until she'd found a brood of bluebirds she'd been charting for a school project tossed casually from the birdhouse one morning, every last chick pecked to death by a sparrow intent on claiming that box, that her nine-year-old brain made the connection. Oh, how she'd cried, watching the parents cheeping softly to their dead babies. She helped her father bait the sparrow trap with millet the next day.

It was harsh, but ... Drew *did* like the martins and bluebirds better: their indigo coloring, their sweet, lisping songs, their graceful flight patterns.

Summer was waning, the crickets and cicadas ramping up their final, urgent serenades to one another like lovelorn drunks after last call. The end of summer used to make her melancholy, but now she felt ready for fall, with its hearty soups and cable-knit sweaters and pumpkin-scented candles. She relaxed into an Adirondack chair near the moon garden to soak in the late-season sun for a few minutes. Goldfinch fledglings, the last of the season's babies, were zooming desperately after their parents, wings fluttering in full begging mode. She watched one hop up to its father, cheeping desperately for some regurgitated seeds, only for papa bird to rudely knock him off the branch and fly away. This was weaning, avian-style. And no matter how many times she saw it, it never failed to crush a corner of her heart.

"He's got a point," her father suddenly said, and winked at her. He was crossing the lawn for the cement patio behind the garage—the only place his wife would allow him to smoke at home.

Sara yanked fistfuls of quack grass sprouting near the retaining wall, not even glancing up when she commented on his mission, "That's right, keep it up. I'm one cigarette closer to my singles cruise with Meredith."

En route, Drew's father held up one hand and mimed a flapping mouth—an invisible Sara puppet.

Observing her parents in their garden, Drew could conclude that the recipe for marital success was this: Work quietly together on household projects. Avoid confrontation, unless in the context of teasing. And have sex often. Last night she heard them doing just that. It was a solid reminder that she needed to stop drifting and move on with her life as quickly as possible.

She watched her father smoking in the shade, shocked by how small he looked. How ... *old*. He wasn't always this old, though sometimes it seemed like it. She remembered him taking all of the girls in her class roller-skating for her tenth birthday; while she jerked around the rink on unsteady skates, her father whizzed past, skating backward, doing jumps, doing the limbo, doing the splits. "Come on, slowpoke!" he'd shout, spinning twice while he zipped past, leaving Drew wobbling in his skate-dust. On his next pass, he'd yell, "Hustle, hustle! Let's see some life!" She would grip her friend's wrist tightly (she tried to make every trip around the rink a couples-only skate, for balance), determined to show no hustling or signs of life lest she fall and crack her head open. That was one of the worst things that could happen to a kid.

Later, she grew to learn that cracking your head open had nothing on a heart cracked in two. And she began to avoid heartache the same way. She became a serial monogamist, making every trip around the rink a couples-only skate with whatever boy glided into her life at that particular moment. A pattern emerged: bad boy, bad boy, long stretch with a good boy. Which was why she settled on Ben. He'd appeared right on schedule after the usual number of bad boys, just as she felt sorely in need of a reliable one. Or at least one who *seemed* reliable, she supposed.

And they were fine for a long time, until they started sleepwalking through their relationship. Drew had been running with a friend in the mornings, coaching the debate team after school and on weekends, grading papers late at night, always exhausted while she and Ben cruised toward the end—too distracted or self-absorbed to intuit what he'd been up to. But when she allowed herself to look back and really see things, the clues were all there. The late hours, his inability to look her in the eye, his utter disinterest in sex, his headaches and mania and stress and depression, all of which seemed real enough. *Of course*, she thought. *Because he was sleeping with a student.*

Goose flesh rose on her arms, and she shivered as the black cloud passed through her. *No more*, she told herself. *It's over.*

She took a deep breath and looked across the lawn at her father, trekking back to the garden. As he passed, he briskly squeezed her shoulder. "You'll be okay."

Though her family had had roots in Wisconsin since the mid-1800s, they were New England in many ways—particularly when it came to the giving of affection and the silent, stoic endurance of misfortune. They didn't discuss ugliness or family secrets. Self-indulgence was frowned upon. The worst thing anyone could be was a whiner.

Or maybe it was a hearty German pioneer thing, part of their farming forebears. A drive to work hard and move quietly forward, each new season an opportunity to till last season's mistakes under and make the soil fertile for better things to come. So maybe the productive silence—which Drew had longed to see replaced with chatty parental meddling in her youth (perhaps the only person in her high school to wish for such a thing)—was where quiet progress happened. A still winter for the soul to transform, prepare itself for new life. And, of course, later you got to celebrate with lots of beer when that new life became a bumper crop.

She joined her parents in the garden. Soon, the three of them were weeding together. Occasionally they tossed clumps of quack grass at one another for comic relief. Mostly they worked silently, the yard quiet save for the sweet burbling of finches.

Ben, you will never heal from what you've done.
But I'm beginning to think I might.

25. GRAHAM

When I look at my married friends, my first reaction is surprise: *Wow! So few?* My second reaction is more objective. Most of the guys, except for one, would lead you to believe they entered the institution of marriage grudgingly. The one who nearly raced down the aisle, couldn't get that ring on fast enough, married a gorgeous bitch who has made it her life's work to nag him into an early grave. The single holdouts, most of whose parents are divorced, love to use the word "settle" in their responses when anyone asks why they haven't gotten married yet. As in, "I don't want to settle. I'm waiting for the right one." Which is amusing to me as the only divorced one in the bunch—having hard-won my cynical stripes—because is there such a thing?

Abby is relaxing with me on the couch, Avis splayed across her lap. We're watching a movie about a sensitive guy with your typical romantic entanglements; he's basically decent but is acting like a dick because he can't commit to his girlfriend, and every so often I'll sneak a glance at Abby. Each time I do, the words *you're settling* echo through my skull. Like there's a little man standing on my cochlea shouting this through a megaphone. I cross my arms, feeling uncomfortably like the asshole on my TV screen.

She catches me glancing surreptitiously over and smiles. "Would you like anything? I'm going to grab a soda." Avis, sensing her comfortable position is about to be disrupted, tumbles from Abby's lap, grumbling the whole way down.

"No thanks, I'm good."

Abby pauses the DVD and goes into the kitchen. My blood pressure begins to climb while I listen to her rummage through my fridge. I suddenly feel possessive of my appliances. I don't want her rummaging through them. I don't want *anyone* else rummaging through them.

Well, not just anyone.

And there's the proverbial and irritating rub.

She returns to the sofa with a Coke and presses Play on the remote. The anti-hero resumes his dickery, and I snag the remote and pause it again. Abby looks over and smiles. "I knew you wanted a soda!"

I take a deep breath. "Abby," and I pause for a long moment, because what I'm about to say could colossally ruin everything. Here is a decent, kind-hearted girl. She treats me well. She likes me. With Abby, there is no drama. I may have no better chance for a reasonable facsimile of love for the rest of my life.

But I don't want a reasonable facsimile. And I'm not in love with her. I'm in love with someone else.

Do you settle? Find the courage to be content somewhere within yourself and cruise into the sunset years with an amiable companion? It's more than most people get. Or do you risk a known, comfortable thing for just the barest chance at what could be the most honest, passionate, *wanted* love of your life?

When I put it like that, there's no contest. "Abby, where do you see things between us going?" Avis is now dragging her soft dog bed out of the kitchen and across the living room with her mouth, all herky-jerky.

She hesitates before answering. "I don't know," she says carefully. "Where do you see it going?"

To be honest, until she asked me that, I wasn't sure. But now I know. I want to be with a person who is unafraid to voice her own opinions when I ask for them, even if she suspects they'll be at odds with mine. Had I not had a near-death experience, had I not been married before, I might have lacked the courage to say what comes next. But life is too damn short. And I finally feel I deserve not to stay with the wrong person simply to keep loneliness at bay.

"Abby, you're a great girl."

Her smile crumples. "Uh-oh."

Avis positions her dog bed and straddles it. She begins to hump it vigorously around the living room. I frown and clap my hands to get her attention. "Avis! Cut that out. You're a girl! You're not supposed to do that." She hops off and pokes at it indignantly with her nose. I turn back to Abby. "Sorry. I guess what I meant was that ... I'm just not sure..." I'm distracted again by Avis, who is repeating her attempt to defy the laws of nature and impregnate her bed. "Would you stop it?" I throw a pillow at her. It knocks her off for a second, and she glowers at me before climbing back on.

A small laugh escapes Abby. "Graham, it's okay. I know what you're trying to tell me."

"You do?"

"Yes. You don't feel about me the way Avis feels about her dog bed."

"Oh, Christ." We both laugh a little. "Abby, I'm sorry. And I'm probably going to regret this, because I really like you. You are so, so awesome. But that's it. I just feel ... I just feel a deep friendship for you. I wish it were more, but that's all there is for me now." *Said the guy in the wheelchair who finally found his ability to tell the truth, and a little self-esteem along the way.*

Her expression hardens, but nearly imperceptibly. "Well, that's really more than most people I know can hope for these days."

It's a sad, grasping kind of rationalization, and I agree with her. "True, but I guess I just want more. At least to start."

She sighs and smiles fully at me. A tender, wise, and heartbreaking smile. "It's okay. I understand. And I think I'm going to go now."

"Are you sure? God, I'm so sorry, Abby."

"Yes. If it isn't there, it isn't there. Thank you for being honest with me." She doesn't hug me, but offers a hand to shake. I press both hands around it to form an awkward hand-hug.

"See you around," she says. Then she leaves me with just the crummy movie and a dog in love with an inanimate object. I feel sick with remorse as soon as the door closes behind her. Avis hops off her bed and runs, panting and happy, through a sunbeam full of dust motes into the kitchen for a drink of water—the canine equivalent of a postcoital smoke. I finish watching the movie, even though it's predictable and puerile, and it lulls me into thinking I did the right thing.

One night not long after this, Drew calls me. She hasn't called me in … ever, perhaps, and every hair on my head begins to tingle. "Meet me at Kohler-Andrae State Park around nine." Her voice is flushed with excitement. "There's something I want to show you."

Love, I think. Because that's what I want it to be.

We arrive within one minute of each other. "Hey," I say, unable to conceal my delight at being here beneath the violet evening sky with her. *Just her, her, her.* Waves rush against the sandy shore behind the dunes, and I have barely enough time to wonder how long it's been since I last walked barefoot on those dunes.

Drew's eyes sparkle in the moonlight. "Come with me." We make our way down a paved walkway, through a patch of dark trees, to a secluded viewing area on a sand dune. One or two crickets are chirping back and forth, setting up a booty call if one of them can make it across the road without being squished. You can see the water from up here, and the moon reflected in it, choppy on the waves.

Drew sits on a bench overlooking the lake, and I park next to her and smile. "So what's up?"

"I quit Lakeside today. It was time."

My enthusiasm takes a hit. "Wow." I feel weirdly abandoned. "Do you have another teaching job lined up?"

She shakes her head. "No, but there might be something for me in Madison. I'll figure it out."

Well, there you have it. I will be lonely for the rest of my days. Cashed in all my chips on a sure thing, poured every dime from that gamble down the drain, but that's life. Always a risk. I try not to let my disappointment show.

"Would you visit me?" She leans over to catch my eye, her expression earnest and hopeful. "If I moved to Madison?"

I shrug and plaster fake cheer on my face. "Yeah, sure. Why not?"

She's trying to read my emotions. After a beat, she adds, "Or maybe we should go to South America."

"What?"

"I mean it. Let's just buy some tickets and go. I've never been to Peru or Brazil." Her voice is full of impulsive conviction and yearning.

"I've never even been to Indiana."

"It's spring in Buenos Aires right now. How young and crazy do you feel?"

"I'm not sure how young I feel, but I can always be talked into crazy." Hope begins to rise in me like a balloon; unfortunately, reality is chasing it with a pin. We'll be lucky to take a trip to the mall together, let alone book airfare to Rio. And I *know* I won't be walking the Incan Trail with her.

I wish she wouldn't dangle these guileless yet hollow invitations before me. Just as I feel that old, familiar despondency begin to settle in, she rubs her arms and looks over one shoulder. "Listen. Can you hear that?"

I strain to listen. I hear a few distant peeps, and the waves washing softly onto the sand over the dunes. "What am I listening for?" I whisper.

"Birds migrating," she says softly, a hint of reverence in her voice. "With a chance for fall out."

I feel a smile spontaneously materialize. "Oh?"

She smiles back, her face pale in the moonlight. "They're migrating tonight from Canada. I saw it on Doppler radar. A huge mass of them. They're flying to Brazil. Central America. Somewhere warmer to spend the winter. Warblers, swallows, tanagers ... right down the Lake Michigan shoreline. It's the Mississippi Flyway, to be even more nerdily specific."

"So what's a 'fall out?'"

"If the weather conditions are just right, like they hit rain or strong winds or even just fog, some or all of them will drop out of the sky and rest here for a bit. That's the fall out."

I love how she sounds like an encyclopedia sometimes. "They do this at night? How do you know that?"

"My dad. The bird nut." Her voice is full of soft affection. You can clearly hear in it how much she loves her father, and even the birds themselves, off to destinations unknown, thousands of miles away. I'd call it plucky, or maybe fascinating—is it something magnetic in their brains that compels this mass migration? The days shortening, the shorter arc of the sun above the horizon that says, *Time to blow this popsicle stand!* But it's more than that. I don't know much about birds, but I do know why these birds are leaving.

Because if they stayed, they'd starve to death.

And suddenly a small miracle happens. Drew reaches across the void, extending her hand for mine, and I take it. We're holding hands. She even lifts mine, presses it against her cheek for a moment. It should feel like a victory, but instead, it feels quiet. It feels like you won the race, but nobody cheers— instead, everyone whispers, "Congratulations." Maybe they're worried the judges will accuse you of cheating and take your trophy away. My heart is full, more content than it's been in years. We hold hands that way, listening to birds migrating by the light of the moon. Older birds making the trip to South America for the last time, fledglings making it for the first. Calling softly to one another to stay in contact through the dark.

"Thanks for taking me here," I say.

She squeezes my hand. "You're welcome. Thank you for everything."

"What did I do?"

She doesn't answer, but scoots closer to me on the bench and lays her head on my shoulder. Strands of her hair flutter against my cheek, but I wouldn't dream of brushing them away.

We stay still yet connected like that for a while, blanched in moonlight, listening to the birds passing overhead, to the waves curling into the sandy shore, until the dank air seeps through our light jackets and chills us. And then it's time to go home. But first we might grab a bite at Country Plate.

SIX MONTHS LATER. SPRING.

In the end, Drew stayed. She found a job long-term subbing for a teacher on sabbatical at a local private school, rented an apartment just three miles from my house.

First floor.

"Do you remember in high school, that night we watched *Good Will Hunting* in my parents' basement?" We're lying on my bed, her head on my bare chest, my fingers absently stroking her hair. *SNL* is on TV in the background, muted.

She lifts her head to smile at me, her cheeks still flushed pink, her hair mussed. "And we drank peach schnapps straight from the bottle. I think I got sick."

"Yeah, sorry about that. God, I wanted to tear your clothes off that night."

"You should have." She's being sweet, not remembering it right on purpose.

"First of all, you had a boyfriend. Second, do you know how terrified I was?"

"Stop it," Drew says, her eyes crinkling. She traces a finger

293

down my nose, across my cheeks. I still feel like pinching myself when she does things like this.

"You were this goddess, my fantasy come to life, and you had your legs on my lap. That's all it took. You made my head spin, and I had no idea what to do with you. It was too much for my adolescent brain."

She pushes up on one elbow to study my face. "I love your nose. Have I told you that?"

"I'm glad nothing happened that night," I continue.

"You are?" She gives me a quizzical smile.

"I was a sixteen-year-old virgin. It would have been over the second you unzipped my pants. You'd have been totally disappointed, and then I'd have to face you in school and you'd be back with what's-his-name. It would have ruined everything."

She runs her finger along my earlobe now, thoughtful. "It's not possible for you to disappoint me." She kisses my cheek. She kisses my nose. She kisses my lips. "It's okay," she whispers, kissing my damp eyelashes. "It's okay."

She nestles into me and I hold her, tucking her hair behind her ear. *This gift*, I think. *This perfect gift.* I turn off the TV and listen to her breathing slip into a slow, regular pattern while she falls asleep. I think about what's possible and what's impossible, and I start to believe. The room is dark, the sheets cool, Drew small and warm in my arms. My heart feels too big for sleep. But soon I feel myself drifting away. Dream that I'm flying.

THE
END

A NOTE FROM THE AUTHOR

I worked in a medium-security men's prison for a few years to help put myself through college; this seems strange enough for any young woman, but at the time, I was so shy I could barely make a phone call without a script. But I needed the money, and more than that, the writer in me couldn't pass on the opportunity. For nine months, I served as sidekick to a phenomenal special education teacher, and when that ended, I took another short-term gig as a clerk for the department tasked with deciding which inmates to ship from our overcrowded prison to private contract facilities out of state. My experiences were a material gold mine, but they alone didn't inspire this story. Some of the credit is also due my parents, who fell in love at the same prison twenty years earlier (Dad was a unit sergeant, Mom a secretary).

They continued to work for the Wisconsin Department of Corrections together for years, which made dinner table conversation pretty entertaining in my youth.

Mandatory Release is built from the ashes of a novel I wrote fourteen years ago: it was called *The Cool Side of the Pillow,* and it sucked royally. That novel has been through more edits and reincarnations than Shirley MacLaine or the recipe for Coke, and the end result is in your hands. It's a tough nut to market, given the setting and genre mash-up, but here you are, reading it! And I thank you for that.

ABOUT THE AUTHOR

Jess Riley lives in Oshkosh, Wisconsin with her husband and crazy Cairn Terrier in a 130-year-old ~~money pit~~ farmhouse. When she's not writing novels, she works as a Grant Writer for school districts nationwide. Vegetarian, gardener, butterfly rancher, movie snob, niece and nephew-spoiler, all-around smartass who cried at the end of *Frankenweenie*. Contact Jess at jess@jessriley.com.

DISCLAIMER FOR THE PICKY FOLKS

Mandatory Release reflects the policies and laws in place during my tenure with the Department of Corrections. Those laws and policies have changed since then and continue to evolve on a daily basis, which makes getting things up-to-the-minute accurate just a bit challenging. Basically, *Mandatory Release* is a fictional snapshot, and I played a little fast and loose with the timeline; so Mom, I love you, but I don't want to hear about the new sentencing rule adopted last week.

MANDATORY RELEASE PLAYLIST

I don't always listen to music when I'm writing the first draft, but I definitely do when I'm editing. And then I miss important typos because my brain is working on an entirely different plane and I'm singing out loud, without even knowing it.

"Ballad of Fuck All" by Malcolm Middleton
The first time I heard this, I actually said out loud, "This is Graham!" The lyrics and melody capture his unique, broken mix of melancholy and longing. So perfect. The fact that Malcolm Middleton has a pretty thick Scottish accent is a bonus, if unrelated to the story.

"Welcome Home" by Radical Face
This song reminds me of Drew's return home to both Laurentide Bay and her parents' house. It's buoyant and beautiful, with soaring key changes and dark, aching lyrics. Goosebump-inspiring.

"Girl Can't Help it" by Journey
This was the song Graham was listening to in the car when he was paralyzed. So of course I had to include it.

"Pursuit of Happiness (Nightmare)" by Kid Cudi
Here's one for both the inmates and my main characters. Everyone looking for happiness, trying to escape from their night terrors with some form of reckless substance abuse. It's fun but really dark. Plus, you have to love that MGMT and Ratatat collaborated on this.

"Comes and Goes (In Waves)" by Greg Laswell
Here's another one for everybody in the book. Graham, Drew, Joe, Brooke, Howard Bell, Leroy, Abby, Sara, even Kevin. It's ultimately uplifting. Makes your heart swell with hope that things might get better after all, that the underdogs might actually win. (Close Runner-Up: **"When My Time Comes" by Dawes**.)

"Violet" by Hole
Oh, this song. It's Drew and Joe. If Common Courtesy didn't play this at LakeFest, they should have.

"Knights of Cydonia" by Muse
Graham is a huge Muse fan. This song is a perfect reason why—nerdily bombastic, building to an awesome head-banging moment and featuring one of the most perfect lines ever: "Don't waste your time, or time will waste you."

"High and Dry" by Radiohead, "The Darkest Side" by The Middle East, "Run" by Snow Patrol, "Little Black Submarines" by The Black Keys and "No One's Gonna Love You" by Band of Horses
Graham could dedicate any of these songs to Drew, and I frequently listened to them while writing his scenes.

"Phantom Limb" by The Shins
I love The Shins. This song makes me think of all of Laurentide Bay—this strange northern town filled with tourists, inmates, and the people who serve them both. It's got a fun, absurd undercurrent, and I imagine Drew and Graham listening to this together and coming to the same conclusions about what it means. Uh, and Phantom Limb? Kind of appropriate to a spinal cord injury.

"Rich/Poor" by Trampled by Turtles

I discovered this band at a bluegrass festival in Utah a few years ago, and was delighted to learn they were from Duluth (and played a lot of gigs in my neck of the woods). I listened to it often while rewriting, because it sets a perfect tone for the story.

"So this is Goodbye (Pink Ganter Remix)" by William Fitzsimmons

It's a more upbeat remix; made me think of Drew finally coming to terms with Ben and moving on.

"Stay" by Rihanna (featuring Mikky Ekko)

It was nearly too popular to make the list, but dammit, it's great. This is Graham's and Drew's song, hands down, even if you're totally sick of hearing it on the radio by now.

"Ruby Falls" by Guster

While the ending credits roll.

One more thing. If you're wondering what Graham's voice sounds like, listen to **"Dear Valentine" by Guster**. That, to me, is it.

ACKNOWLEDGMENTS

Major gratitude and love to my beta-readers and some of the best friends a girl could ask for: Trish Garner, Stephanie Elliott, Mary Hennessy, Nicole Waltemath, Coree VanThiel, Leeann Busse, Danielle Younge-Ullman, Eileen Cook … thanks as well to Betsy Sundquist, Jeff Lee, Casey Miller, Madeline Martin, Emily Berghorn, Mary Martin, and Scott Van Pay.

Writing can be a lonely business, so I also owe thanks to some amazing authors: Suzy Soro, Karen McQuestion, Jen Lancaster, Sarah Pekkanen, Dina Silver, Dee DeTarsio, Kathie Shoop, Malena Lott, all of the incredible women on the Girlfriends' Book Club blog, the Debs, and my local writer pals December Gephart and Nikki Kallio. I am so grateful for your behind-the-scenes friendship and support!

I was on the verge of stuffing this novel back in the drawer when my editor Jim Thomsen said the nicest things about it and basically talked me off the ledge (though he didn't know it).

Thank YOU for taking a chance on this crazy mash-up of lad lit and chick lit. Thank you to all the book clubs who have read my books, to my friends and family for putting up with me when I'm obsessed with a project, but mostly my husband Jason. You make it all possible.

CPSIA infor
Printed in th
LVOW04s1
413544

4 081877